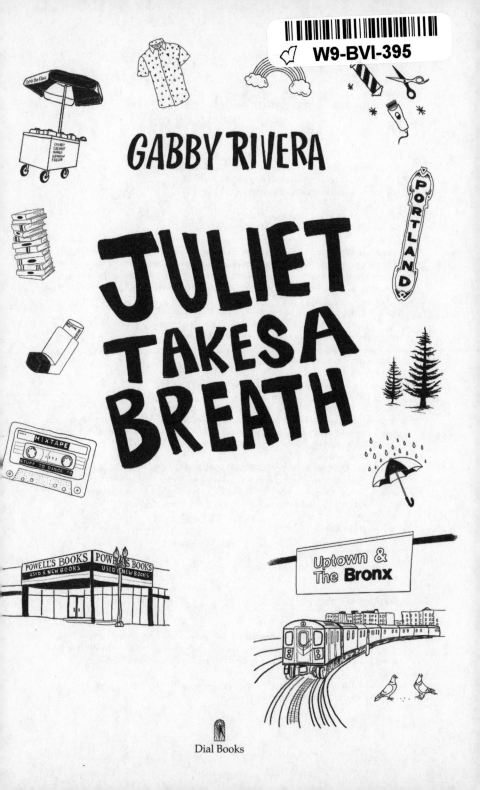

GABBY RIVERA

JULIET TAKES A BREATH

Dial Books

Dial Books
An imprint of Penguin Random House LLC, New York

First published in the United States of America by Riverdale Avenue Books, 2016
Published by Dial Books, an imprint of Penguin Random House LLC, 2019
Dial Books paperback edition published 2021

VISIT US ONLINE AT PENGUINRANDOMHOUSE.COM.

THE LIBRARY OF CONGRESS HAS CATALOGED THE HARDCOVER EDITION AS FOLLOWS:
Names: Rivera, Gabby, author. | Title: Juliet takes a breath / Gabby Rivera.
Description: New York : Dial Books, an imprint of Penguin Random House LLC, [2019]
Summary: "Juliet, a self-identified queer, Bronx-born Puerto Rican-American, comes out to her family to disastrous results the night before flying to Portland to intern with her feminist author icon—whom Juliet soon realizes has a problematic definition of feminism that excludes women of color"
—Provided by publisher.
Identifiers: LCCN 2019019851 (print) | LCCN 2019022383 (ebook) | ISBN 9780593108178 (hardback)
Subjects: CYAC: Lesbians—Fiction. | Puerto Ricans—Oregon—Fiction. | Feminism—Fiction. | Authors—Fiction. | Prejudices—Fiction. | Internship programs—Fiction. | Coming-of-age—Fiction.
Classification: LCC PZ7.1.R57645 Ju 2019 (print) | LCC PZ7.1.R57645 (ebook) | DDC [Fic]—dc23

Manufactured in Canada

ISBN 9780593108192

10 9 8 7 6 5 4 3 2 1

Design by Cerise Steel
Text set in Palatino

To Christina Elena Santiago, aka Nena

We will always be homegirls coming up in the Bronx on the hunt
for 32 flavors and then some.

To the round brown girls who are told they aren't enough, who
move in the world uncertain if there's room for their bodies,
selves, and hearts.

Take all the room you need, camarada.

Make no apologies. Fight hard. Love on each other.
You are a miracle.

PALANTE * PA'LANTE (adverb)

Puerto Rican slang, also used in Latin America and other parts
   of the Caribbean. Contraction of *para adelante*, meaning
   to move forward.
A call out into the world for our people to always keep it
   moving.

PREFACE

Dear Harlowe,

Hi, my name is Juliet Palante. I've been reading your book Raging Flower: Empowering Your Pussy by Empowering Your Mind. *No lie, I started reading it so that I could make people uncomfortable on the subway. I especially enjoyed whipping it out during impromptu sermons given by old sour-faced men on the 2 train. It amused me to watch men confront the word "pussy" in a context outside their control; you know, like in bright pink letters on the cover of some girl's paperback book.*

My grandma calls me la sin vergüenza, the one without shame. She's right. I'm always in it for the laughs. But I'm writing to you now because this book of yours, this magical labia manifesto, has become my bible. It's definitely a reading from the book of white lady feminism and yet, there are moments where I see my round brown ass in your words. I wanted more of that, Harlowe, more representation, more acknowledgment, more room to breathe the same air as you. "We are all women. We are all of the womb. It is in that essence of the moon that we share sisterhood"—that's you. You wrote that and I highlighted it, wondering if that was true. If you don't know my life and my struggle, can we be sisters?

Can a badass white lady like you make room for me? Should I stand next to you and take that space? Or do I need to just push you out of the way? Claim it myself now so that one day we'll be able to share this earth, this block, these deep breaths?

I hope it's okay that I say this to you. I don't mean any disrespect, but if you can question the patriarchy, then I can question you. I think. I don't really know how this feminism stuff works anyway. I've only taken one women's studies class and that was legit because a cute girl on my floor signed up for it. This girl made me lose my train of thought. I wanted to watch her eat strawberries and make her a mixtape. So I signed up for the class and then she became my girlfriend. But please don't ask me about anything that happened in that class afterward because love is an acid trip.

Feminism. I'm new to it. The word still sounds weird and

*wrong. Too white, too structured, too foreign; something I
can't claim. I wish there was another word for it. Maybe I
need to make one up. My mom's totally a feminist, but she
never uses that word. She molds my little brother's breakfast
eggs into Ninja Turtles and pays all the bills in the house.
She's this lady that never sleeps because she's working on a
master's degree while raising my little brother and me and
pretty much balancing the rhythm of an entire family on her
shoulders. That's a feminist, right? But my mom still irons
my dad's socks. So what do you call that woman? You know,
besides Mom.*

*Your book is a refuge from my neighborhood, from my
contradictions, from my lack of desire to ever love a man,
let alone wash his fucking socks. I don't even wash my own
socks. I want to learn more about the wonder of me, the lunar
power of my pussy, my vadge, my taquito, that place where
all the magic happens. You know, once people are quiet
enough to show it reverence. I want to be free. Free like this
line: "A fully realized woman is at all times her true self. No
soul-crushing secrets or self-imposed burdens of shame, these
create toxic imbalance, a spiritual yeast infection if you will.
So step out into the fresh air and let that pussy breathe."*

*I've got a secret. I think it's going to kill me. Sometimes
I hope it does. How do I tell my parents that I'm gay? Gay
sounds just as weird as feminist. How do you tell the people
who breathed you into existence that you're the opposite of*

what they want you to be? And I'm supposed to be ashamed of being gay, but now that I've had sex with girls, I don't feel any shame at all. In fact, it's pretty fucking amazing. So how am I supposed to come out and deal with everyone else's sadness? "Sin Vergüenza Comes Out, Is Banished from Family." That's the headline. You did this to me. I wasn't gonna come out. I was just gonna be that family member who's gay and no one ever talks about it even though EVERYONE knows they share a bed with their "roommate." Now everything is different.

How am I supposed to be this honest? I know you're not a Magic 8 Ball. You're just some lady that wrote a book. But I fall asleep with that book in my arms because words protect hearts and I've got this ache in my chest that won't go away. I read Raging Flower and now I dream of raised fists and solidarity marches led by matriarchs fueled by café con leche where I can march alongside cigar-smoking doñas and Black Power dykes and all the world's weirdos and no one is left out. And no one is living a lie.

Is that the world you live in? I read that you live in Portland, Oregon. No one I know has ever been there; most people I know have never left the Bronx. I refuse to be that person. The Bronx cannot own me. There isn't enough air to breathe here. I carry an inhaler for those days when I need more than my allotted share. I need a break. I know that the problems in the hood are systemic. I know that my neighborhood is stuck in a sanctioned and fully funded *cycle of poverty, but damn if this place and the people here don't wear me down. Some days it feels like we argue to be louder than the trains that rumble us home. Otherwise our voices will be drowned out and then who will hear us? I'm tired of graffiti being the only way to see someone's mark on the world—the world that consists of this block and maybe the next, nothing farther. There aren't even enough trees to absorb the chaos and breathe out some peace.*

I'll trade you pancakes for peace. I heard that you're writing another book. I can help with that. Let me be your assistant or protégé or official geek sidekick. I can do all the research.

Seriously, some of my best friends are libraries. If there's room in your world for a closeted Puerto Rican baby-dyke from the Bronx, you should write me back. Everybody needs a hand, especially when it comes to fighting the good fight.

Punani Power Forever,
Juliet Milagros Palante

PS: How do you take your coffee? This will help me decide if we're compatible social justice superheroes or not.

PART ONE

WELCOME TO THE BRONX

CHAPTER ONE

WOLVES, FALCONS, AND THE BRONX

"We are born with the power of the moon and the flow of the waves within us. It's only after being commodified for our femaleness that we lose that power. The first step in gaining it back is walking face-first into the crashing seas and daring the patriarchy to stop us."

Raging Flower: Empowering Your Pussy by Empowering Your Mind, Harlowe Brisbane

THERE WAS ALWAYS train traffic ahead of us and that Saturday was no different. The delay between the cell-block-gray train car and my redbrick house on Matilda Avenue, mi casa, was long enough to merit the *Assaulting an MTA Officer Is a Felony* sticker on the wall. Without a heads up, I was sure we'd all be busting heads and windows open on the 2 train to the end of the earth, aka the North Bronx. Any wait period that lasted longer than two songs provoked collective teeth-sucking, eye-rolling, and a shared disgust for the state of New York, public transportation. I always wondered what would happen if the white people didn't all get off at 96th Street. Would it make my commute home to the hood easier? Would the MTA give any more of a damn? Good thing I had a pen, my purple composition notebook, and headphones blasting *The Miseducation of Lauryn Hill* like it was my j-o-b.

The train was elevated after 149th Street and Third Avenue, so for almost one hundred blocks the view of the sky existed only above the train station—but no one ever seemed to look up that far. I'd looked through metal bars my whole entire life just to get a view of both the sidewalk and the sunshine. Past the train, there were clusters of electrical wires and telephone poles that looked ready to burst into flames or fall over from a gust of wind. This was my Bronx: the North Bronx, the split between the Bronx and Westchester County, the difference between the South Bronx and the part of the Bronx that no one ever traveled to.

"We apologize for the inconvenience and thank you for your patience," said the automated white male robot voice used by the MTA. *Thank us for our patience.* Like, save the gratitude and get me home. I was leaving that night for Portland, Oregon, and I still had to finish the mixtape I was making for my girlfriend, Lainie, who was already away at her internship with the College Democrats of America. On top of all that, I had to pack, shower, get ready for my good-bye dinner, come out to my family, and then hopefully still be able to hug my mom so hard that I would feel her on my skin for the whole summer. I didn't have time for the train to be stalled.

"Seven times three is twenty-one, seven times four is twenty-eight." Across from me, a young girl and her mom, both wearing bandanna dresses and head wraps, reviewed times table flash cards. Three dudes stood in the doorway. They bragged about their conquests over "some bitches from last night." When boys talked, it sounded like feral dogs barking. They fiended for attention, were always aggressive, and made me wish I could put them down.

Raging Flower was both book and shield. I pulled it out, sighing mad loud. The main boy gave me a look. Whatever, papi culo. I couldn't even with dudes lately. All they did was talk smack about how good they laid down the pipe. Anytime I ignored them I was both a *bitch* and all of a sudden *too ugly* or *too fat* to get it anyway. Neighborhood dudes sure knew how to slime and shame a girl in one swift move. Reason number five hundred and fifty-one *Raging Flower* was so necessary. Reading helped me gather myself, reminded me that I had a right to be mad. It felt like my body was both overexposed and an unsolved mystery.

"You must walk in this world with the spirit of a ferocious cunt. Express your emotions. Believe that the universe came from your flesh. Own your power, own your connection to Mother Earth. Howl at the moon, bare your teeth, and be a goddamn wolf."

Ferocious cunt. I circled that phrase in neon-purple ink. Was I a ferocious cunt? By tomorrow night, I'd be in Harlowe's home, not on the train in the Bronx. I had planned my escape—chose to come out and run off into the night. What kind of wolf did that make me?

I needed air. I wasn't ashamed of myself. I wasn't ashamed of being in love with the cutest girl on the planet, but my family was my world and my mom was the gravitational pull that kept me stuck to this Earth. What would happen if she let me go? Would my family remain planted to terra firma while I spiraled out and away into the void?

The train lurched a little. The mother-and-daughter duo beside me packed up their flash cards and got off. The train doors closed with a high-pitched two-note signal.

At the corner of 238th Street and White Plains Road in the Bronx, the 5 and 2 trains split ways. I got off the train and stood on the corner, staring at the fork between the elevated train tracks. A bent, corroded metal rainbow, it curved above and beckoned the 5 train in another direction, away from Mount Vernon and into the unknown. But nothing likes to be split in half so when the 5 train hit that bend, sparks flew out and landed like mini-meteors on the sidewalk. The wheels ground hard, metal on metal, and sent out a screech: a torturous yell that could be heard for miles. The sound shredded the fibers of my bones. I felt it in my cavities, heard it in my daydreams.

The sun was setting over the neighborhood. Jamaican men

stood in zigzag patterns on the block, shouting, "Taxi, miss?" No insurance, some without a license, but damn if they didn't get a person where they needed to go. I dipped around them and made a left toward Paisano's Pizza Shop. Black and brown bodies were in full motion. A solid line of people shuffled in and out of the liquor store. It was owned by Mrs. Li. She sent flowers to my uncle Ramon's wake when he died two years ago from cirrhosis. Sirens sounded as ambulances rushed to the nearest emergency to transport the bloody and wounded off to Our Lady of Sacrifice Hospital.

The block was never silent.

We lived loud and hard against a neighborhood built to contain us. We moved like the earth pushing its way through cement sidewalks.

I pulled a dollar out of my pocket. "Robert," I said to the man crouched in between the liquor store and Paisano's. He didn't move. Jacket over his head, he stood still as death. Robert existed in a plume of crystal-white smoke. "Robert," I said again, louder. The jacket shifted, his wide brown eyes peered out from the sleeve.

"Hey, ma," Robert said, not blinking. I put the dollar in his coat pocket. He nodded thanks and pulled the jacket back over his head. I didn't know how else to reach out to this man who'd been smoking crack in between the same two buildings for almost twenty years. Even on Christmas morning, he stood like a sentry dedicated to crack rock. I've asked him if he needs anything. All he's ever asked for was a dollar. That was our relationship. I nodded and kept it moving, past his smoke spot, past the row of cab drivers, past the seventeen-year-old girls snatched up for prostitution and their eighteen-year-old pimps. I was almost home. Good thing too 'cuz those dudes from the train were *still* talking mad loud behind me. Why were they on my ass? My cell phone buzzed in my pocket. Mom.

"Nena!"

I yanked the phone from my ear. "Yes, Momma?"

"Pick up some recao, cilantro, and tomato sauce for the sofrito. Oh, and something sweet. I love you."

"Love you too," I replied, still keeping the phone a safe distance from my ears. I learned a long time ago that you never told Momma she was shouting.

Everything in the Imperial Supermarket was mad suspect. The fruits and vegetables were often moldy. A pack of sesame candy I bought had a roach in it once. And man, I hated buying chicken there too. Every package of meat had a grayish tint to it, and the aisle itself often smelled like blood. But it was the only market we had within walking distance from the house. Momma was going to get her sofrito ingredients. I just had to be diligent and examine everything, as per usual. Figured I'd start with the easy stuff and pick up the tomato sauce first.

The group of bro-dudes from the train found me in the canned vegetable aisle, and one of them said, "Hey, mami, you lookin' good. What's up with your number?"

I didn't answer him. I focused on the sixty-five-cent tomato sauce in my hands. He moved in close behind me.

"I *said* you lookin' mad good," he repeated, his breath harsh on my neck.

My back tensed up. I cracked my middle knuckle with my thumb. Every way this group of man-boys could possibly assault me flashed through my head. A bolt of fear snaked up my spine. I squeezed the can, wishing I was bold enough to clock him with it. I shrugged hard and turned around. His friends had moved in closer, forming a little semicircle around me. Fucking dudes, man.

"Whassup? You too good to say hello?" he asked, smiling.

"I'm gay and not interested," I blurted out.

My whole face went hot. Why did I say that? Jeezus. With fluorescent lights above me, stained white tiles under my feet, and a circle of machismo incarnate around me, there was nowhere to run.

"That's a damn shame. Maybe you just need this good D right here," he said as he grabbed his crotch. He stared at me and gave himself a good up and down stroke. His eyes had a hard glint to them. His tattoo-party tattoos showed from beneath his beater: a lion on his right arm, a crucifix on the left, and the name *Joselys* across his neck.

His boys gave him a pound. They laughed, salivated, and tightened their circle around me. I stepped to the right, and he moved in my way. They laughed again.

A woman pushing a stroller bumped right into him and cleared the way for me. Her three kids clamored through too, breaking their formation. Thank God.

Tomato sauce in hand, I got the rest of the items Mom needed and headed for the checkout line. I kept my arms crossed over my chest best I could. This halter top was half a size too small but made my tetas look amazing. Maybe too amazing. I should have worn my other jeans. Or cargo shorts and a baggy T-shirt. I got way less static when I dressed that way. These tight-ass jeans felt like a reason. Funny, I felt really good when I left the house this morning. I thought I looked cute.

My shame seeped into a frothing rage. The type of rage that can't be let out because then you'd be that crazy chick that killed three dudes in the bodega and no one would even light a damn candle for you. I wondered what dudes like them really expected of girls like me in those situations. Like, did they want me to drop to my knees in the middle of the supermarket and orally worship their Ds? And damn, was it really so wrong to wear something that made me feel confident and sexy-ish? I prayed that la Virgen would get me out of the hood forever.

I'd never said I was gay out loud to anyone I didn't know. What was happening? Was I practicing? God, now those dudes were always going to know me as Dyke on the Block. I imagined that they'd be offering me their "good Ds" forever. I hated that damn Imperial Supermarket. Home, home, I had to get home. Just had to lock the doors behind me and breathe.

My head seemed like the safest place to be most of the time. Maybe that's a bit hyperbolic. I felt safe in my house. Our three-family home on Matilda Avenue was my redbrick fortress, cemented together during the 1930s when someone decided that this would be a good neighborhood for families, specifically Jewish ones. My grandma, Amalia Petalda Palante, moved into this house pregnant with my father and married to her third husband, my grandpa Cano, in 1941. They were legit the only Puerto Ricans on the block. Everyone else was either Jewish or Italian Catholic. But according to her, "A los Judios y los Italianos no les importaba que éramos puertorriqueño. They cared that we kept quiet and made sure the front of our home was clean." I'm sure it didn't hurt that my grandma was hella light-skinned and brought food to her Jewish neighbors on the left and the Italians on the right. Bricks were used to build the house, but it remained standing because of her: because she scrubbed its floors 'til her knuckles bled, because she planted hydrangeas in the front yard as an act of solidarity with her neighbors and because she didn't let anyone tell her that Puerto Ricans couldn't live there.

I climbed the steps to our home and ran into the kitchen. Mom and Grandma Petalda held court over food simmering in calderos and pilones filled with mashed garlic and spices. I dropped the requested items for sofrito onto the counter and kissed them both on the cheeks. They snuggled me. Grandma wore her favorite purple bata and wooden chanclas. My mother was dressed in loose-fitting blue jeans and a souvenir shirt from our last trip to Miami. They were deep in dinner preparation mode, so it was easy to head up to my room. All I wanted to do was finish Lainie's mixtape and be weird with Lil' Melvin, my kid brother. I didn't even care that he was already in my room, slobbering over a book and some TWIX bars.

"Don't ever be an asshole on the streets. Don't ever tell girls that you wanna grab their bodies or corner them in supermarkets while you touch your junk," I said, kissing his chubby cheeks. I stole one of his candy bars and ate it to keep the tears away.

"I'm re-reading my old Animorphs 'cuz Mami threatened to throw them away. So definitely not on team macho-douchebag. Acting like that is uncouth and also gross, sister," Lil' Melvin said, looking up from his book. "Rabid animals get put down. Those types of heathens should, as well. Glad you're home. Time for you to play me those depressing white lady songs that you're adding to Lainie's tape." I hugged him tighter than usual and went to work.

I obsessed over which Ani DiFranco song to add to Lainie's tape. When we first started dating, I had no idea who Ani DiFranco was. Lainie, shocked to baby-dyke hell, made it her mission to convert me. And yo, it took a lot of work. Ani was crazy white girl shit. Her music evoked images of Irish bagpipes and stray cats howling in heat. Her garbled singing voice made my eyes water, and I couldn't ever be sure of what she was singing about. But with enough practice and encouragement from Lainie, I broke down Ani's gay girl code and understood that I too was just a little girl in a training bra trying to figure shit out. Lainie's mixtape needed some Ani. Lots of Ani. Enough Ani to make Lainie think of me all summer long. Five Ani songs in, I added some Queen Latifah, Selena, and TLC for balance. I wrote the names of songs and artists in black Sharpie. The mixtape was for her and only her, but I still played Lil' Melvin every song twice. If he approved, he would hold up the Live-Long-and-Prosper salute. If not, he would give me a theatrical thumbs-down. The idea of leaving him for a summer made my heart ache.

Lil' Melvin believed in the possibility of humans shifting shape but only into other mammals. He also knew months ago that something dark and sad was brewing inside me. I cracked one night after a fight with Lainie and told him that she was my *girlfriend* girlfriend and not just a friend. He put his chubby hand on mine and offered me an unopened package of TWIX. It was the best offering of acceptance a fourteen-year-old boy could provide. He knew tonight was the night I'd planned to let the family know that I was a big old homo. The Animorphs book series entered his life at the right time. A little shape-shifting and fantasy all helped in him being down for me and open to the possibilities of this evening. "You sure about this, sister?"

"It has to be tonight, brother. I'll die if I don't speak up, but they'll kill me if I tell them." I decorated the *i*'s in Lainie's name with black bomb stickers. I'd never made a girl a mixtape before. Lainie was my first girl anything. I'd written a free verse poem about her in the margin of my purple composition notebook.

It worked better in pieces, so I used it as love filler for the liner notes of the mixtape.

"I doubt they'll kill you. It's not like Mom and Dad are cyborgs that'll disintegrate you with death rays." Lil' Melvin slid one TWIX bar into his mouth and measured the other. If they weren't the same size, he'd e-mail Mars and complain about their apparent lack of quality control.

"Duh, brother, but I mean, like, die in my soul." Eighteen songs and one Floetry skit all accounted for on the inside of the CD case. Making a mixtape was way easier than announcing to the world that you're a lesbian. I added more bomb stickers and glued a picture of Lainie and me at Lilith Fair to the back cover.

"Spiritual death is unlikely, Juliet. Your soul would just find another creature to attach itself to and then you'd be a falcon or something. And no one cares if falcons are gay," he said. Lil' Melvin: philosopher, letter writer, concerned citizen, and TWIX coupon hoarder. He rolled over on the bed and pressed his forehead against mine, his soft belly resting on my arm. "Let out your lesbionic truths, sister."

"*Lesbionic.* I'm keeping that word forever." With my hands folded behind my back, I looked up at my Virgin Mary wall clock, and for a second I thought she smiled at me. Lil' Melvin slipped back into his Animorphs coma.

The smiling faces of Selena, Ani DiFranco, TLC, Salma Hayek, and Angelina Jolie gazed down on me from the walls like patron saints on stained-glass windows. Surely they understood why I wanted to come out. They waited confidently, knowing that eventually I'd just have to do it. It'd be nice if one of them could have said something.

Could I really go downstairs and get this demon off my chest? Was it possible to exorcise yourself? I paced back and forth, following the worn path in the dark red carpeting. Prayer always freed people from possession in the movies. What kind of prayer made parents the people you needed them to be? If I went through with it, I wouldn't be able to take any of it back. I wouldn't be able to rewind my life to before Lainie or the movie *Gia*.

I watched Lil' Melvin eat TWIX bars on my bed and read his book. Maybe he was right, maybe Mom and Dad really wouldn't care that there was a gay falcon in the family.

What was left for me to fear anyway? I'd been a nervous wreck since coming home from college. I'd avoided my parents and their questions the same way my parents avoided Jehovah's Witnesses knocking at our door: turn off the lights, turn down the TV. No confrontation; just wait for them to go away.

Dinnertime with the family sent me into panic mode complete with angsty silence and a carnivorous burden; I felt like if I didn't act soon enough, we'd all be consumed by it. And really, all I could do was play awkward, nerdy, fat-girl, closeted-lesbian dodgeball with the questions directed at me.

"No boyfriend, nena?"

"No, too busy with student government. Oohh, are you making arroz con maíz? That's my favorite."

Dodge. My portrayal of the aloof-but-diligent daughter should have been nominated for an Oscar, or at least a Golden Globe. But

ceived pats on the head and plotted ways to get my
into the world. And by plotted ways, I mean, acted
atic scenarios in my head a la Grandma Petalda's
⸻⸻. ʏⁿad to tell them and it had to be now.

My mother, Mariana, and my father, Ernesto, sat at the head
of the table. Grandpa Cano had built it out of red maple wood
before I was born. Grandma Petalda sat wedged in between Lil'
Melvin and me. Across from us were my titi Wepa and my titi
Mellie. Everyone came together for me; this was my good-bye-
for-the-summer dinner. Grandma Petalda and my mom spent
three hours making arroz con maíz, alcapurrias, and bistec encebollado. Leaving the Bronx was cause for celebration. Doing it
by way of an internship with a published author and for college
credits merited an all-your-favorite-foods dinner. No one in my
family knew exactly where Portland, Oregon, was—anywhere
north of the Bronx was "upstate" and outside of New York was
considered "over there somewhere"—but none of that mattered.
Better to make food and have a send-off for the first-born granddaughter, me, Juliet Milagros Palante. This was how we said
good-bye. We ate Puerto Rican food and used outdoor voices to
tell perfectly exaggerated stories while loving so hard it hurt. The
act of eating was a good excuse for me to daydream and wallow
in what-ifs while Titi Wepa's latest cop story filled the air.

She looked each of us in the eyes while gesturing with her fork,
and said, "So I see this asshole rob an old lady by Yankee Stadium
and I go, 'Hey, I'm Officer Palante, get down on the ground now,'
and he says, 'Whatever, bitch,' and takes off running. 'Cuz I'm

a chick, he thought he'd get away. I might have tits, but I've got brains too. And I knew he was gonna go down River Avenue. So I took One Hundred and Sixty-Second and bing boom, I caught him. Got him down on the ground and cuffed his ass. These punks, they don't think ahead. They've only got one move. Not me, baby, my brain has all the moves. Every woman needs a plan A, B, and C," Titi Wepa said. She slapped the table to bring her point home and clinked beer bottles with Titi Mellie.

Her story made me think of my plans. I definitely had an A and a B, but definitely not a C. Plan A: I could sit there and keep eating and when dinner was over I could get in the car with the whole family, go to JFK, say a tearful good-bye at my gate, and just leave. No big gay announcement. Nothing to put this perfect night of mine off balance. Plan B: tell them I like girls and get it all off my chest so that my lungs wouldn't feel so damn tight and just maybe I wouldn't need my inhaler so much. Red pill or blue pill. Down the rabbit hole or remain asleep under the tree, dreamless and stuck. This dinner could be a straight line, if I wanted: no bumps, no bruises, turbulence-free.

Lil' Melvin was reading his Animorphs book under the table. Less than interested in Titi Wepa's latest cop tale and more connected to the idea that he too could one day morph into an animal.

"I bet you wouldn't be so good at chasing falcons, Titi," Lil' Melvin said without looking up from his book.

"You don't chase falcons. You shoot them," Titi Wepa said. "And I've got a nine millimeter for that."

"Boring. Animals don't have guns. Now, Titi, if you could fly and you flew after a falcon and caught it, then that would be the coolest thing ever." Lil' Melvin shoved a forkful of yellow rice and corn into his mouth.

Titi Wepa stared at him, coughing, shaking her head. Dad got her a glass of water. Mom snuck around behind my chair, dropped a second alcapurria onto my plate. "So quiet tonight. Don't be nervous. Idaho isn't so far away." She kissed my cheeks and sat down at the end of the table.

"Oregon, Mom. Portland, Oregon," I said, swallowing pieces of fried plantain and spiced beef. I picked up Lil' Melvin's falcon cue, took a deep breath, and dove into my confession. "So, a group of boys cornered me in the supermarket and told me they had the best you-know-whats in the world. So annoying."

Titi Wepa and Titi Mellie laughed like I'd said something funny. My father looked up from his second plate of food and shook his head. Grandma Petalda sucked her teeth. "Boys today have no class."

"Ay, please, they just don't know how else to say they like you," Titi Mellie said, her neon-pink halter top trying its very best to keep all of her bits under wraps. Titi Mellie's lipstick was the same shade of pink as her halter top, her acrylic-wrapped fingernails, and her hair scrunchie.

"Like me? Oh stop. No boy on the block is talking about his junk to me because he likes me, Juliet, as a person," I said, as my heart beat so damn fast I felt like I was going to faint or die, "Besides, I told him I was a lesbian and he backed off."

I kept my eyes fixed on the image of the Virgin Mary hanging in the kitchen.

Titi Wepa clapped her hands. "Ah, the dyke-n-dodge trick. I've used that so many times. It's a classic. Gotta be careful though, sometimes that revs up their little pingas even more." Titi Mellie nodded her head in agreement as if the wisdom of the ages was being passed on to me.

"Ay, you know we don't use that kind of language at the table," Mom said, standing up again, refilling my father's plate for the third time. Her hips swayed under a Puerto Rican flag apron. "Why didn't you just tell them that you have a boyfriend?"

She had her questions and I had mine. "Why lie? I don't have a boyfriend. And I think I'm a lesbian," I said. My words felt like they were being sucked out of me. They lingered in the air above our red maplewood dining room table, compact and ready to be tucked away. I thought for sure there'd be an earthquake of some kind after my revelation. Nope.

Titi Wepa added some salt to her bistec encebollado. "If not having a boyfriend made people lesbians, Mellie would be running her own parade," Titi Wepa said, her mouth full of food. Lil' Melvin snorted, his laughter bubbling up around the table until even Grandma Petalda joined in.

"Okay, enough of this crazy talk," she said, smiling. Mom raised her glass of sweet pink moscato on ice. "Tonight Juliet is leaving the Bronx and going away for an amazing internship. Let's toast to her college career, her brave spirit, and to making all of us so proud." Everyone around the table raised their glasses and looked at me. In each of their faces, I saw different versions of who I was. This was all happening way too fast. How had I lost my moment?

"Stop. Everyone, just stop," I said as I pushed my plate away. "Thank you for all of this but listen to me. I am gay. Gay, gay, gay. I've been dating Lainie for the past year. This isn't a joke. I've been wondering for weeks how to tell you all, and this is the best I've got. I'm definitely a lesbian."

No one moved or laughed, no glasses clinked. From the window, the sounds of the 2 and 5 trains screeching away from their shared track filtered into the dining room. Grandma Petalda was the only one still eating. I set free the elephant, the falcon, or whatever kind of animal spilled its truth onto dining room tables. Was this what ferocious cunts did? I didn't feel ferocious. The smoldering discomfort that rose in my chest was humidity—thick, oppressive humidity.

There was nowhere to look. Titi Wepa polished off another beer. Titi Mellie checked the length of her acrylic nails. Mom stared at me from across the table.

"It's this book, isn't it? This book about vaginas has you messed up in the head and confused," she said, looking past me, anywhere but at me. Her voice heavy but not angry. My father reached out for her hand and held it.

"No, it's not *Raging Flower*. I love Lainie. It's never felt like this with a boy," I said. Tears betrayed the tiny bit of strength in my voice. Lil' Melvin bowed his head low, his cheeks flushed. He nudged his knee into mine and kept it there. I pushed my plate of food aside. Mom and I stared at each other, and I felt like I was falling.

"But, Juliet," she said, "you've never had a boyfriend, so how would you know? All you know are these neighborhood boys. You haven't given any of the boys at your college a chance. You might like Lainie but it's not the same thing. I promise you that."

"Love. I love her. You don't know anything about my feelings."

"I know you better than you think I do, and this isn't you, Juliet."

Mom got up from her seat, pushed her chair in, and walked upstairs to her bedroom. No door slam, no stomping feet on the stairs. She ghosted and left us at the dining room table without a word.

It was 8:00 p.m., and my plane was scheduled to take off from JFK at 11:30. I wondered if it would become a one-way trip.

Grandma Petalda cleared the dishes and put food in glass containers, ending my good-bye dinner. Titi Mellie gave me a quick hug and told me that a good boyfriend is hard to find but that I'd grow out of this lesbian thing. Lil' Melvin exited the dining room to play *Final Fantasy*. My father kissed my cheek and left the table to go talk to my mother. All I heard from upstairs was unintelligible whispers that almost became shouts.

Titi Wepa and I sat across from each other. I'd never seen her so still. Wepa's wild brown curls were gelled back into a severe cop-style ponytail. She studied me, her dark brown eyes meeting mine. "Okay, lesbian, it's time to take you to the airport. Get your stuff, let's load up the car."

The house felt too small for me. My father emerged from the bedroom and helped bring down my bag. Still no sign or sound from Mom. Dad's face was gray like worn asphalt. Tension lines in the corner of his eyes conveyed grief, stress, sadness, something other than his usual men-don't-show-their-feelings type of face. After loading my gear into Titi Wepa's Thunderbird, he held me. It was the longest hug I'd ever received from him. I wondered what they had said about me behind their closed door. Grandma Petalda stood in the doorway; she beckoned me over.

"You are what you are, Juliet. You are my blood, my first-born granddaughter. I love you like the seas love the moon," Grandma Petalda said, pulling me into her soft belly. "You will be back. This is your home. Now, go say good-bye to your mother."

I was about to argue with her, say something like, "I can't come back here, Grandma" or "She doesn't want me anymore"—something final and dramatic. But I checked myself. I saw our family in her eyes; she wasn't throwing me away. I kissed Grandma's cheeks, smelled the adobo still on her skin, and felt waves of Grandpa Cano flow through her. She released me, and I ran up the stairs to my parents' bedroom.

I made it to the door, raised my hand to knock, and then stopped. My mom was in there, and she wasn't making any effort to come to me. Maybe she didn't want me barging in on her, maybe she didn't want to see my face. I slumped to the floor, feeling like I'd destroyed everything.

"Mom," I called out through the closed door. "I'm sorry I ruined dinner. I didn't know how else to tell you about Lainie. I didn't know how else to say any of it," I said, my chest wheezing. "Titi Wepa's taking me to the airport now. I love you so much, Mom." I took a puff from my yellow inhaler. The small screech of release it made filled the air around me. I waited, listening for movement, for any sound of life reaching out from the other side of that door. The hallway walls were lined with pictures of our family. Pictures from the day my mom and dad got married in City Island hung in wooden frames. My dad rocked a short trimmed Afro and full beard with his baby-blue ruffled tuxedo. My mom looked like a statue of the Virgin Mary; she was covered in lace and purity, smiling like she knew in that moment what the rest of her life would be like and it was already everything she'd imagined.

From under the door, Mom slid a worn photo of us into the hallway. In the photo she held me in her arms, the Hudson River behind us. My arms were outstretched toward the sun. I turned the picture over and in black ink she'd written *Mariana and Juliet, 1987, Battery Park*.

"Whenever I look at you, I see that baby. You'll always be that baby to me, so forgive me if I can't accept what you've said tonight," Mom spoke, still on the other side of the door.

"Aren't you going to hug me good-bye?" I waited for her answer. I just knew if she'd open the door and wrap her arms around me, it would all be okay.

"Call us when you get to Iowa so we know you're safe."

"Portland, Mom."

"You know what I mean." I heard her get up from the floor and walk over to the bed she shared with my father. I heard the bed frame creak and knew she was lying down. She wasn't going to come to me and I couldn't go to her. I held the picture of us against my chest and rested my forehead against the door for a moment. *Dear God, please help us.* I walked downstairs and away from my mother.

Titi Wepa's Thunderbird hummed in the driveway; Bon Jovi's "You Give Love a Bad Name" blasted from its speakers. I climbed in and took a deep breath. A TWIX bar slapped against my shoulder. "Don't worry, sister," said Lil' Melvin, getting into the backseat. "The Force is strong with you." I kissed his chubby fingers and said, "You're my falcon-brother soulmate weirdo."

Titi peeled out of the driveway, windows down, her ponytail swinging in the wind. Our redbrick house grew smaller and smaller in the rearview mirror as we sped off to the airport. Titi Wepa ran a red light, blessed herself, and kept her foot on the gas pedal. After a few blocks, I couldn't even hear the trains rumbling anymore.

CHAPTER TWO

LA VIRGEN TAKES THE WHEEL

TITI WEPA DROVE super fast, like a surge of adrenaline released into the bloodstream. Each lane of traffic was an algorithm for her to solve using agility and the need to be faster than everyone else. As a proud, shield-carrying member of the NYPD, this was how she'd been taught to drive in order to save lives; no alternative existed, so we flew. The only thing out of the ordinary was her silence; Titi's lack of one-liners and profanity-laden nicknames for the drivers around us created a deep void. I wondered if she was repulsed by my confession or if she thought I was a coward for spilling and running. Lil' Melvin sat quietly in the back, nighttime erasing his ability to read. He was also out of TWIX bars. I kept my eyes on the sky and looked for the moon.

When we were little kids, Mom and Dad took us on massive summer road trips to visit Titi Penny, Mom's only sister, in Vero Beach, Florida. We'd drive down, our minivan divided into two sections: one for sleeping and the other for everything else. Lil' Melvin and I fought over the last cookie in the snack bag while trying to outsmart each other in games of I Spy. Dad drove the entire way, focused on the highway numbers and how many miles he could squeeze out of each gallon of gas. But the best part—the part we'd beg for—was when Mom told us stories about her and Titi Penny spending summers in Puerto Rico. Their mom, my grandma Herencia, sent them to stay with La Perla, her sister. Mom and Titi Penny chased lizards and hunted for coquis. They practiced arching their eyebrows to the heavens with La Perla's makeup and learned the drinking songs that the male suitors sang to their great-aunt in the moonlight. Puerto Rico seemed so far away, almost made up, but somehow the stories got us to Florida faster. The car rides and all Mom's stories gave us a loving transition into our summer adventures.

But this one, this joyless, motherless ride to the airport was nothing like those trips to Florida. As we sped along the Bronx River Parkway, the moon had still not shown itself. I wished it would emerge and offer a blessing. My heart ached, so I texted Lainie even though I knew she probably wouldn't reply until tomorrow. She'd started her internship in D.C. with the College Democrats a week ago, and we hadn't found a moment to talk. My phone buzzed against my thigh, I flipped it open hoping it was Lainie. Instead it was my cousin Ava:

Yo prima, heard you're a big old out loud lesbiana. Viva la Revolución. Call me.

Ava made me laugh. Everything with her was "Viva la Revolución," even small shit like Pop-Tarts coming out of the toaster on time and catching the bus. But damn, word traveled quick, like the bochinche plague. Mom must have called Titi Penny and oh my God, now the whole family was going to know about me, and what if Portland became the only safe place for me in the world?

Titi Wepa swerved across three lanes to catch the exit for JFK. Her tires screeched hard as she pulled into the Southwest departing flights drop-off zone. Around us taxicabs and shuttle vans loaded and unloaded hordes of baggage-laden souls. Everyone traveling to or coming from the ends of the earth in search of family, friends, self-discovery, and a shared desire to be anywhere but where the hell they had been.

Titi Wepa didn't move. She stared hard at me and said, "You were born in the middle of the night on a Monday, September sixth, nineteen eighty-three. I'll never forget that day as long as I'm living and breathing. My brother came out of the delivery room—first time in my life I'd ever seen him cry—and told us you were a baby girl." Titi wiped her eyes. "I've loved you from that moment and I always will. I don't care if you're gay or if you shave your head or . . ."

"Or if you become a falcon," offered Lil' Melvin from the backseat.

Titi Wepa laughed. "Or if you become a motherfucking falcon. I'm your titi and nothing will ever change my love for you. Now get the fuck out of my car." Her black mascara ran down her cheeks.

I reached over and pulled her into a tight hug. "I love you too, Titi. I love you times infinity." She kissed my cheek and left a dark red lipstick stain. I took a deep breath, inhaling her Cool Water perfume and the new car smell that emanated from the blue, tree-shaped air freshener. I wanted to bottle all of her up and take her with me. I got out of the Thunderbird and grabbed my purple-and-black Adidas duffel bag from the trunk.

Lil' Melvin popped out behind me, chocolate still crusted to the corners of his mouth. My brother, my baby, a gray-eyed boy version of me, I took him all in at the curb. We faced each other, and he pressed a brown paper bag into my chest.

"Don't open this until you need to, sister," he said, shifting his weight from one foot to the other.

Confidential was written on the bag in black marker. "Okay, weirdo," I said, grabbing him by his side chub. "Take care of everyone and mostly yourself. Love you." I ushered him into Titi's Thunderbird and shut the door behind him. Waving, I watched them drive off into the throng of vehicles. Once I lost them amid all the other red taillights, I stuffed Lil' Melvin's brown paper bag into my backpack. I stepped through the doors, trying not to cry, feeling both wrecked and excited.

Every night that week, I had dreamed about Portland. Extended, epic, Technicolor dreams where white lesbians appeared like faeries to welcome me as I landed in the middle of a lush forest clearing. They draped wreaths of Oregon grapes and flowers around my head, my hips, and all over my body. The faeries gathered in a circle around me and swayed in rhythm to the trees and the winds. The white angels sang in harmony about couscous cures for all ailments and aligning our periods with the ancient cycles of the moon.

I'd stood there, staring, and tried to use my phone to call Ava so she could swoop down and bring her brown revolution to save me. Wide-eyed, I'd lit a cigarette, looking around to see if I could catch a taxi or something. My phone never worked, and I couldn't call Ava or hail a cab in the woods of my dreams. I'd wake up and peek over at the map of the United States on my wall, just to make sure Portland was a real place. I mean, if no one I knew had ever been there or even heard of it, then I had a right to wonder whether Portland, Oregon, existed or not, right?

Coming out had taken over my brain space these last few days, but before, when I had a little extra breathing room, all I thought about was how Portland was going to be different from the Bronx. I assumed that I'd have to go vegetarian or at least limit my meat intake to chicken and bacon, the most under-standable can't-live-without-them types of meat. Harlowe wrote about not eating meat in *Raging Flower*.

"Red meat comes from what the patriarchy calls 'the indus-trialization of food' but in reality, it's the separation of humanity from their own food production and from Mother Earth. It's also wholly dependent on the enslavement of other individuals and animals. That terror and disregard for life seeps into our souls and bodies with every bite. It's an absolute poison to the pussy. Don't believe me? Go down on a meat-eater and tell me if you can't taste the sadness."

I definitely couldn't "taste the sadness," but I'd never hooked up with a vegetarian, so I couldn't really compare and contrast. *Vegetarian* was another word that I couldn't connect to. The idea of living with Harlowe in Portland pushed me to create room for ideas outside of my everyday life. Like, anything was possible in that space with her; if she wanted me to be vegetarian, I would. If she wanted me to howl at the moon with a bowl of period blood on my head, I'd at least give it a try. Things that I'd normally laugh at became possibilities from the moment I began reading *Raging Flower*. Portland could be anything I wanted it to be.

I imagined that Portland would be a place without bullshit. No piles of garbage lining the blocks, fermenting in the hot sun. No doped-up hoodrats trying to fight each other on the train. No young dudes trying with winks and hollers to stick their things inside every girl who passed by. No one getting shot on the street by cops. Just groups of young, gay weirdos being able to chill and be free without hassle from anyone. Yeah, everyone would probably be white, but white people seemed to totally be okay with gay stuff and just being different in general. It had to be a utopia if Harlowe lived and wrote *Raging Flower* there. It had to be more soul-affirming than the fucking Bronx, right?

Sitting at gate 14, I texted Ava back:

No revolution here, just sad lesbian me leaving on a jet plane. Life is weird. Call you when I get to Portland.

Still no message from Lainie. Her mixtape was packed in my duffel bag. Her parents didn't know she was gay or that we were in love. They just thought we were super-close new college friends.

I'd wanted to say good-bye to Lainie in her twin bed: late at night, deep inside of her, with my lips pressed against her collarbone. But no. Lainie felt it'd be inappropriate and a little odd if I slept over the night before she left for D.C. Instead, we went shopping at Banana Republic—the only store she ever shopped at—so that she could have a new wardrobe for her political summer. After the mall, we said good-bye in secret. Seated across from each other at a greasy, podunk Hartsdale diner that hadn't changed its appearance since the 1970s, our elbows resting on paper placemats advertising local businesses. We shared an order of fries. Lainie dipped a french fry into a puddle of ketchup. "Scenes just aren't a thing in my family," she said. "It's not like we'd be able to kiss and be cute at the airport, like in front of my parents. Please don't be upset."

"I'm not upset, Lanes," I replied, touching her foot with mine. "I get it. I'm just going to miss your face. That's all."

Her heart felt far away from mine, like they were beating in different time zones or different dimensions of love. I should have asked for her to fight for us and to shed some fucking tears over a summer apart. If I was gonna spill my truth to my family, then so should she. But I didn't have those words—didn't even know I wanted those things—until after she was gone.

All I wanted was her in my arms all night, but the clanking of dishes, the smell of stale coffee, and the absolute hetero-vibe of Westchester kept me so aware of how unattainable that was. Where could our type of love grow anyway?

After dinner, we made out in the parking lot, in the backseat of her mom's Corolla. Kissing was its own good-bye. Her lips found my lips. Our love was safe if we kept it on our tongues and in between our teeth. When we came up for air, Lainie said, "Let's make feminist, power-lesbian mixtapes and fall in love all over again."

"There's absolutely nothing else worth doing, babe," I replied, holding her hand over my heart. She smelled like all the reasons I didn't want to say good-bye, not even for a summer.

Portland, Lainie, Mom, Harlowe. Harlowe, Portland, Lainie, Mom. I was sitting at the airport, waiting for my flight, and those four elements of my life banged around in my head, fighting for space. Mom didn't hug me good-bye. Lainie still hadn't called me back. Flying off into the unknown, alone and feeling so raw, pushed my anxiety into overdrive. My chest tightened up. I took deep breaths and heard a familiar wheeze in my lungs. Airlines should assign buddies to everyone flying solo for the first time. Fumbling in my bag for my inhaler, I checked my phone again. Still nothing.

"Now boarding Flight 333, New York to Portland, Oregon," called the Southwest gate attendant, her voice snapping me back to earth. I called Lainie again. It went straight to voice mail, so I left a message.

"Sweet babe," I said, smiling big despite my anxiety, "I'm about to board my flight. Lainie, I know we're gonna change the world. Like on some fuck-the-patriarchy-forever type of love revolution. Call me tomorrow. Te quiero mucho."

We were going to be Thelma and Louise, minus the part where we drive off a cliff. Like Thelma and Louise if they were renegade feminist lesbians who had totally taken women's studies classes on purpose. Lainie and I were going to do the damn thing.

The takeoff terrified me. I prayed to la Virgen. It wasn't something I did all the time; showing reverence was one thing but reaching out to her was something way more sacred. I was fucking scared. I needed some all-powerful woman to tell me everything was going to be okay. I closed my eyes and whispered the prayer I learned as a kid, the one I'd hoped she'd written for us: "Hail Mary full of grace, the Lord is with thee. Blessed art thou among women. Blessed is the fruit of thy womb, Jesus. Holy Mary Mother of God, pray for us sinners now and at the hour of our death."

With or without hugs or sweet words from Lainie, I was off into the world, off to see this Portland, this Harlowe. I slept on the shoulder of Mary: a deep, warm sleep. No dreams and no wheezing lungs.

PART TWO

YOU HAVE NOW ARRIVED IN PORTLAND, OREGON

CHAPTER THREE

THE PUSSY LADY

HARLOWE. HARLOWE. HARLOWE. The excitement of finally meeting her had built up so deep inside me. I sat in the PDX baggage claim, waiting for her, itching to see her face. I stared at my watch and counted seconds. I walked around the conveyor belt. Scenarios of what Harlowe would be like flashed through my mind.

In one version, Harlowe would arrive with a pack of Amazonian dykes, covered in war paint and body glitter, chanting lines from *Raging Flower*. She'd march toward me and lift me to the heavens, presenting me to the goddesses. In another, I imagined Harlowe seeing me from across the crowded airport and leaving me there. I'd beg the airline to let me fly home, back to where I really belonged. With each scenario, I attempted to assuage the building anxiety in my chest that Harlowe might have forgotten to pick me up. It was already thirty minutes past our designated meeting time. Each minute that ticked by made me doubt my decision to come here.

Why did I decide to travel across the country over a few e-mails and love for a book?

What did I really know about Harlowe Brisbane? She was the woman *DYKE* magazine referred to as the "Pussy Lady," and she was the woman who invited me into her home and shouldn't I have asked a million other questions before coming? What if she was one of those people who was capable of inducing a riot or commanding the attention of a flock of feminists at a rally but couldn't handle the normal shit, like picking up their dry-cleaning or a scared Puerto Rican baby-dyke from the airport?

Thirty minutes. In thirty minutes, I'd lost myself to anxiety and daydreams and nearly sprang out of my flesh when Harlowe appeared five inches from my face and asked, "Hey, are you Juliet?"

My mouth opened, but the words I was going to say evaporated. Every clever and adorable, awkward thing I'd prepared vanished.

"Harlowe?" I asked, mouth dry, heartbeats eclipsing all other brain functions.

She nodded fast, smiling big. Harlowe wrapped her arms around me and pulled me into her chest. The scent of patchouli and tobacco enveloped my nostrils.

"Oh, Juliet, you're here," Harlowe said, still holding me. She kissed my cheek and hugged me tight enough to lift me off the ground. "Sweet girl, your aura smells so fresh," she said, pausing to take a look at me.

Harlowe kept her palms on my shoulders. We admired each other for a moment. Her bright flaming red hair was cut short and her eyes were a deep blue. Taking her all in quelled my anxiety and gave me a moment to take a deep fucking breath.

"I've told the whole world about you," she said. "And thank goddess for your sweet-smelling aura because otherwise this entire experience might be way more difficult, you know?"

Never in my life had I been excited about having an aura that smelled good. Who knew they even had a smell?

She led us out of the airport. We walked into the parking lot under an inky-black sky littered with stars. The way she held my arm reminded me of the way my mom had walked me to my dorm room on college move-in day. She led me with a gentle directness, with the purpose of taking me to something new. This moment with Harlowe felt like that; I ached for my mom.

Harlowe's pickup truck was Pepto-Bismol pink and covered with hand-painted daisies. I stared at it, feeling the magnitude of the distance between the Bronx and me. Vehicles like this didn't exist in my neighborhood. I kept thinking of things to say to Harlowe; thinking, not speaking. Absorbing the moment was more important: this sky, this truck, all the things that felt so different. I wanted to always remember what it felt like to be next to her.

"Did you notice that there's no moon tonight?" Harlowe asked. She started up the truck.

Inside there were stacks of envelopes addressed to Harlowe, bits of letters, crumpled up pieces of paper.

"I was wondering where it went," I said, peering up at the sky from the passenger side. I hadn't seen the moon in the Bronx either. I wondered if my family could see the same sky.

"Yes, no moon, which means that you've brought in a new lunar phase," Harlowe said, navigating the twisting lanes of airport road. She drove stick shift while smoking a hand-rolled cigarette. "Like, at this very moment, the sun is shining so bright that it keeps us from seeing the moon. You must be the sun, Juliet."

Harlowe slapped my knee in excitement, and I started to cry. How was I the sun when I couldn't even be the daughter? An empty highway stretched before us. I gripped the yellow inhaler in the pocket of my faded blue jeans. I couldn't breathe.

"Oh my god, I didn't mean to hit you, lunar cycles excite me and then I get all handsy . . ." Harlowe searched for the right words.

"No," I gasped. "You're fine. I've never done anything like this, and I've never been this far away from home." I admitted all this between wheezing breaths. Harlowe reached across me and rolled down the window. "I literally just came out to my family before I left for the airport and, like, my mom didn't say good-bye and now you're telling me that I'm the sun."

"Breathe, girl," she said, her palm once again on my shoulder. "New moon means you get a fresh chance." Harlowe touched my cheek, still puffing on her cigarette. I took a puff from my inhaler.

We drove under the moonless sky. The quiet between us was soft, no pressure. I let out some of the bits about my mom. Shared words with Harlowe about how maybe I was an emotional runaway and how one of my secret hopes for this trip was to find my real bravery, to feel it when I walk and not just when I send e-mails to strangers.

"Can we listen to the mixtape I made for my girlfriend?" I asked, digging into my book bag. "Because of what you said about creating a female-centric world in *Raging Flower*, I only put chicas on it." I wiped my cheeks and showed Harlowe the mixtape.

"Play it. Thank goddess, the only singing man I can deal with is Bruce Springsteen and that's because my dad grew up in Jersey," she said. Harlowe pushed the CD into the opening and Queen Latifah's melodic voice swept in on rumbly speakers. *Just another day, living in the hood, just another day around the way.*

With the windows rolled down, everything floated away into guitar riffs, beat drops, and her asking me the names of newer female musicians. All the weird self-doubt and wheezy feelings in my lungs smoothed over and I felt calm.

We pulled up to Harlowe's house well past the witching hour. The cypress tree in front of her home glowed in the dim light of the streetlamp. *America is an enormous frosted cupcake in the middle of millions of starving people* was written in chalk on her front steps. Her yard swirled with hydrangeas, rosebushes, overgrown sunflowers, and grass gone wild.

Harlowe lifted my bag off my shoulder, led me through the

garden, and up her chalk-covered steps. She paused in front of her door and put her hand on the frame.

"Blessed house, thank you for shelter," she said as she tapped the doorframe three times and stepped inside the house. Her actions made me wonder if she had spirits in the house. I tapped the doorframe three times too, just in case.

It floored me that the doors weren't locked. Anyone could have run up into this white lady's house and stolen everything. There weren't bars on the windows. Harlowe didn't even have a big scary dog. I'd never gone to someone's home and not seen them unlock it. My dad locked the door to the house when we were sitting in front of it getting some fresh air "just in case."

It was late and I was tired; I couldn't even process the extent of her hippieness.

We walked up a set of narrow steps and into her attic. Wooden beams stretched along the sloped ceiling. She plopped my bag down on the floor next to a queen-sized mattress with a lamp and a small bookshelf at its side. Harlowe walked toward it.

"This is your spot, sweet human," she said, turning to me and yawning. "It's so late that it's too early for anything else but sleep, right? We'll talk about all the things in a few hours. Welcome, Juliet." Harlowe hugged me again and left me there in the attic.

I sat on the mattress and looked around. I'd made it to Portland and was inside Harlowe Brisbane's home. Holy shit.

CHAPTER FOUR

CLUELESS

SOFT GRAY LIGHT fell in from the windows. It felt like I'd just gone to sleep. Still under blankets, I checked the time. 11:15 a.m. Well at least it wasn't the butt crack of dawn. The attic stairs creaked and I wished Harlowe's attic had a door. I fished for my tank top in the blankets and slipped it on. I poked my head out from under the white comforter just in time to peep Harlowe's red hair making its way up the stairs. She stopped at my bed in a deep squat like someone who's never had to balance the weight of her belly on her knees.

"Good morning, sweet human," she said. Harlowe's big blue eyes caught my sleepy browns. I reached for the joint in between her callused fingers and took a pull.

I coughed hard on the exhale.

"Wait, don't you have asthma?" Harlowe asked. She turned to me, all neck and eyes, like a pigeon on the stoop.

"I do indeed," I said. I took another hit and didn't cough. "But weed helps me feel less anxious, so I trade a little cough for some Zen, know what I'm saying?"

"Boy, do I," Harlowe said. She stood up fast and spun around. "Juliet, I've been listening to your mixtape all morning, and it got me thinking about your internship. And I finally know what you're going to help me with." She looked at me with wide eyes and this grin, this let's-make-a-batch-of-vegan-cookies-and-be-best-friends-forever grin. I laughed but felt a twinge in my chest. We'd planned this almost three months in advance and she'd only figured out what I was going to do this morning?

She said, "Your mixtape is all songs by women. All women come from faeries, goddesses, warriors, and witches, Juliet. But we don't know anything about the women who birthed those women. We don't know who our ancestral mothers are. I want you to help me find them. We have to tell their stories before they disappear forever amid all the violent and whitewashed history of men. My next book is all about reclaiming our mystical and political lineage. And you, Juliet, you're going to be the faerie hunter, minus the guns or actual hunting."

"You really think all women come from faeries?" I was a little blazed but not "faerie hunter" blazed. I wasn't even sure if I was fully awake.

"Of course I believe that, Juliet. I mean, where else would we come from?" Harlowe responded. "Certainly not from the rib of some 'fraidy-cat snitch named Adam."

"Ooohh!" I howled. 'Fraidy-cat snitch.

I pulled out my purple composition notebook and wrote down her words. This was my internship and her second book. Last thing I wanted to do was mess up.

"How does one go on a faerie hunt?" I asked.

"Well, first, you need clues, and I've got a box full of them," she said.

I wondered what in the world of half-baked hippie white lady she was talking about. Clues.

Did she really have clues for this? Was I just a little too high all of a sudden?

Harlowe stood up and walked toward the corner of the room. The dust of incense sticks covered the floor in a light film. Harlowe dragged a box from against the far wall and left it at my feet. She went about the room, lighting candles and incense. Her cardboard box was dented and stuffed with scraps of paper. They'd been ripped out of lined notebooks, pulled from magazines; names were written on all of them. Mixed in with the fragments of paper were pictures of women. This box looked like the inside of Harlowe's pickup truck.

"These are clues to the lives of our unknown and underappreciated women. This box of wonderful shit is the beginning of a masterpiece," Harlowe said, tapping my knee. "I'm in no rush, though. Discoveries are not lightning quick."

I sifted through some of the names and pictures, in awe of the sheer number of them. Who were these women? I didn't recognize any of their faces. How could I be nineteen and not know any of them? I'd always done all my homework, read all the books assigned in school, and yet, here was a world full of possibly iconic ladies I knew nothing about.

"Where did all the names come from?" I asked.

"Anytime I read something about a fierce woman I'd never heard of or came across a bold woman I wanted to know more about, I either wrote down her name or ripped out whatever pages mentioned her," Harlowe answered. "I stuffed all my findings into this box. I knew one day it would come together. I didn't know how, but I knew it would. And here you are."

Harlowe stood up. She slid into a warrior pose, hands clasped together over her head, one leg bent, the other extended behind her. "Come to me with questions at any time, but right now let this sink into your skin and your intrepid spirit. Get a feel for how you want to start and go with it. I trust you," Harlowe said as she exhaled to the heavens.

Before I could think of anything else to say, she left. I looked at the box and reached for my inhaler. Panic always started in my lungs first and then spread to nervous fingers, knuckles that had to be cracked, and a heartbeat that wouldn't slow. During these moments of panic at home, I'd find Mom's lap and rest my head in it. She'd run her fingers through my hair and calm all the internal noise. It was noise that told me I wasn't good enough or I wouldn't have enough time to finish whatever I was working on. Here in Harlowe's attic, the noise was still the same, but I was on my own.

The box full of unorganized notes and the unstructured independent research time were a surprise. The logical part of my brain knew it'd be okay, but that wasn't the part in charge. I was all Virgo and no clarity. I needed some control over my environment or a good head rub. Maybe a file cabinet with items listed in alphabetical order.

I was laid back on the outside but a nervous, asthmatic panic baby on the inside. This wasn't how I'd imagined our working relationship. I thought that I'd be at her side and we'd fight patriarchal crime together, like some type of intergenerational, interracial Cagney and Lacey. But this busted-up cardboard box full of women-centric raffle tickets and some heartfelt words about having faith in me doing this on my own? That was my internship? How were we going to be the greatest writing and research team the world has ever known?

Why hadn't she prepared something solid for me to do? She'd been on the call with me and my women's studies professor, Dr. Jean. We'd all discussed how this internship would "advance my understanding of feminism as a tool for social change" and writing bomb-ass books about pussy. And it's not like she didn't know about the research paper I had to write so, like, again, why was she acting so brand-new? Wasn't this important to her too?

My mind raced with questions. Perhaps I could work around this. Witches and warriors and faeries were fun things, right? It's not like I was hanging out with bougie young Democrats all summer. I didn't know how Lainie was able to make that commitment. It seemed like a slow, boring death to me. This thing with Harlowe could be great. Maybe. I took a pull off my inhaler and still couldn't relax. My lungs expanded and the wheeze lifted, but my hands twitched. I opened one of the windows and crawled out of the attic onto a small ledge. The warm Portland sunlight washed over my skin.

I dialed Titi Wepa. Her ringback tone was that Lisa Lisa and Cult Jam song "Can You Feel the Beat."

"Juliet," Titi Wepa answered, coughing and shouting into the phone. "I was just about to call you. You doin' okay out there?" Freestyle music blasted in the background over honks and sirens. Titi Wepa was always driving. The world needed her to be in constant motion, for there was always someone in distress, someone who needed a little Wepa.

"I'm good, Titi. Just chillin' in Harlowe's attic," I answered, making no attempts to hide my melancholy.

"That woman has you in her attic? Has it been checked for rats?" Titi Wepa asked in her Seven on Your Side wannabe-news-anchor voice. "I mean, because you know if anything happens to you up there, I swear to God, my lawyer will be calling that lady up so quick her fucking head will spin. You know me, J. I don't play." The sounds of traffic in the Bronx filtered through her end of the phone and into my ears.

"No, Titi, her attic is mad cool. It's filled with candles and books. Mad comfortable, and rat-free," I assured her, smiling a little. "That's not what's bothering me."

"Talk to me, J. What's going on?" Titi Wepa lowered her music and told some other driver to "stuff it out his ass."

"Harlowe told me what exactly she needs me to do and it's

impossible," I said. "This morning, she pulled out this box with all these little papers about women and I gotta document who they are and that's, like, my whole internship. And yo, I mean these are scraps and random pictures of women that no one's ever heard of and I'm magically supposed to find them," I whined into the phone.

Titi Wepa coughed again hard. It turned into a coughing fit. She'd been coughing like that after she spent a few months as a first-responder at Ground Zero. I didn't say anything. She hated the attention her cough generated.

Titi Wepa caught her breath and said, "So this lady, Harlowe, breaks down what you gotta do and now you don't wanna do it?" Wepa asked with a mix of attitude and incredulity.

"Titi, Harlowe's asking me to work with scraps and faeries and weird shit . . . C'mon," I pleaded, trying to put her back on my side where she belonged.

"No, no, you said your piece," Titi Wepa said, stopping me. "J, you're the one who flew all the way over to wherever the fuck you are without having discussed this with her beforehand."

"Portland. I'm in Portland, Oregon," I muttered. Thick gray clouds rolled across the sky.

"Whatever. Listen, you're the one who tracked her down and asked her for this opportunity, and I know you get anxious and wheezy—you've been like that since you were a kid—but you can't let that stop you. Juliet, it's just a puzzle and there are a million ways to solve it. So find your own and get it together. Call me if you need another kick in the cojones. I love you,

Juliet," said Titi Wepa. Our conversations always ended with Titi Wepa telling me she loved me in her tough Bronx accent.

"Love you too, Titi," I replied, trying to maintain some control over the emotions flooding my insides. Tears welled up in my eyes. The unconditional love in her voice leveled me.

Titi Wepa could always love-bully me into being calm. She and my mom existed in this polar opposite energy field. Wepa was the fire starter, the one who stood in your face and pounded her fists on the table until her truth was heard and her love was felt. Mom rubbed worried heads, found nervous hands under blankets, and held them while she cooked pots of rice and beans. I should have called Mom, but I was afraid that her bedroom door would still be closed.

Titi Wepa was right. I crawled back into the attic. I opened the box and picked out a scrap with the name Lolita Lebrón on it. I had no idea who she was, but I liked her name. I grabbed another name from the box. *Sophia/Wisdom* was written on green construction paper without a last name. Maybe it would all be okay? With Mom and Wepa in my heart, Lolita and Sophia in my hands, I decided to be brave and embrace what I came here to find, even though I had no idea what that was.

CHAPTER FIVE

SIN ROPA

SOPHIA AND LOLITA were out there in the world somewhere. I wasn't convinced that I could find out who they were, but I had to try. I had to do something that didn't involve thinking about the lack of phone calls from Mom or Lainie. I hoped that diving into this world of unknown women would help me forget the women in my life who were absent. I pressed the slips of paper with their names into my composition notebook, stuffed it into my book bag, and descended the attic steps.

In Harlowe's kitchen I was confronted by a naked Filipino dude, about my age, maybe a little older. He stood in the window frame, so tall that his spine bent like a crescent moon to fit. His presence startled me. Was I still in Harlowe's home, or had the dimensions switched on me? Wishbone thin, his arms and legs were long and poised to move. He turned and held my gaze from the windowsill. I'd never seen a flaccid penis before in real life. It reminded me of the fat slugs that would emerge after heavy rainfall and slide along our driveway at home. I wondered if they all looked like that. Were they supposed to be so thick and rubbery looking? I realized I was staring at him, right *there*. I blushed hard and turned my face away. I was caught between embarrassed laughter and nervousness.

"Phen, did you ask Juliet if she's okay with your nudity?" Harlowe called from somewhere.

Phen gazed down at me without altering his humorless expression. "Juliet, are you okay with my nudity?" he asked.

I blinked first and looked away. Well, at least I was in the right dimension. "I'm good, yo. Be as naked as you wanna be," I said, walking around him to fill my water bottle at the sink.

"You could be naked and free too, Juliet," Phen offered. "You must first let go of your internalized fear of nudity and the societal pressures placed upon women to have perfect figures. The choice is yours." He grabbed an apple from the table and chomped into it.

"My internalized fear of nudity?" I asked. "I didn't know that I had one. So you're the naked guy and the judgmental guy all in one?" I folded my arms and looked at him hard.

Footsteps padded into the kitchen where the naked Filipino and the unimpressed Puerto Rican were having a stare down. Harlowe breezed in wearing a Big Bird–yellow ultra-fluffy robe. Her feet were bare, and she carried a coffee mug that read *Praise Witches*. "Phen, I'm feeling the energy in this room and the goddesses are telling me that your naked phallus is disrupting our ovarian flow. Now if today were Wednesday, I'm sure your phallic energy would be in sync with our yonic organisms, but it's Sunday and that sure as hell ain't the case. Maybe cover up just a little?"

Phen shot me the deadliest look, biting deep into his apple.

"It's because of her, isn't it? You've never made me put on clothes before, Harlowe. I don't see why I have to get dressed because she's not enlightened enough to handle my nudity."

I stiffened. Kids in the Bronx always told me I was too weird or white-acting to be Puerto Rican. Now this Phen dude was telling me that I was too indoctrinated by mainstream society to be down with nakedness. I didn't even know what to say. Can I live, yo? Harlowe took note of my anti-response and rallied to my defense.

"Phen, if the goddesses tell me that the energy is off, then I must submit to their will. No matter what other entities are in my presence," Harlowe said, without malice. She picked up her copy of *The Mountain Astrologer* and continued. "Second, Juliet is my guest. It would be in the best interest of all our energies if you got to know her before passing any judgment."

Harlowe turned back to her mountain astrology magazine. I poured myself a bowl of Granola O's with a heavy helping of Harlowe's fake milk and hoped for the best. I added Phen to the long list of jerks I navigated on the daily. Harlowe hadn't mentioned anyone else living here or visiting. Perhaps Phen landed unannounced and would leave soon. I hoped that was true. My thoughts went back to Lolita, Sophia, and finding the nearest library. Did Portland have a subway system? Why hadn't I asked about that?

Phen grabbed a lilac sarong from behind Harlowe's chair and wrapped it around his waist.

The outline of taut muscles along his stomach and hips made me wonder if he was a dancer. Phen was kind of beautiful, like, for a judgmental random naked guy.

I touched Harlowe's hand with my finger and said, "I've got two names in my book bag and I'm ready to do some work. Got any tips for navigating the transportation system and finding a library?"

"Juliet, you might want to wait for your aura to sync up with the city and with mine before you start. I gave you all the information today so that it could start to sink into your pores and your soul," she said, rolling a cigarette, "not so that you felt pressured to start. Give yourself time. You'll know when your aura is ready."

Phen sucked his teeth. "What does she even know about auras?" he asked.

Harlowe whipped her head around. "Jealousy does not become you, Phen." Harlowe once again sipped from her *Praise Witches* coffee mug. "I think it would be an exercise in patience and understanding if the two of you ventured out into Portland," she said, as if pulling this idea from all the alleged energies swirling around the room.

Phen and I looked at each other. Neither of us said a word.

The absolute last thing I had any desire to do was spend the afternoon with Phen and all his judgment. I wanted to wander alone or with Harlowe, not with him. What if he found out that I really didn't know anything at all about auras and that I was panicked about not knowing what a synced aura felt like? I didn't come to Portland to hang out with boys. There were enough boys in the Bronx and I didn't ever want to deal with them either. Well, except for Lil' Melvin, of course.

Harlowe pulled out a purple jar with a metal clasp and a soft velvet pouch from the cabinet above her stove. She flipped open the jar's lid to reveal a small mountain of bright green bud.

This was not your typical dry-ass bag of regs littered with seeds and stems that you got from so-and-so's cousin up the block. No, this was manna from the weed gods. These nugs glimmered in the light with shiny crystals and red fibers that crisscrossed their fatness like electrical wires. The smell alone got me geeked. Harlowe removed a glass pipe from the velvet pouch. It was clear along the mouth and turned blood orange the farther it got to the bowl.

"These are my trees and my Saturn-ruled smoking pipe," Harlowe said, voice melodic and calm. "Juliet, whenever you want to partake, feel free. Use as much as you want, whenever you want. All I ask is that you use my instruments with care and return them to a safe place. Saturn doesn't always want to be kept in the cupboard. She will let you know her desired resting place."

I felt honored, excited. It was nice to not be in some white boy's dorm room trying to clear a five-foot bong while listening to Dave Matthews with everyone chanting, "Toke! Toke! Toke!" The three of us took hits off of Saturn.

Phen blew out a slow spiral of smoke. "Harlowe," he said, "maybe I should also take Juliet to Powell's so she can see where the reading is going to be?"

Harlowe slapped her hand on the table. "Yes, oh my goddess, how could I forget? Juliet, another part of your time here will be helping me prepare for this mega reading I have at Powell's for *Raging Flower*." Her grin was wide, dimples flashing wild. Harlowe's face was open to the world; it pulled in all the light from the room. Her excitement was infectious and brilliant. I breathed it in with the weed smoke. *The* Harlowe Brisbane needed my help with a reading at a fancy bookstore.

Phen brought up the first time he met Harlowe. It was at an open mic night in Olympia. Harlowe read excerpts of what would become *Raging Flower*. I watched them exchange easy remember-whens. I munched on my cereal and hoped I would know Harlowe like that one day.

Researching badass women in history and organizing a book reading worked for me. The two components made sense. Readings at school were often all-white—boring. People read things about the silences in the trees and most nights some privileged wannabe "outsider" white boy claimed the open mic to lament the fact that no chicks would bang them. LGBTQ events didn't feel like family yet, either. Even the letters themselves made me feel like I was hovering above a movement and not connected to it via blood and tissue. The on-campus LGBTQ group called itself the Gay Brigade. I always needed a few drinks to loosen up and feel comfortable in my skin at their events. I was like one of one Latinas in the group anyway. Mainly, I went to snuggle up with Lainie in public, surrounded by other self-identified homos. A reading from *Raging Flower* in Portland with real-life adult gay people sounded like it could break open my chest. Whatever Harlowe needed me to do, I'd do it.

Phen looked at me and placed his hand on my arm. "Juliet, I apologize for being rude and for imposing my nakedness on you. I would feel blessed if you let me take you around Portland."

Through the haze of our morning smoke-fest, I saw him as a misfit in a sarong, an equal. "No worries, man," I said. "I'd love to bounce around this city with you."

CHAPTER SIX

PGPs AND BIG PUNISHER

WE CAUGHT THE TriMet bus on East Burnside and 16th. Phen wore a tattered red Che Guevara T-shirt, ripped army-green work pants that cut off right below his knees, and dusty black combat boots. His tall frame made it look like he had robbed a militant ten-year-old of his clothes. Thick little me had on my favorite Baby Phat jeans and black-and-white *BX* T-shirt. I wore red plastic-framed glasses and had my labret pierced; glasses because I was a nerd with bad vision and the labret in an attempt to hide both of those facts. Oh yeah, and let's not forget the crisp Jordans.

They'd be broken in perfect by summer's end.

Waiting at the bus stop we looked like a streetlamp and a fire hydrant out for a day trip. A bus pulled up, and Phen ushered me in first. My nose twitched and eyes watered. *What the fuck?* A stench I had never known assaulted my olfactory sense. I couldn't comprehend how a bus full of white people smelled so bad. Didn't they have mothers? When I was eleven and my chubby chest turned into actual breasts, Mom swooped in, handed me some Dove deodorant, and gave me the lowdown on covering up.

"Nena, from now on you must always wear a bra. Your breasts will get bigger, like mine and Grandma's. You must protect them. Trust me, eventually you will need the support as well. Men in public or even in the house should never be able to see the outline of your tetitas or the poke of your nipples. Put your bra on the second you wake up in the morning. Men can't handle seeing those things. It makes them crazy. Remember, they're just not as smart as we are, mama. From now on, you must shower every day and always wear deodorant and perfume. I do not want my little girl to be stinky. You are too pretty for that."

Boom. Instant knowledge of appropriate feminine hygiene. This must have been a busload of no-shame-having motherless children because there were loose sagging tits, sweat stains, and BO running free like locusts. Some of the men on the bus looked like normal white guys, but their beards were thick, unkempt, and their T-shirts were yellowed from sweat. I didn't understand them. What kind of white people were they?

Back home, my brother and my cousins hit up Butta Cutterz, the local barbershop, once a week to get tight shape ups. My older cousins wore the best colognes too. Real talk, sometimes the hood stinks, but I was not prepared to find myself in the middle of a sucio fest here in Portland.

I parked my curvy ass in an open window seat and counted how long I could hold my breath. Phen was unfazed, and, judging by the ocean-deep sweat marks under his pits, he felt right at home. I sat there breathing all crazy and feeling demasiado grossed out. How was I supposed to survive here? These Portlanders were an entirely different breed of white people.

From an all-girls Catholic school in Westchester County, New York, to the private liberal arts college I attended in Baltimore, Maryland (yay scholarships!), I was used to the buttoned-up, wealthy, Casper-skinned whites who always spoke in their library voices and used words like *sassy* and *spicy* to describe me. I was used to white people who embodied the suburban American dream. White people like Lainie's parents, who wished their daughters weren't friends with me but tolerated it and engaged me in discussions about affirmative action and how I benefited from it. White people who informed me that my fellow Latinos were "genetically more violent" than the average white boy all while inviting me to their summer home on the Cape. I was comfortable with white people who only sweat during a friendly game of tennis with their law school buddies. Those law school buddies would often have sons who would try to seduce me in secluded walkways and darkened corridors in other wings of their giant homes. They were careful to avoid their perfect cheerleader girlfriends while putting the moves on me. Flawed as the set-up was, those were the blanquitos I knew. The devils you know and whatnot. These cats over here made me wish I had santos to pray to for guidance. I didn't know how to navigate hippie white.

A storm cloud of hypocrisy slid over me. I felt kind of sick. My mother didn't raise me this way. Who was I to assume that these stinky-ass people had no home training? Or that they were any worse than the other uppity whites I was more familiar with? Who was I to judge how these hippie-types chose to live in their own bodies? I closed my eyes and breathed in these new people. Still stanky. After a few long minutes, I got used to the rawness of it and filed the smell in my brain as *earthy*. I could do earthy. I swiveled around and went back to scoping everyone. Some of these hippie white girls looked summer-sweet, like the type you make wild love to lakeside somewhere surrounded by dandelions, possibly on hallucinogenic drugs. *Damn that girl in the corner is beautiful with her brown dreadlocks, blue eyes, and grass-stained overalls.* She smiled at me, and I couldn't help but grin back. Beautiful-hippie-stranger girl reached for the yellow tape to indicate her stop and a Chia Pet of pit hair popped out from under her arm. I choked and spun back around to look out the window. Being open-minded about everything earthy was going to take a hot minute.

Phen stared at me, unsmiling. He crossed his arms over his chest and asked, "So, Juliet, how do you identify? What are your preferred gender pronouns?"

"I'm sorry, what? How do I identify what?" I asked, my voice quiet. I wanted to ask what a preferred gender pronoun was, but Phen's face, his raised eyebrow, his entire manner kept me from feeling comfortable. The way Phen asked—so casually, like this was common knowledge—made the air between us shift into a hazy thickness.

Phen half rolled his eyes, "Oh c'mon, do you identify as queer? As a dyke? Are you trans?" he asked, spitting phrases at me, amused by my ignorance. "And PGPs are so important even though I think we should drop preferred and call them mandatory gender pronouns. So, are you she, he, ze, they?"

I shrugged and said, "I'm just Juliet." I chewed my pinkie nail, looking down at the floor.

I was surrounded by hippies and the only person in the world who knew my name on this bus was sitting across from me speaking another language. His disdain slid into my heart and carved a space for itself. Trans? Ze? PGPs? Those words weren't a part of my vocabulary. No one in the Bronx or even in college asked me if I was a ze or trans. Was that even how they fit into sentences? I felt small, constricted, and stupid, very stupid. Phen dangled these phrases over my head. He was waiting for me to jump up and beg to be educated, beg for him to explain the world he inhabited.

"How did you even get here?" Phen asked, unblinking. "Harlowe told me she didn't need any help this summer because she found you, some Internet fan girl." Phen rolled a cigarette with organic tobacco and dye-free rolling papers. "I bet you're not even really gay. You're just feeling trendy because you go to some liberal arts college."

I started to tear up. I stood and walked to the back of the bus. Phen wasn't going to see me cry or take pleasure in my silence. The moment to retaliate passed by, leaving brass-knuckle bruises on my ego. His queer questions brought back memories of Puerto Rican kids asking me if I knew all the words to Big Pun's part on "Twinz (Deep Cover '98)." Pun spat lyrics so twisted they choked the tightest vine-tongued wannabe. But for some reason this song was the test: Are you Puerto Rican enough, Juliet Palante? Do you know the words? Are you down with us? Or are you just a white girl with brown skin?

Dead in the middle of Little Italy, little did we know
That we riddled some middleman who didn't do diddly

No, I didn't know the words. No, I didn't know my gender pronouns. All the moments where I was made to feel like an outsider in a group that was supposed to have room for me added up and left me feeling so much shame. Burning hot cheeks, eyes swollen with tears that were all the words I couldn't say—that's what my shame looked like. I wanted to run. The world is filled with enough room to flee at any moment. In any situation, there's a window, a crowbar to blast through a locked door, or even the ability to just jump across the roof or down an entire flight of steps; there's always some way to escape.

After a few more stops, the bus driver announced that we were in downtown Portland. Two white lesbian moms on the bus—one had her blond hair twisted into frayed dreadlocks and the other wore their baby wrapped behind her back in kente cloth—exited in front of me. I followed them, not alerting Phen, not making a sound, just moving. There were fewer trees and more concrete in this part of Portland. I stood at the intersection and just as I picked a direction, a hand landed on my shoulder from behind. I whipped around quick, ready to fight.

"Juliet," Phen said, jumping back. "I almost lost you." He lit the smoke he'd rolled on the bus.

I sighed and said, "Listen, dude, you don't have to babysit me, okay? I'm from New York. I can navigate Portland." I walked past him heading down West Burnside with no idea where I was going. Phen followed me, silent. Our steps were awkward, like the steps taken while trying to make up after a public fight with your girlfriend. I wondered what he thought, if he knew that he'd been some weird word snob to me on the bus. I had no idea why he was here with me in this moment. Would Phen slow down my aura's ability to sync with Portland? Since when did I start thinking about my aura as an entity that existed? Feeling light-headed and disoriented, I stopped in the middle of the sidewalk and inhaled all the hippie air my lungs could take in.

We stood at the corner of Northwest Tenth Avenue. Powell's Books beckoned to us in red, black, and white, like a flag for a new America. One that's educated, homegrown, and all about sustaining local book culture. "New and Used," its storefront promised, assuring the world that information would not be discarded; that we could find what we needed within its doors. It looked like the Salvation Army of bookstores, and who doesn't love a little dig through salvation?

Phen folded his arms behind his back and spoke in a soft voice. "When I need information not regulated by our genius-crippling government, I come here."

I stared at him and asked, "Are you going to be nice to me now? Like, can I get a break?" For a moment he was too real to look at, radiant in an angry sort of way. Phen had the kind of beauty that boys with attitude and slim bones get away with. They're the type of boys that writers like Allen Ginsberg fell in love with and bled out poetry for.

He held the door open for me. "I wasn't mean to you. I asked you two questions. You chose to not answer them. Being nice is worthless. You're existing on a different plane of consciousness."

I didn't respond. He wasn't on my consciousness level either. The doorway to Powell's loomed and his judgments of me drifted into the dust. Aisles and aisles of wooden bookshelves created a labyrinth in which nerds like me could lose themselves possibly forever. We walked inside and I almost crashed into a life-size cardboard cutout of Harlowe Brisbane. A copy of *Raging Flower* stood on a large metal easel. The caption above her face read: Portland's own Harlowe Brisbane brings her Raging Flower to Powell's Bookstore! reading and q&a Thursday, July 24th at 7:00 p.m. Make sure to RSVP. About a hundred copies of *Raging Flower* sat in stacks of ten along a mahogany table.

"Intense, right?" Phen picked one up and flipped through it. "Portland dykes worship her and the local literati can't get enough Harlowe. I'm surprised you haven't received death threats for landing such a coveted internship."

"I had no idea that Harlowe was such a phenomenon," I said, staring at cardboard Harlowe's face.

"Juliet, right now in this town and along the West Coast, Harlowe is the white lady authority on pussy, feminism, healing, and lesbianism. Even non-queers love her. You've got so much to learn, chica." He leaned against the row of her books, shaking his head. Phen turned in the direction of other similarly dressed boys and disappeared into the abyss of books.

Phen used the phrase *non-queers*. As much as I wanted to dive into his language and understand his words, I also refused to bite. The way he used words felt like bait. He wanted to enlighten me, to educate me. I didn't want to experience Portland or obtain a queer education that way, not from some smug dude. His energy drained me. I didn't like the way he said *dyke*. Maybe he was allowed to say it by association, but he wasn't an associate of mine.

I focused on cardboard Harlowe. Seeing her immortalized was surreal; it gave me a moment of unexpected reverence. Like when you're watching someone perform and you're holding your breath 'cuz you don't want them to mess up because what they're doing onstage makes you feel like you're in church; it felt like that. I stood in front of her, not moving. This must be what it's like to be a writer, a real one, not one that leaves graffiti tags in the margins of their notebook, not one that scrawls illegible notes and poems into something that stays forever tucked away.

Raging Flower was out in the world and by default, so was Harlowe.

I stood alongside cardboard Harlowe and wrote in my purple composition notebook.

* Ask Ava about ze, trans, PGPs, non-queers, and use of dyke by non-dykes(?).

* Cry a little to Ava. Ask if Mom's talked to Titi Penny.

* How do I identify? As in myself? Identify self. Is that possible beyond 'hello my name is'?

* What would it be like to be a real writer like Harlowe?

I didn't want to forget the important things. Maybe other people would ask me those questions here and not having an answer the second time around would be my fault. Perhaps other Portlanders or queers or whatever the people here were, maybe they'd all question me and egg me on to prove myself, my gayness. Or Phen could just be one huge bastion of unchecked ego. I kept that in mind as I roamed through the aisles of bookshelves.

My phone vibrated in my back pocket: Mom. I picked up without hesitation. I loved her and wanted her to love me back and not care that I was gay. I needed her voice and her support. I needed her.

"Hi, Mom." I said.

"Juliet," Mom said, quiet, her voice smooth. "You didn't call me. Is everything with the flower book lady going okay?"

"Yes, Mom," I replied. "She's great. Everything is fine." I walked in circles, focused on her voice. I brushed away single tears. They came without a sound. Her voice had that effect.

"Good, okay, I'm glad, nena," Mom responded, pausing before adding, "You know your titi Penny had a lady friend once and she was very nice. This was right before she met your uncle Lenny. We didn't talk about those things back then, but I knew. I could tell by the way she looked at her that it was different than just being friends. I've seen you look at Lainie the same way."

Her words made my legs weak. I pressed my back against the nearest wall and slid into a sitting position.

"You knew about me and Lainie?" I asked, hand on my inhaler.

"I'm your mother, Juliet. It's my job to know everything about you," she said. "But it worries me. I'm not happy with it. I don't understand. I didn't understand with Titi Penny either. But I'm sure it's a phase, just like it was with her."

"Mom, it's not a phase," I said. She had me glowing for a moment and that one word took it all away. I needed her to understand that this part of me wasn't going to change.

"Nena, you don't know that," she replied with a hushed sharpness in her voice. I heard Lil' Melvin calling to her through the phone. She yelled to him that she'd be down in a minute. "Juliet, you don't know who you are yet. You will grow out of so many things; you have already. Now I gotta go watch my *Buffy*. Call me, nena; no more of this sending texts business."

I said okay. She said okay and then she hung up.

In less than five minutes, Mom dropped some family truths and tried to find some common ground. At least I think she did. But nothing was resolved. She didn't say that she loved me. But she had to still love me, right? Why didn't she say it? Why didn't I? It wasn't a phase. I wasn't going through some phase. Okay, so maybe I went through a Backstreet Boys phase and there was that time I only ate chicken tenders and french fries for a few months. Legitimate phases. Being in love with Lainie wasn't one of those things. Not at all.

No matter what, I was glad that my mom called. It meant that her door wouldn't be closed forever. I maintained my position on the floor in a corner of Powell's and people-watched. Phen walked over with a few books under his arms.

"A peace offering," he said. He bent forward and placed a copy of *A People's History of the United States* in my hands.

I thanked him. Phen offered a hand and helped me up. He led us out and held the door for me as we exited. I didn't know what to make of his judgment and his impeccable manners. I tucked the book into my bag and braced myself for more time with him.

Phen worked his slim arm through mine so that our elbows linked. He ran us through the streets until we came to a thudding halt on Southwest Morrison. He announced that we were in Pioneer Courthouse Square. It sprawled out before us; clusters of hippie folks all around. We parked ourselves at the top of some steps.

A group of guys in open-toed sandals and cargo shorts played hacky sack. Phen ran down the steps and joined them. I remained at my perch just taking everyone in. At the bottom of the brick stairs, a couple sang while they played acoustic guitars. The square was filled with people and dogs off leashes; there was even an anarchists' corner. It felt like Washington Square Park in the summertime, minus the frenzied pace and designer suits. Bustling and free: a place to smoke trees and fall in love with someone wearing too much eyeliner and not enough deodorant.

Phen hacky-ed his heart out as the hours passed. I wrote about my conversation with Mom, made notes about Titi Penny having a girlfriend. I wondered if she'd tell me about her if I asked. Or if she'd be weird about it. Would Ava know? Phen waved up at me. I could see his pit stains from where I sat. I waved back. Like, did he want me to watch him play this dumb kick-a-bean-bag game? I remembered the book he gave me as a peace offering. Maybe this was how he attempted a fresh start. I watched him play for a while; he was kind of pretty to look at.

I sat up with a start. We still hadn't checked out the library. I grabbed our bags and ran down the steps. I tossed his at him. He and the hacky sack dudes were passing around some beers in brown paper bags. Phen was less than concerned about the library.

"It's probably closed by now," he said while smoking a clove with his beer. "We're going to go to an action for union rights. You should come and learn some things."

I sighed at him. "I don't know, Phen. I wanted to check out the library and I don't know your friends. I'd rather go back to Harlowe's."

"Everyone is a spiritual comrade, Juliet. Just come with us," he replied, with a quick eye roll.

"I-I'm not sure," I stammered. It was all dudes and me; dudes I didn't know and we'd be going somewhere unfamiliar.

"Whatever, Juliet, so much for 'I'm ready for anything.' You have no sense of adventure or curiosity about other people," Phen declared, his hands on his hips. His friends watched us. They said nothing.

Phen, all sorts of worked up, said, "You're not ready for Portland." He nodded to the guys, and they all walked off.

"Phen," I called out. "Which bus did we take?"

"Figure it out," he said without turning around.

The sun set over the Willamette River and I was alone. He

left me. I couldn't get over it. Yes, I was from the Bronx, but I'd always been surrounded by my people. My titis wouldn't have left. My friends on the block wouldn't have left me either. We stick together. We don't generally troop around solo in the Bronx. Roaming in a pack protects against predators and police. I retraced my steps to Powell's Books. From there I crossed the street and found the bus that would bring me to Harlowe's house of wonders. I felt sick inside. I didn't want to go to Harlowe's. What was I doing here? I'd been in Portland for less than forty-eight hours and I'd been judged, dismissed, and abandoned. Also, I hadn't seen one other Latino. No faces like mine; nowhere to breathe easy.

The bus pulled up and I got on, weary in my bones and feeling like my heart was frayed. If I were home and some dude pulled what Phen just pulled on me, one phone call would have Titi Wepa and Titi Mellie on the scene ready to bust his ass. But in Portland, I had no one, just me.

Harlowe wasn't gonna throw blows for me and the one kid who should have been my friend just ditched me in an alleyway. And, like, does anyone really want to chill with random boys besides straight girls and other random boys? Like, am I crazy for not wanting to crack open a hot can of PBR and find a union action? What the hell was a union action anyway?

Disillusioned, I settled into my seat on the bus and watched the alien streets roll by. Opposite me an elderly Black woman filled in a crossword puzzle from one of those big puzzle books. My mom swore by those books. She always had them in the car when we took trips. I settled into my seat a little easier. Three young Mexican dudes sat together in front of me. One of them held a boom box in his lap. Green Day's "Basket Case" played on low. I smiled and took a deep breath. Fresh air breezed in from the open window vents. My fists unclenched. I closed my eyes and reminded myself that I could handle anything. I was from the Bronx.

I got myself here. I deserved this internship. No jealous boy could take that from me. And damn, I should have said that to his face. Ha. As if I ever said things to people's faces in the moment. All the right words found me later, much later, sometimes just in my dreams. In the moment, I have always gone blank and felt scared, like guts clamping shut, mouth filling with pre-vomit bile. A complete mess. Why did people have to be mean anyway?

I needed to confront Phen. Oh God, I was already sweating about it. If we were going to share space for the entire summer, he was going to have to chill and cut me some major slack. An ambulance passed by, lights on, no sirens. I counted four rainbow flags hanging from outside people's homes while trying to figure out the best way to talk to Phen. Did I storm into Harlowe's, shoulders back all sorts of hype, ready to throw down? Nah, I couldn't be cool like Titi Wepa if I tried.

I was gonna have to nerd it out somehow. Maybe write him a letter? No. I put all my honest soft everything into letters. And I couldn't offer that to Phen yet. I was nearing Harlowe's.

I didn't want to leave the bus. I wasn't ready to step back into that house. Phen wasn't there, but he would be at some point. Three blocks from Harlowe's street, I decided to ride the bus until its wheels fell off or until the bus driver called out last stop. Harlowe's house passed by my window. Only the light in the attic was on. I imagined Harlowe smoking and writing, staring off into her own world. I didn't pull the yellow cord. Her house faded in the distance.

I didn't know where I was headed, but I didn't care. It was 9:15 p.m. on a Sunday. I've ridden subway trains at 4:00 in the morning in New York City, with drunks nodding off on my shoulder and kids starting fistfights. If I could handle my city no problem, why was I having palpitations on this bus thinking about a one-on-one with Phen? Farther out from Harlowe's, the streetlights began to disappear. I stared out into the darkness. A do-over. I'd ask Phen to talk on the porch and we could start over. I mean, Harlowe kinda put him up to taking me around, maybe it was all weird 'cuz we didn't decide to link up on our own. Or maybe he was just a jerk. Either way, I was going to set things right for myself. And if he couldn't handle hearing me out, then pa'carajo con el.

"Last stop," called out the bus driver. I froze and realized I was the only person left on the bus. I raced to the bus driver, shaking with nerves and without a coin in my pocket.

He sighed and said, "Come with me." He patted my shoulder and walked me to the next bus; it was the last bus of the entire night. They waived my fare and I hugged him. At first he stood there uncertain, but then he hugged back and it was nice. We made the slow, dark trek back to Harlowe's. My entire day had been one of retraced steps and unresolved issues. But it wasn't over yet and I had a plan.

The kitchen lights at Harlowe's were on when I got to her house. Head high, shoulders back, I readied myself to ask Phen to talk.

"You just left her downtown all by herself," Harlowe said, her voice tumbling onto the porch from the open kitchen window.

I shrank to the ground and sat right below the window.

"She's not a baby, nor is she my responsibility," retorted Phen. "I invited her to come with me and she declined. So if she's out there lost, it's her own damn fault."

My whole body flushed red. Prickly heat bumps popped up on my neck.

"I'm troubled, Phen," Harlowe said. "This isn't you. What's going on?"

"Don't you get it?" he said. "I'm right here and you chose her to do research alongside you. I know your work. It should have been me."

The windowsill creaked above me. Smoke from Harlowe's organic cigarettes filled my nostrils. I held in a cough.

"That's not it," Harlowe replied, "and we both know it. She's not coming back, Phen. I'm sorry to say it but . . ."

"You don't know that," Phen replied, as the sill creaked again.

They were both sitting at the kitchen window, smoking.

"It's been three years and I haven't heard a word from her," Harlowe said.

"That makes two of us," Phen said in a low voice.

"You can't take the pain of your mom leaving out on Juliet or anyone else," Harlowe added. "Not in my house and really not anywhere else."

The inhale and exhale of cigarette smoke whirled above me. No one said a word. I kept my back against the wall of the house.

"I miss her so much; when you two were together everything was so good and easy," Phen said. "Whose mom just up and leaves? Here's the only place she'd come back to."

Hot wet tears were not slipping down the side of my face. Nope. Totally wasn't crying. Jeez, mom shit was messing everyone up. Bendito, now how was I going to confront him? A reckoning still needed to happen, but maybe it didn't involve a sneak attack. I kept my booty low to the floor and slid off the side of the porch. I popped back around and came right up the front steps.

"Y'all, I navigated the bus home," I said, smiling at both of them.

"Yeah, you did," Harlowe said. She slipped out the window and gave me a smoky hug.

Phen stood behind her watching us then looking down at his bare feet. I stepped away from Harlowe.

"Think we could get a minute?" I asked.

He nodded. Harlowe gave us both long intentional looks before she bowed her head and went inside. I laughed despite myself. Phen laughed too. The tension in my chest eased up. I took in full breaths without any tightness.

"Dude," I said, "I really wanna like you. But what's up with all the weird mind games and judgment? I'm not dealing with it all summer. Whatever you have to say to me, say it, and let's be done with it."

My heart pounded in my chest, eardrums, back of my throat. Lord, the *fwthoomp* of each heartbeat was all I heard. I hated this part. The moment when someone might flip out or be regular, that part always made me anxious.

"I'm not nice," he replied, lighting a smoke. "And you're so fucking nice and you mean it. Caught me off guard."

"Stop, c'mon," I replied, rolling my eyes. "You also tried to make me feel small for not knowing things. What gives?"

"It's an easy way to cut people down," Phen said with a shrug. "And a bad habit."

He took a long drag off his cigarette and offered it to me. I shook my head.

"This internship belongs to you," he said. "Shouldn't have made you feel otherwise."

"I worked my ass off to get here," I replied. "Waitressing, three nights a week working at the Alumni House for work-study. I applied for two grants using the word *pussy* multiple times in each."

"Doing the universe's work," Phen said, brushing his hair out of his eyes. He looked over at me. "Sorry for being a rat."

"Truce," I said, and offered him my fist. He tapped his against mine.

We sat on the porch and watched the stars. He wrote in a palm-sized leather journal. I propped my purple composition notebook against my knees and did the same. Edith Piaf's voice wafted onto the porch from the record player in the living room. We wrote for a while in silence. I texted Lainie and kept an eye on Orion's belt. It was the only constellation I knew by heart.

"I'm leaving in the morning," Phen said. "Haven't told Harlowe yet."

"Please don't say it's 'cuz I didn't know PGP things," I said, hand on my chest.

"Not everything's about you, Juliet," he said. Phen turned around and rolled his eyes real slow. "It's union organizing stuff."

I served him the exact same eye roll. He laughed.

"Good luck," I replied.

He nodded and tipped two fingers in my direction. I headed inside, notebook under my arm. Took a glorious shower and made my way up to the attic. Harlowe typed without rest in the corner. She was still there in the morning when I woke up. I lay there listening to the deep clicks of her keys, like a pianist she glided over them. After a while, I made my way into the kitchen. Harlowe's half-empty tea cup sat on the table next to a note from Phen.

Harlowe,

*I'm chasing after ghosts in Portland. My energy's
taken a massive hit. Need to shake off this mean and
re-center. Blessings to your continued takedown of the white
supremacist heteropatriarchy.*

Evolution and respect,

Phen

My cheeks flushed red. Phen was gone. Our conversation from
last night rushed over me. He up and did it. Harlowe's pack of
American Spirits sat on the table, crushed up. Her typing trickled down the stairs in hard clicks and long pauses. I still didn't
know what PGPs and zes were. But at least now I knew they
were a thing.

Maybe the universe had done me a favor by having Phen go
shake off his mean or whatever. Doing things alone made me
feel like the whole world could see that no one else wanted to be
with me. But I had to remember that I got myself here. I didn't
need anyone to hold my hand, even if I was hyperventilating
half the time.

CHAPTER SEVEN

CELESBIAN SKIN

A FEW STREETS away from Harlowe's house was Blend Coffee. I used the walk to give Lainie another call. It rang once and went to voice mail again. Her phone was being so weird. I left a message and kept walking. The crunch of beans grinding and the rich smells of coffee and hazelnut welcomed me to Blend.

The cement walls were spray-painted lime green. A cork message board was on display near the entrance: *Nanny needed for gluten-allergic kids* and *Vegan Buddhist looking for drum circle.* The artwork on the wall boasted local artists. They didn't just sell coffee at Blend, they sold Portland. Bronx bodega coffee served in blue-and-white cups was too many miles away to miss. I ordered an iced coffee with milk from the young white girl with tribal tattoos and a septum piercing. I wasn't sure if she was gay, but she was wearing an Ani DiFranco T-shirt, so it felt safe to assume she wasn't straight.

"We're waiting on our milk delivery. Sorry. But we do have soy milk," she said, looking apologetic and adorable.

I froze. Ugh, it was hard enough drinking Harlowe's almond milk (how do you even get milk from almonds?) and now I was being offered soy milk.

"I've never had soy milk before," I said. "I feel like around here that must sound crazy, right?"

"Maybe a little, but you sound kinda like you're not from here," the cute barista said, leaning over on her elbows. "New York? Brooklyn, maybe? And just try the soy."

"You're good. Close—the Bronx," I replied, gazing up at the chalkboard menu, avoiding eye contact. "I'm here as an author's research assistant. And sure, soy sounds great."

"Sweet. Done." She turned around to grind coffee beans. "Assisting anyone I know?"

"Harlowe Brisbane," I said, ignoring my buzzing cell phone, "She wrote *Raging Flower: Empowering Your*—"

"The pussy book lady," she exclaimed, spinning around, coffee beans tumbling to the floor. "Like *the* Harlowe Brisbane? No shit?"

Some of the other lesbians in the coffee shop perked up.

The front door burst open.

"Billie, this chick is working for Harlowe Brisbane!"

Billie, head shaved and slim as a pipe cleaner, carried glass bottles of milk in a crate. "No fucking way, I love her. Think maybe we could get her in here for a reading one day?"

I turned and saw a few women staring at me, waiting for my response.

"Umm, maybe," I replied as the cute barista girl slid me my drink. "That'd be mad cool. I'll ask her." I reached for my wallet, sliding my phone back into my pocket. "How much again?"

"Don't worry about it," Billie said, holding a fist out. "Just ask Harlowe about that reading."

I bumped Billie's fist. "No doubt," I said and headed to the very back of Blend, away from all the inquiring eyes.

Harlowe Brisbane is a bona fide celesbian . . .

I checked my texts and there was a message from Ava:

Chica, call me, text me, anything me. Are you a hippie
Portland dyke yet? Besos.

Would I ever be a hippie dyke? Did I even want to be that? Sitting on a red vinyl chair at a table that was a giant ceramic mosaic, surrounded by gay women and alternative-looking folks, I didn't know how to answer Ava's text, so I called her.

Ava spoke fast in between cracks and snaps of her gum. Her enthusiasm for all the things she'd heard about my life in the last few days poured through the phone. I told her about Phen and the cardboard Harlowe. We talked about my crash-and-burn coming out situation. For every detail she already knew about me, Ava added one about herself. I told the family I was a lesbian. Ava said she'd been dating a boy, then a girl, and was doing the whole "casual, low-key, college, no labels thing"—her words, not mine. I asked her how Titi Penny and Uncle Lenny took her coming out.

Ava said, "Prima, I didn't really come out. I'm just living, and they're down for however I'm living in the moment, you know?"

I didn't know, but I wanted to. I wanted to be that cool. How could three years make such a huge difference in whether one was a nerdburger or the coolest low-key, no-labels cousin? In an attempt to up my coolness, I told Ava about the free coffee and how excited the lesbians who worked at Blend were about me being there. I felt like I could be friends with them. In essence, I'd found my people. Ava popped a tight bubble with her gum.

"Juliet, what makes you think those white chicks are interested in being your friend?" she asked quietly.

"Free coffee equals friendship, Ava, come on," I replied.

"They're down for Harlowe. They're down for each other. They're not down for you, Juliet Palante from the Bronx, you know?"

"Yo, Ava, I don't think it's that serious. Everyone is super friendly. Like, it's nice to just be surrounded by other people who aren't straight or so hood that they're constantly checking your hood pass. It's comfortable here. And honestly, I could use some friendly faces." The ice melted in my coffee. I waited for her approval.

"I get that. Still, you should come to Miami and spend some time with me. I'm always going to be down for you," Ava said.

"I know, cuz. I doubt I'll be able to take a trip to you this summer. I'll be here until August," I said with a sigh. I wondered when I'd be able to find time for a visit.

"Listen, watch out for those white girls, okay?"

"Okay, cuz," I replied, shaking my head.

Ava told me she loved me and made me promise to keep her updated on everything. I sipped my coffee and wondered when she'd gotten so militant. *Watch out for those white girls, okay?* Like, what was that? Were we in a scary movie or something? White girls could be annoying, but mostly they were just harmless. Sometimes it was easier to be around white girls anyway; all the things that made me weird in my neighborhood seemed cool to them.

I was welcomed at Blend. Harlowe had opened up her home to me. The Harlowe Brisbane connection gave me access to other lesbians, their friendliness, and this free coffee. Was this my aura syncing up with the world around me? Harlowe deemed aura-syncing a necessary component of this internship, so why not rock with it? I expected a tingling or some sort of frontal lobe pressure. My family never talked about auras. Maybe auras and the Holy Spirit were connected in some way? Because there was always talk about El Espiritu Santo, even if just as an exclamation for something outrageous. I wanted to feel something, something that said "Okay, Juliet, this is your aura, get ready, we 'bout to get crazy."

My asthma attacks always came with warning signs. My lungs would burn slow, a tiny Pentecost behind the rib cage. This built tightness, as if the bronchi were filled with smoke. Each breath more labored until the crackle wheezes pierced through each gasp. The wheezing was the worst; it's the sound lungs made because they ached. It's the sound of damaged goods filtering in and out of your chest, past your ears, back into your psyche. My attacks were brought about by cold weather, infections, and unmanaged emotions. I knew these symptoms well. Were they connected to my aura? If my aura got super strong, would it take my asthma away? I wondered if la Virgen dealt with auras too.

There was so much I still didn't know. I'd come in confident. My letter to Harlowe burst out of me in one night, 'cuz I just had to believe Harlowe Brisbane would listen. She'd know what I was talking about when it came to feminism, racism, inequality, and family stuff. But I wanted more, I wanted the world that included all those words Phen used. Stuck, bouncing around with them, it dawned on me to check *Raging Flower*. Maybe I'd missed all the radical pronoun terms amid all the discussion about vaginas and feminism and the dismantling of the patriarchy forever. If Harlowe didn't write about it, then maybe I wasn't just some lost little gay kid who didn't know anything.

I looked in my bag and realized that I'd left my notebook in the attic. With watered-down coffee and a whirring aura, I left Blend, nodding at the baristas, wondering what it'd be like to be their friend. My friends at college were a mix of theater nerds and student council kids, and most were Lainie's friends first. I spent a huge chunk of my freshman year awkwardly courting her, but dating Lainie didn't make me feel like an official lesbian. Being around other gay people made me feel nervous, like someone was going to see us out in the world and we'd be targets.

But the folks around us didn't flinch; Blend was vibing like any other coffee shop. Nobody stared at the girl couples holding hands like they did when Lainie and I did it at the Galleria. There weren't any preachers shouting about the sins of Sodom like they did on my train rides home. The stress of being outed or attacked in public lived under my skin at home; I didn't have to look over my shoulders here. None of that was present. I wanted this life. The meet-up-with-your-other-gay-friends-for-coffee-because-it's-totally-no-big-deal-and-no-one's-mom-is-mad-at-them life. Was this what it was like to be openly gay and at ease in the world?

Walking to Harlowe's house, I saw a young, brown-skinned woman wearing a tie-dye bikini top and jean shorts bike past. She smiled and waved. I waved back. No helmet, her face free of stress. No car alarms blaring or police sirens declaring ownership of neighborhoods and the bodies within. The wail of the Bronx was constant. But this neighborhood, East Burnside, offered wide-open sidewalks, trees bursting toward the sun, and houses that didn't have bars on their windows; it offered a melody. I wanted my mother to come here to know what a quiet neighborhood could sound like, what peace sounded like. Mom and I might even be able to hear each other speak and really listen. We could set our words on these sun-drenched branches and let the breeze guide us to resolution. For a split second, I wondered if there was a price to pay for this type of peace.

CHAPTER EIGHT

ON THE ROAD TO POLYAMORY AND GOD

I WAS ABOUT a block away when a black pickup truck pulled up alongside me. The window was rolled down and Harlowe's face popped out across the driver's side. Harlowe called me "sweet human" and motioned me over to the truck.

"I want you to meet Maxine," she shouted, waving her hand at me.

I walked faster toward the truck. The tension between my shoulder blades eased. Couldn't hide the big grin that slipped over my face and radiated off my body. What a joy to see Maxine: confident, Black, and vibrating with good-ass energy. She got out of the truck and hugged me, towering but so gentle.

"Good to meet you, sis," she said, giving me a soft pat on the back. There was a hint of Southerner in her voice.

"So good to meet you. I love you," I said, my eyes flying wide open. "Your bow tie, I love your bow tie!"

My heart thumped in my chest. Did I really just . . . ? Sure did. Sigh. Was it my fault that her glittery purple bow tie popped perfectly against her skin? Maxine stepped back from the hug and kept a hand on my shoulder.

"Thanks," Maxine said. "I made it myself. Could show you how to make one if you want."

She motioned me toward the truck. Her biceps and perfect dimples made my hips dip to the side, like I'd been waiting for her. I had to catch myself. Gosh, what kind of malcriada was I, getting cute shy around Maxine while I had a girlfriend?

I nodded, digging my toe into the dirt. "I'm not like the make-things type," I said. "Harlowe, do you want the middle?"

"Nah, I like the window for smoking," she said, patting the spot next to her between the two of them.

"So what type are you?" Maxine asked, slipping in next to me. She started the ignition. Her black jeans were faded and ripped at the knees.

"I'm the watch-you-do-it-'cuz-I-hate-messing-up-in-front-of-people type," I said.

Maxine nodded but stayed quiet. Harlowe rummaged through an old CD book. Why did I always make everything weird?

Squeezed in between them, my D-cup breasts filled the space in front of me and pushed farther out than Maxine's or Harlowe's chest. I was both uncomfortable and so proud; I've always loved my breasts. I've loved them for the way they defied gravity: full, brown, perfect. They held court over my soft belly, another part of me that I was always aware of, another section of thickness that announced itself by daring to exist. My thick, soft everything was a direct contrast to Maxine's muscular and firm build. Her solid shoulders were wired into lean limbs knotted with firm muscles and flawless skin. I felt tight all over, hyperaware of every inch of my body. I licked my lips, craving something sweet. What was happening? I had to get it together.

"I've gotta go to the library today, Harlowe." I explained about my notebook being home and wanting to find the library myself. I talked until I was the only one still talking. They laughed and Harlowe told me that my aura couldn't have synced so fast. She twirled a few wild strands of her red hair around her fingers. Maxine smiled at me.

"From what I've heard, you might really dig this Octavia Butler–inspired writer's workshop," she said. "But you also shared that you're a sit-and-watch type, so maybe not."

"Yeah but writing's mad different," I replied. "I can write and not worry about who's looking at me or if I'm going to let people down."

"So we're going then," Maxine said, making a hard left on a yellow light.

My body slid into Maxine's. I froze. She didn't shift or push me over. I didn't even think Maxine noticed the difference between when our thighs weren't touching and when they were. But I did. The AC pumped out weak blasts of semi-warm air. I felt ungodly hot. Maxine smelled so good, like shea butter and incense.

Harlowe eyed me for a moment, smiling, like she could sense

the embarrassing crush-like feelings in my brain. I thought she might call me out, but instead she rested her head on my shoulder. I sighed, relieved, and Maxine caught my eye. I turned away so fast, fast enough to not let out any stupid doe-eyed grins. Someone had to talk, otherwise this tension of fluttering beats in my chest was going to kill me.

"So, like, how did y'all meet each other?" I asked. "Is there a really juicy love story or a good friends thing or what? Tell me everything."

They laughed and leaned forward a bit to meet eyes. Harlowe and Maxine went back and forth for a minute deciding who would start off. Maxine cleared her throat.

"It was at the Oly Queer Punk Festival. Maybe ninety-eight or ninety-nine," Maxine said. She stroked her chin as if there was a beard or goatee under her fingertips. "I think Gossip played for the first time that night."

"Yes, Beth stripped down to a white lace garter belt and a cone bra," Harlowe added. "You were reading Audre Lorde in between bands breaking down and setting up. All those bodies pressed together, and there you were reading in the middle of it. Unbothered. Beautiful."

"*Zami* is one of the finest pieces of written work ever," Maxine said. "I read that book in bathrooms, on buses, everywhere. And in the middle of the chaos at that show and all those pages was you."

"Some moony-eyed, hippie white girl that wouldn't, and still won't, leave you alone," Harlowe added, turning to face me.

"This was before *Raging Flower* and before Max's MDiv. and before we were primaries, poly, before any of that. It was the love boom."

It became clear to me that if I didn't start asking for clarity in the moment, my notebook would be filled with contextless phrases and words that the Oxford dictionary might not even have definitions for. I cleared my throat and asked, "What's a poly primary emdiv?"

Maxine laughed. I laughed too, even though I wasn't completely certain what the joke was.

"Sounds wild when you put it all together like that, huh?" Maxine said. "Poly's short for *polyamory*, which is just a queer way of saying you're open to multiple partners."

"Oohh, like that HBO documentary about the middle-aged white people throwing swing parties in their mansions," I said, nodding with excitement.

"Umm, sort of but not quite." Maxine furrowed her brow. "I mean maybe for some folks it's like that, but for us, it's allowing room for intimacy with other folks independent of our relationship," Maxine said. She tapped her thumbs on the steering wheel.

"So Harlowe would be your main chick," I asked, thinking of the way boys on the block talked about girls.

"Right, but there aren't any side chicks in this scenario because one person isn't hidden from the other," finished Maxine.

"Huhmm . . ." I exhaled, thinking all of that over. Polyamory.

Shit sounded a little like a hippified way of rationalizing outside booty or not being able to commit or something. But I liked the idea of mutual respect and honesty.

"So, like, if Harlowe met someone mad cool, you'd be totally fine with her hooking up with them?" I asked, eyebrow raised. "That seems suspect. How do you deal with jealousy?"

"We embrace it," Harlowe jumped in. "We're all curious and beautiful humanoids. So why not just acknowledge that sometimes we're gonna get hot for someone else's mind, spirit, and sexy bits? Why not own it and discuss it as two adults? One person can't be someone else's be-all and end-all every single minute of every single day."

"My mom is for my dad," I said softly, missing both of them hard.

"Maybe that works for them. It works for a lot of people," Maxine replied. "But to me, as a queer person, I have the freedom to create any type of relationship model that works for me. And what's sexier than abolishing heteronormativity while I do it? That radical power lives within every single one of us."

"Whoa," I said, because that's all I could say. All of Maxine's words about love left me spinning. I wanted to ask a million more questions, but I thought about Lainie instead. I imagined her trying to poly me and me being like, "Hell no." I wanted to ask Titi Wepa if she'd ever been in a poly thing. I wanted context from some other place that these types of things existed outside Portland. I'd never ever heard of a polyamory thing happening in the Bronx.

"Whoa is fucking right, sweet Juliet." Harlowe nodded, her bright blue eyes fixed on Maxine. She reached behind me and rested a hand on her shoulder.

"Oh, and what's an emdiv?" I asked, as the phrase popped back into my head. "Is it a type of poly something?"

Again, Maxine and Harlowe laughed, like the way my aunts laughed when I asked them questions about sex. They laughed as if they were related to me and it was okay to find delight in what I didn't know.

"MDiv. is a master of divinity. I'm a professor of theology with a focus in Black womanist liberation theology," Maxine explained.

"Holy shit, you can get a master's in divinity?" I asked, impressed. "That sounds like some superhero stuff, like being a god or something. Are you a preacher too?"

"Nope," Maxine said.

"So what's the point if you're not bringing people to God?" I asked.

"We're all gods, Juliet," Harlowe said, blowing smoke out the window. "No, let's be real. There's only one God and He ain't me, you, or Maxine."

Maxine poked my thigh and I froze, again.

"I'm going to assume you were raised Christian, either Pentecostal or Catholic." Her hand rested on my thigh. Blood rushed to my head and my cheeks.

"Uh, uh, yes, Pentecostal Protestant," I sputtered.

"Okay," Maxine said, giving my thigh a small squeeze.

"That's where the one God thing comes from and also why I won't be a preacher. You want answers. Make your own religion out of doubt and curiosity. Don't go running after one God."

"Well, why not? Why not run after one God?" I asked. "I mean, obviously there are other gods in other religions and stuff, but I think it's all based on one God anyway. It's just the interpretation that's different."

"Yes and no. The only thing we can really do, Juliet, is develop our own sustainable theodicies. You know? We need to create our own understanding of divine presence in a world full of chaos. My God is Black. It's queer. It's a symphony of masculine and feminine. It's Audre Lorde and Sleater-Kinney. My God and my understanding of God are centered on who I am as a person and what I need to continue my connection to the divine," Maxine explained. She took a long breath. "It's everyone's job to come up with a theodicy. One that has room for every inch of who they are and the person they evolve into."

Harlowe snapped her fingers in agreement, the way people do when the spirit hits them at poetry slams. I wanted to tell Harlowe and Maxine about the time I met God. But I didn't; I couldn't. It was better to enjoy this silence. I tried to tell Lainie once. All I did was say that I knew for sure that God was real and it set off her debate team skills. You know, after she laughed and gave me that are-you-serious-babe? face. She deconstructed the reasons why attempting to make God exist past the realm of faith and into the realities of the human world was absurd. We lay on her futon in the middle of her dorm room, surrounded by tea light candles. She argued that God couldn't exist because God wasn't made up of anything solid. God couldn't be touched. God couldn't walk into a supermarket and buy a gallon of milk. Lainie had a million reasons why God wasn't real in the way that she and I were real. She explained that God was at best an elevated spiritual feeling and at worst one of the most brutal myths people have ever created.

I let her talk and clamped my mouth shut. I held my truth in my throat. That moment between us hurt me. I kept that hurt to myself. I locked it inside my chest cavity. I laughed off its existence in front of Lainie. And then I fucked it away using her body and that futon as transport. I hadn't thought about it since. In the truck with Harlowe and Maxine, it resurfaced. I wanted to blurt out all the wonder and magic, every detail of meeting God, but I didn't.

It wasn't the right time and I didn't know if there'd ever be a right time. Quiet settled in among the three of us, between our hips and shoulders and uncrossed ankles. Harlowe flipped through a CD case, found what she was looking for, and slid a CD into the player. I checked my phone and still no call or text from Lainie. I was about to text her again when Harlowe raised the volume on the stereo.

A white girl rock song I'd never heard before blared through the speakers. The lead singer screeched and wailed about a rebel girl who was the queen of her world. She sang about hearing revolution when the girl talked. Lainie and I read *Raging Flower* at the same time. All she could talk about was the feminist takeover of society. I put my phone away. This song was the universe's way of giving me a little piece of Lainie. Something inside of me clicked, like I was exactly where I needed to be in my life right in the truck with Harlowe and Maxine. Lainie was at her internship. She'd call. She always did. We were all rebel girls here. I fell asleep against Harlowe and didn't wake up until we got to where we were going.

CHAPTER NINE

AIN'T NO PARTY LIKE AN OCTAVIA BUTLER WRITER'S WORKSHOP

THE THREE OF us walked into a small classroom. There were about fifteen other people already in the room. Maxine was greeted by a woman draped in flowing, brightly colored clothes. Her limbs jutted out from between openings in the fuchsias and limes in her fabrics. Her locks wrapped around themselves into a high, full bun. Maxine and the woman embraced. Their hug was deep with room for soft hellos and murmurings of "you look so peaceful."

Maxine turned to us. "Zaira, this is Juliet, Harlowe's research assistant and houseguest. Juliet, this is Zaira."

I extended my hand. Zaira reached for it and pulled me gently into a hug. "Welcome, Sister Juliet," she whispered against my temple.

I hugged back hard. "Thank you."

Zaira's embrace was like having motherhood and a fortress

wrapped around my body. "Hello, Harlowe," Zaira said, taking one half step toward her.

"Zaira, it's good to be here. I love your open workshops," Harlowe said, and met her halfway. They held hands and forearms, smiled big, admired each other with respect. They didn't hug. I thought it was weird but only for a second.

Maxine and Zaira walked off, nestled together, greeting other folks around the room.

Harlowe paused, watching them move through the space. I stood by Harlowe.

We found seats toward the back, near a very small cluster of white women. I sat on the outskirts of their group next to Harlowe. But I realized that they were the outsider group. Black and brown women of all shades and sizes organized and worked this space. The energy in the room was warm and loving, like that plate of food your mom brings back for you from a party at your aunt's house. It felt like home, sort of. The styles of the women here were different from back in the Bronx. People didn't look hard here or worn down. They looked like they worshipped the sun and bathed in buttermilk. It made me feel like this writer's workshop was actually the official meeting of hippies of color or some shit. Just sitting there watching everyone made me view my people through a whole different lens, like we could be hippies too and that wouldn't make us any less Black or brown. I could dig that.

The power and confidence that radiated from Zaira permeated the bright classroom. She let go of Maxine's arm and walked to the front of the room, clasped her hands together, inhaled deeply, closed her eyes, and exhaled. All eyes were on Zaira. She smiled wide and opened her hands, palms facing up.

"Hello, beautiful women writers. Welcome to Honoring Our Ancestors, the Writer Warriors Workshop series. Thank you for your presence. I'd like to ask all of you to turn to your neighbor, look her in the eyes, and say, 'Thank you, sister, for sharing your time and essence.'"

I almost laughed, but the silence and reverence in the room pushed that laugh back into my chest. The woman next to me breastfed her baby. Such a beautiful and weird thing, breastfeeding. The mom held her child with one arm and reached out to me with the other. She said, slightly breathless, "Thank you, sister, for sharing your time and essence." I repeated the blessing, holding her hand and her child's hand.

Zaira blessed her neighbors on both sides. "Ashe, everyone. I'm Zaira Crest, founder of Black Womanists United, and we are here to celebrate the legacy of our sister Octavia Butler, one of the greatest writers of all time. Octavia gave us worlds caught in post-apocalyptic struggles, narratives billowing with critiques of the way racism and brutality are ingrained in white American society and culture, a culture that we must also navigate and reclaim. Octavia gave us the means to do that via a genre where there are no limits.

"This writing series is for the empowerment of Black women and femmes and the development of a Black womanist, Afrofuturistic writers' group. Blackness isn't limited to African

Americans here. We welcome our Afro-Latinas también y toda la gente morena, negrita, el color de la noche y de café con leche. Many of our meetings are closed to non-Black, non-POC individuals but members of the group expressed interest in offering open sessions. White allies, we ask that you respect this space, own your privileges, and remain open to your own journey. We welcome all women here and hope that we can all find or further cultivate our relationship to Octavia Butler's work and to the world of science fiction. In this series of workshops, we will also produce an anthology of sci-fi short stories with a social justice lens from writers of color. Thank you, sisters, for sharing your time and essence with us all."

Zaira was a force. Her words enveloped the room and while she spoke, all attention was on her. She gave us a minute to take it all in. I had mixed feelings, but only about the sci-fi part.

Science fiction was actually the worst. One Christmas, my parents decorated the entire tree in Star Trek ornaments, complete with a Spock tree topper that told us to "Live long and prosper." *Trekkies* wasn't a strong enough word for them. They also loved the *Star Wars* trilogy and every single 1950s sci-fi show ever created. And now here I was, somehow at a science fiction workshop. Hope no one minded me dying of boredom and awkwardness.

Zaira asked us to stand. We stood in a circle, holding hands. She implored us to find a sound within our bodies and memories, hold it in our hearts, and then share it out loud. She counted to three, and the women in the room opened their mouths releasing secrets, deep hums, and the sounds of prayers. Nothing came out of me. I held the hands on each side of me. I moved my mouth as if I was participating and that felt hella awkward too. The cacophony died down. Zaira called for it again. Once more, I pretended to make noise. Zaira watched me, read my lips, caught my lack of give, and let it go. The ice-breaker ended. Respectful silence followed. Zaira introduced two women, Aleece and Ruby, to the group. They read excerpts from *Parable of the Sower* and *Kindred*. Trippy shit, for real. I wrote the titles down in my notebook. Zaira and her team then asked us to brainstorm terms we associated with science fiction.

Words written in pastel yellows and pinks filled the black-board. *Asteroids, Milky Way, immortality, corporate colonization, gamma rays, meteor showers, parallel universe, queer futurism, no air, Gaia, geeks, moon colonies, lunar pulls, aliens, abduction, time travel, apocalypse* . . . We were asked to choose one word or phrase and write our science-fiction-loving hearts off. I wanted to leave, smoke a cigarette, and call Ava about this new-wave hippie brown people thing. Maybe she knew about it. But the affirmations and the weird humming got to me. Instead, I remained in my chair and wrote. My words were: *heavy metal, android Latinas,* and *time warp.*

Forty-five minutes later, a chime went off indicating the end of the writing exercise. Zaira encouraged the group to share a section of their work with the person they exchanged the greeting with. The mother turned to me, her child asleep in an orange stroller.

"Do you want to go first?" I asked.

"No way, go for it," she replied. She reached for my hand. "My name's Melonie, by the way, and this is my son, Nasir," she said.

"Juliet," I replied. We shook hands like we were already friends, none of those awkward jerky movements. It was smooth like passing slang through gossip.

I swallowed, just a little nervous but sort of excited too. Sci-fi was another notch in my belt of geekery on this trip.

But I pushed forward and read from the short story I titled "Starlight Mamitas: Three Chords of Rebellion," in which three Boricua sisters from New Brooklyn, year 3035, formed a heavy metal band called the Starlight Mamitas. They sold bionic quarter-waters and titanium Jolly Ranchers on the train to make money for lessons and instruments. On the night of their first real practice ever, a giant meteorite hit their mid-atmosphere apartment complexidome and . . .

That's where it ended.

Melonie stared at me. She flashed a huge grin, showing off beautiful full lips and a Madonna gap in her teeth.

"Wait, no fair. I want to know what happens next!" Melonie exclaimed, her voice breathy and deep. Her son wiggled in his stroller.

"So, I did it okay?" I asked. My heart beat fast. "Like, it's not stupid?"

"Nope, not at all, sister. You should definitely submit that to the anthology."

"Ahhh, no way! Thank you. That means a lot. I've never written sci-fi before."

Nasir woke up and gurgled next to us. His small baby fingers tapped my hand. Melonie cooed at him and then looked at me.

"Don't be afraid of anything. Submit your story but most of all submit to joy. That's what I'm teaching this boy right, here, isn't it, Nasir?" she asked, looking from me to him.

I tucked her words into my chest. Maybe this little story could be something great.

Melonie shared her piece and it was all about robots taking over the banking industries. They thrived on the evil souls of corporate bankers. It was heavy but rad. I wondered if moms were allowed to date. 'Cuz in another life I'd ask her out and then maybe she'd keep reading to me.

Zaira announced the end of the workshop. The room erupted in hugs and kisses, as if we'd all given birth. Melonie pulled me super close and whispered, "Submit that story, girl." She kissed my cheek and turned to baby Nasir.

Harlowe, Maxine, and I left the workshop after more hugs and rounds of introductions. I was exhausted. The workshop was beautiful, but I definitely needed some low-key chill time. I wasn't sure where I'd get any of that. The three of us passed two young white women who had been in the workshop with us. They were near the water fountains. I paused for a sip.

White Girl #1: "I loved the workshop, but, like, I don't get why the white ally thing has to be such a big deal, like why do we have to be the quiet ones? All our voices matter, you know?"

White Girl #2: "Exactly! It's like in my feminism we're equals. Why does any group have to have the dominant voice? I know reverse racism isn't technically real, but, like, this kinda felt like that."

Maxine and I rolled our eyes. I didn't really know what was wrong with what they said, but it felt weird. Their tone and the fact that this was what they took from the workshop felt strange but, like, whatever; white girls say dumb shit sometimes.

But Harlowe spun around and addressed them. "It's not about having a 'dominant voice.' It's about women of color owning their own space and their voices being treated with dignity and respect. It's about women of color not having to shout over white voices to be heard. We are the dominant force almost all the time. White women are the stars of all the movies. White women are the lead speakers in feminist debates, and it's little white girls that send the nation into a frenzy when they've been kidnapped. So if for, like, one or two hours in a small classroom somewhere in Oregon, a group of women of color have a workshop and have decided to open it up to us, we should be fucking grateful and not whining about how we're not the most important or equally as important. Our entire existence is constantly being validated and yeah, we have lots of shit to deal with because of the patriarchy. But for goddess sake, check your privilege. We're the ones that need to give women of color space for their voices."

At that last line, Maxine walked off. The two white girls stared at Harlowe, eyes wide.

White Girl #1: "Oh my fucking goddess, are you Harlowe Brisbane? The *Empowering Your Pussy* lady?"

I stayed for a minute. But I felt that weird thing again, like when the white girls first opened their mouths; something felt wrong. I didn't understand what Harlowe meant about "giving us space" for our voices. I left her to deal with her groupies. What was I supposed to do anyway?

Harlowe must have schooled those girls right, because it took her forever to meet us in the truck. Once again I sat in between them, but this time there was no cozy cuddling. None of our thighs touched. It was hard to keep my round everythings contained but I put in the effort. Harlowe was all angles. Pointy knees crossed over the other. Legs pressed into the passenger side door. Head practically out the window. Maxine drove sitting straight up, not taking an inch of extra space. The windows were down on both sides. The low roar of wind flowing into the car mimicked the tension between us.

"After years of workshops and endless conversations about race, you still manage to center whiteness," Maxine said finally, eyes on the road.

Her statement whipped through the car. I shrank lower in my seat, wishing they didn't have to look around my body to see each other.

"I'm white," Harlowe said, stopping hard on that *T*. "No matter how I said it, you're going to experience the white supremacy first. We've talked about this, Max."

I bit my bottom lip, tried to keep my eyes from going to wide. I could fix lots of things, but my face wasn't always one of them.

"You said, 'We're the ones that need to give women of color space for their voices,'" Maxine replied, tapping her fingers on the steering wheel. "Y'all don't need to give us anything."

Harlowe shifted her whole body, knees bumping into mine, to face Maxine.

"Max, I honor your statements. I still have much to learn," Harlowe said, her voice going low. "And also, we've talked about how you're extra sensitive around Zaira too."

Maxine stiffened at the mention of Zaira. The vein in her neck flexed. She swallowed hard, like when I'm about to say something reckless but still have the wherewithal to hold it in. Maxine turned her head to the side and cracked her neck.

"We'll finish this later," Maxine said and turned to me. "Apologies if we've made you uncomfortable, Juliet."

I looked at Maxine and then Harlowe.

"Uh, no worries," I replied, staring back down at my thighs in the dark.

Maxine and Harlowe didn't talk for the rest of the ride home. Just as we pulled up in front of Harlowe's, I got a text from Lainie. My heart fluttered and despite being tired and cranky, I smiled. There she was. We were gonna be okay. I left Harlowe and Maxine in the truck and raced into the house. I plopped on the bed, ready to read her text and call her back and talk on the phone all night long because we were due. It was gonna be so cute.

I looked closer at my phone and resisted the urge to fling it across the room.

Got your messages. Call me tomorrow.

Two basic-ass sentences. That was it. I read them over and over again for a full ten minutes. I pressed the call button and dialed Lainie's number. Maybe she had a free second. I'd catch her in that free second and get to say goodnight at least. The call went straight to voice mail. I hung up. That night I tossed and turned, I dreamed that Max and Harlowe were arguing about the dimensions of the universe. In the dream, Lainie's phone went straight to voice mail too.

CHAPTER TEN

GEEKERY AND A GIRL

I CALLED LAINIE the second my eyes popped open. Once again, it didn't ring. I sighed hard before the beep and left another message. I made a few dad jokes and put all the casual Tuesday-morning chill I could muster into my voice. On the inside though, my stomach churned and I ran through our last conversations in my head. Had I done something wrong? Or was she just so invested in saving the world one Democratic policy change at a time and I was the needy girlfriend who couldn't handle not hearing from her for a few days?

I slumped down the stairs, sliding my back along the rail. The smell of cinnamon and sweet potatoes wafted from the kitchen where Maxine stood, spatula in hand, in front of the stove cooking breakfast.

"I made extra if you want some," Maxine said, already grabbing another plate from the cupboard.

"What? Thank you so much," I said. I smiled and shrugged a little. "Morning hug?"

Maxine wrapped me up in her strong arms and hugged me tight. I hugged back, hard. It was good.

"How'd you know I needed one of those?" Maxine asked, her dimples flashing at me.

I peeked out the window and noticed Harlowe's pickup wasn't out front.

"'Cuz I needed one too," I replied, getting some coffee going.

I filled their small coffeemaker with El Jefe espresso. Set the flame on high and left it to boil. I heated up almond milk, nutmeg, and cinnamon in a small pan. Steam whooshed out of the espresso machine as the coffee brewed within. Maxine scooped sweet potatoes and mushrooms onto our plates. She fried some okra on the stove.

"I think my girlfriend's avoiding me," I said, pouring the coffee into the heated milk.

"So's mine," she replied, setting our plates on the table. "But white privilege makes it easy to play the victim, so I'm home making breakfast and not out chasing after her."

I knocked the sugar over at *white privilege*.

Maxine laughed. "Speak of the devil."

"That's not right," I exclaimed. I laughed too.

"Maxine," I asked, "what should Harlowe have said differently last night?"

She served the okra over the sweet potatoes. "Why don't you

try and answer that?" she replied. "Did any of it feel wrong to you?"

I stuffed a bite of okra into my mouth to give myself some time to think. Had any of it felt wrong? Since I'd arrived in Portland, all I'd amassed was questions. Questions about words and phrases, queerness, POC spaces, and whiteness. All of it swirled in my head, and I didn't know what to do with it. All of it seemed black and white and rich and poor and queer and weird. And hell yeah, it had.

"Harlowe made it seem like those white girls had to give us something," I replied, turning my head up a little. "Like, as if we couldn't do our thing without them?"

"See, you get it," she said. "Space isn't theirs to give to us. Nor is Harlowe separate from those girls. They are her. She is them. White allies need to keep that distance out of their community education."

"Damn but, like, at least she said something, right?" I asked.

Maxine raised an eyebrow, shaking her head. Her rich full laugh wrapped me up. These sweet potatoes and mushrooms weren't chorizo and a side of tostones, but they were love. I joined in with my wheeze laugh. Her shoulders heaved up and down with each breath. She'd fit right in at the breakfast table back home. Maxine dabbed at her eyes with her napkin. In all love and seriousness, she slowed down and looked me square in the eye.

"You know just saying something is good enough until it isn't. At all."

I nodded. I wondered if Maxine had known that or was just starting to realize it. Maybe even just then at the table between sips of coffee with me. And here I was all hurt because my girlfriend wasn't calling me back. We finished eating and washed dishes together. She offered me a ride to the library and I agreed. Maxine turned up Etta James's "A Sunday Kind of Love" as we hit the corner in her pickup. I re-read the slips of paper I had in my notebook on Sophia and Lolita. Etta James turned into Prince singing about the beautiful ones. Maxine waited for me to step into the library before taking off.

THE MULTNOMAH COUNTY Central Library seemed massive compared to the one at my school. It hummed with palpable excitement. I was a beast in the library. Libraries were where nerds like me went to refuel. They were safe havens where the polluted noise of the outside world, with the bullies and bro-dudes and antifeminist rhetoric, was all shut out.

Libraries had zero tolerance for bullshit. Their walls protected us and kept us safe from all the bastards that never read a book for fun.

I wandered around for a bit and found myself in the reference section. The smell of the room reminded me of our basement at home. There was an oversized *Webster's Dictionary* on top of a pedestal in the middle of the room. Curious, I made my way to it and flipped it open. I looked up Sophia and found the following:

* Sophia is a female name derived from the Greek word for wisdom.

* Sophia (∑οφία Greek for wisdom) is a central term in Hellenistic philosophy and religion, Platonism, Gnosticism, Orthodox Christianity, Esoteric Christianity, as well as Christian mysticism.

Christian mysticism? I could practically feel Harlowe doing a dance of menstrual joy. I kept Lolita Lebrón in my pocket and focused my search on Sophia/Wisdom. Using one of the open computers, I searched for the history of Greece and the origin of *Sophia*. Four potential book leads popped up. I went over to the help desk and asked an elderly librarian with purple streaks in her hair where I could find books about ancient Greece. She sent me to the back of the second floor. Electrified, my quest appeared surmountable and exciting. I found the Greek history section and was so immersed in research that I didn't notice the girl shelving books until we bumped shoulders, hard. My notes and all her books fell to the floor.

"Sorry 'bout that," she blurted out. "There's always so much to put away, I get a little lost in my head."

"No problem." Distracted as well, I crouched down and gathered my things. Some of my papers were mixed in with hers; I sifted through them.

The girl dropped down to collect her books. She smelled like vanilla lotion and **citrus** perfume. I looked up and she was hella foxy. Like jet-black hair, thick bangs, green eyes, olive skin, tattooed wrists kind of foxy.

"Um, I'm Kira and when I'm not bumping into strangers, I work here as a junior librarian. So if you need any help, please feel free to ask," she offered, gathering her books from the floor. "I owe you one."

"Thanks, I'm Juliet," I said. My brain started to get a little fuzzy taking in all of her. I knew my mouth was still open, but I couldn't close it because I couldn't think.

"Juliet," Kira said. "I've never met anyone with that name before. I like it."

"Yeah, um, my mom was super into the 1968 movie version of *Romeo and Juliet*," I said, heart beating fast, cheeks turning red. "And then I think I was also conceived at a later date while my parents were watching that movie and so as a joke and because of my mom's love of that movie, I was named Juliet, which I'm thankful for because my little brother's name is Melvin."

Kira laughed and all the pressure I felt mounting inside me because she was pretty and sweet wiped itself away.

"Well, Juliet, maybe you find me later and say good-bye before you leave, okay?"

I nodded and walked off wondering what it'd be like to spend the rest of the day talking to Kira. I forced my big, silly grin down and turned back to the Greek history books. Hours passed between pages. One of the first things I learned about

Sophia was that she was anchored to the word *philosophy*. She was also linked to Christian religious traditions, according to some of the texts, but none of the mentions were specific enough.

I was suspicious of the Bible. It had never been particularly forthcoming when it came to stories about women. Mary Magdalene wasn't really a hooker, and Eve didn't force Adam to eat that apple. What did painting women as untrustworthy or whorish have to do with God's love anyway? Those stories weren't even about women directly. They were stories about men in which women had side roles as the mother or the second wife or the daughter-for-sale. The fact that I grew up in a religious household and had never heard of Sophia further proved to me that the people interpreting the Bible were misogynists and didn't care about anything a wise woman had to say. Christianity wasn't budging an inch on this quest of mine.

There were allusions to Sophia's existence, but nothing real. My stomach rumbled. It was almost dinnertime and I still hadn't done any research on Lolita. The last book stared me in the face ready to take me down. I flipped it over, bored, and with bleary eyes burned through its glossary. Nothing, nothing until Sophia, page 48.

Sophia is the feminine representation of the wisdom of God.

Oh shit. I read that line over and over again. I read page 47 in order to lead myself into the scope of page 48. Sophia was divine wisdom manifested as a feminine force. God had a feminine side? Or was she an entire entity? Like the Holy Spirit? Was Sophia the Holy Spirit?

"Attention, the library will be closing in thirty minutes," blared the PA system. Jolted straight out of my thoughts, I scooped up the books I needed and ran to the copy machine. I dropped change into the first machine and copied page after page of Sophia-based information. A few paper jams sucked up some of my time, and I cursed at the machine.

"Watch out. That one's a little sensitive," said a voice from behind me. I turned around and it was Kira.

"So should I kick it?" I asked, trying not to stammer or embarrass myself. "What's the secret?"

"It's more of a hip check." Kira met me halfway and bumped her hip against the coin slot.

The copy machine rumbled again and printed. "Why aren't you just checking them out?"

"I don't have a library card."

"Well, next time you're here, come find me. We'll take care of that."

She walked away. I watched her walk away and at once I wanted her Doc Martens and her attention. Whoa, nope, I needed to slow all the way down. I shook out my hands. Kira was super nice and totally cute. But she was helpful because it was her *job*. Nothing else to see there or daydream about. That wasn't even the point. I was Lainie's girl and she was mine. The copier lid came down with a harsh snap. The people next to me looked up. I rolled my neck at them and shrugged. Somehow, I managed to get it together. I made the copies I needed without breaking the whole damn machine and left the library.

My phone vibrated in my back pocket. I sucked my teeth and pulled it out ready to start something. Lainie. I gripped the phone in my hand and picked up.

"Babe," I gushed, "I'm so glad we finally caught each other!"

"Yeah, me too," she said. "Is everything okay?"

"What do you mean?" I asked, finding a spot near the bus stop to wait.

"You've called and texted so many times, I just assumed there was some kind of emergency," she said.

"No, we just hadn't talked since I left home and I missed you," I replied.

She sighed. "Juliet, I'm really trying to be present during my time in D.C.," she said. "And you reaching for me every five minutes is distracting to say the least. You can understand that, right?"

That last statement stunned me like a middle finger flick to the neck. She checked me right in my soft spot, the place where I let myself reach out for her. I shouldn't have said I missed her. I sat down on the concrete against the slim metal bus stop pole.

"Lainie, I'm sorry. I . . ."

"It's okay," she said. "I gotta go anyway. There's this group thing that folks in my caucus have to attend. Call me with the real stuff. I love you."

The words spilled out of her mouth too fast for me to gather them or offer her my own. There was a click and then dial tone only. The bus pulled up. Its doors opened and shut as handfuls of folks moved in and out. I sat there on the sidewalk as a dozen or more buses came and went. A few hours passed before I yanked myself up from the floor and started the slow trek on foot to Harlowe's. All the lights were off by the time I made it back. I fell asleep sweaty and anxious going through all my text messages to Lainie, wondering what I'd done wrong.

CHAPTER ELEVEN

ORGANA-PON

"Know your period as you know yourself. Touch the wobbling blobs of blood and tissue that escape and land intact on your favorite period panties. Note the shades of brown and purple and volcanic reds that gush, spill, and squirt out announcing themselves. Slide fingers deep inside your cunt and learn what your period feels like before it's out of your body. Masturbate to ease cramps and meditate to soothe the spirit. Connect to your blood cycle. Build sacred rituals around your body during this time of renewal."

Raging Flower: Empowering Your Pussy by Empowering Your Mind, **Harlowe Brisbane**

•

OH FUCK, I leaked. Springing up, blanket and all, I tripped over my feet and landed hard on my bottom. The blanket fell to the side and there it was: a bright, candy-apple-red first-day period stain. *You've got to be kidding me.* I was an entire week early. I heard movement downstairs and panicked. I felt nauseous, my underwear was blood-soaked and the stain on the bed made my stomach drop. You just didn't bleed on someone else's mattress. Gross. God, I didn't think Harlowe would beat me with a chancla, but I couldn't imagine her being excited about it. All of me was mortified. At least now I knew why I dedicated myself to sitting on the sidewalk at the bus stop for hours yesterday.

The bathroom was downstairs. So were my soaps and access to water or bleach.

Blood dripped down my thigh. Fuck. I had to clean or hide or something. I dug into my book bag and found a three-day-old bottle of water and my deodorant. Panicked, I figured they'd help clean it up somehow. I poured what was left in the bottle onto my blood spot and scrubbed it with the deodorant. Cramps flowed down my lower back and along my ovaries. Fists clenched, scrubbing back and forth over the stain, I must have looked deranged. I refused to stop scrubbing even when I heard footsteps coming up to the attic. Maybe I could get it out . . .

"What the hell? Are you okay?" asked Harlowe.

"Just, um, you know, cleaning the mattress." I hid the deodorant behind my back, knees tightly pressed together. I was a sticky, aching mess, and I hoped Harlowe would just drift away and give me time to collect my dignity.

Instead, Harlowe hunched forward on bent knees. "Did you bleed on it?"

"Yes, and I'm totally sorry, and if you've got some bleach . . ." I looked at her and quickly looked away. I wanted the floor to devour me and save me from the rising levels of shame pulsing through my body.

"That's incredible." Harlowe grabbed my shoulders and hugged me. "Don't you see that it's a blessing?"

The mangled and bloodstained deodorant stick fell out of my hands.

Harlowe looked at it and laughed. "Not sure if deodorant was the right way to go. What we need is some salt and water for this ceremony."

"Ceremony?" I asked. "Are you going to make me gargle with my period blood? 'Cuz I don't think I can handle that right now."

"No, I'm not going to make you gargle with your period blood," Harlowe assured me, laughing. She walked to the other side of the attic and found me a clean towel. "But what an idea that is. I'll have to look into it. No, the salt and the water are to clean up the stain on the mattress. And as for ceremony, periods should always be celebrated."

She handed me the towel. I wrapped it around my waist. Harlowe went to the kitchen and returned with a container of sea salt and a cold, wet rag. She sprinkled salt onto the bloodstain and handed me the rag. Pun most likely intended.

"Scrub the stain," she said. "Not because I have a problem with it, because I don't, but scrub so that you know how to get rid of menstrual stains when you need to."

I ran the rag over the salt, over the stain. After a few scrubs, the bloodstain on the mattress disappeared.

"Whoa, that's some magical shit right there. I'm a week early and once again, I'm so sorry." I held the towel tight around my waist and made my way to the stairs. Harlowe followed. I ran into the downstairs bathroom and shut the door behind me. Harlowe stood outside the door.

"You're early because our cycles have synced! Don't be alarmed, Juliet. My cycle is probably going to mentor yours."

"So will your period get my period some narcotic-level painkillers or are we just going to ride out the gnarly cramps with some hope and faerie dust? Stupid cramps, it's like they don't show up until you've seen the blood, you know?" I said, agitated.

"Stupid cramps? Juliet, your body is going through an extreme transformation. It is purging itself of the beginning of life! My goddess, it's that type of thinking that keeps us bound to bleached tampons and toxic placebo painkillers. I never use that shit, Juliet. Meditation and masturbation are the only ways to relieve cramps. I'm convinced painkillers make your cycle worse, anyway. Wait, is it weird that I'm standing outside the door? I'm just so honored that you got your period in my house. Goddess, the energy is going to be great."

I stood arms wrapped around my chest, knees and thighs pressed together in an attempt to keep my non-alpha period from sliding out. *Fuck, this isn't my house. There's nothing in this bathroom that even looks remotely like Tylenol and I'm not masturbating in her bathtub.* I stood in the tub, still wrapped in that towel, still wearing bloodstained underwear. The thought of bleeding on her floor or getting blood anywhere else kept me frozen. Also, the idea of spending my morning running around after bloodstains with salt and cold water didn't hold any appeal.

"Harlowe," I said, voice weak, cringing, "I have tampons in my bag upstairs, I think. And, like, I have cramps and I kind of want to die right now. This is, like, first period ever level of embarrassment, just FYI."

"Don't worry, Juliet. Let me help. I can bring you your tampons or my sacred period ritual kit," she said from behind the door. "Which would you prefer?"

What a fucking question.

"I don't ever want to be the person that turned down a sacred period ritual kit," I said, settling into Harlowe's bathtub. I heard her move away from the door and head up the stairs. I hunched over and held onto my knees, thinking about the first time I got my period.

For an entire week, a whole month before I turned twelve, I hid, stuffed, pushed my underwear into a side pocket of the suitcase I'd packed to visit Titi Penny and Cousin Ava. I hoped no one would find them. I didn't want to ruin our mini-vacation— the one time Mom, Lil' Melvin, and me went away without Dad. They couldn't know that I was dying, not yet. The brown, sticky stains on my underwear were a sure sign that I had some sort of cancer or blood disease. Yeah, I knew about periods. Mom gave me a period talk and she talked about her period all the time.

Ava already had her period and told me things about it, like how much it hurt. But periods were supposed to be red, like apples and fire trucks, not brown like peanut butter. The dark brown smearable spots gathering between my legs were obviously signs that I was going to die, so I stuffed the underwear deep into that suitcase. Hoping and literally praying to God each night to keep me alive one more day.

I'd made it to Thursday. I was brushing my teeth in Titi Penny's bathroom when Mom burst in holding three pairs of rolled-up dirty underwear in her hands. I dropped my toothbrush on the floor. We stared at each other, the water still rushing into the sink. I ran to her, crying, and apologized for hiding the fact that I was dying. I told her that I'd been praying all week, but still the brown globs of death spilled forth. She held me close, laughing, running her fingers through my sweaty black curls. She promised I wasn't dying. I didn't believe her. I told her it was okay, that I was a big girl and could handle the truth. She knelt in front of me on Titi Penny's tiled bathroom floor and promised to God that I was not dying. Not only was I not dying, I'd in fact become a woman—an actual woman—and those brown stains were my period. She told me that periods can be brown, purplish, dark red; they can be watery or thick. She made me promise not to hide things from her again. Especially if I thought I was dying. I promised Mom that I'd always tell her the truth. She bathed me, brought me fresh clothes, and taught me how to use a maxi pad. I went from feeling mortified to feeling magical.

Harlowe returned, arms filled with goods. A period Santa Claus. She lit white candles and red candles around the porcelain tub. In the corner of the bathroom, she burned a cinnamon incense stick, offering its smoky sacrifice to a Virgin Mary candle. She ran warm water into the bathtub while I was sitting in it. The water warmed my toes, calmed my senses. Harlowe spread rose petals and drops of lavender oil into the water. She poured a bit of violet-infused soap in there as well. It bubbled up around my ankles. Harlowe offered a hand to take the bloody towel and I handed it to her. She exited the bathroom so I'd have some privacy. I slipped off my pajama shirt and bloody underwear, sank deep into the water, and soaked in the quiet and the bubbles. This sacred period ritual felt good and weird. My mom would have loved it.

Harlowe brought me a cup of peppermint tea. She presented me with comic books and a packed bowl full of fresh bud. She pulled out a gray, cloud-shaped box from the wooden cabinet and put it on top of the closed toilet lid. Harlowe sat down on the floor, back to the tub.

She read the label on the box to me. "'Organa-pons: Mother Nature's way of absorbing your essence. Organa-pons are made from unbleached, uncompromised cotton, helping women everywhere lessen their carbon imprint during menstruation.'

"Not sure what you use, but Organa-pons are an option. But let's talk about your cramps. Right now all of your heat is centralized in your ovaries, and that's what makes you feel like someone is stomping on your lady bits. Drink tea to balance your core temperature."

This was Advanced Bleeding, course level 300.

"Soak in the flowers. They add the vitality of the Earth to your aching body. I'm going to leave you be now. If you need anything, give me a holler." She added a few more rose petals to my bath. Harlowe touched my shoulder and left, shutting the door behind her.

Sinking back under the water, I concentrated on the floating petals and thought about the power of their energy. Could I bring that into my body or was that just hippie talk? The petals seemed to drift in rhythm with the pulse of my heartbeat. I resurfaced, rose petals on my head. The peppermint tea warmed my chest, my abdomen. My trust in Harlowe transformed from words into a full body experience. Harlowe's energy pulsed all around me. It was almost like the energy from the writer's workshop but focused on me. The time to believe in auras and faeries and all that other crazy shit had arrived, and I needed to either get with it or go home. I wasn't going home. I sank back under, moody and thoughtful, and let the bathwater swallow me whole.

I heard a tap on the door. Harlowe entered; she placed a pair of my shorts, a T-shirt, and an oversized yellow towel on the toilet and stepped outside. I finished up in the tub, inserted one of her bizarro Organa-pons, threw on the comfy clothes she'd left, and met her outside the bathroom door.

Harlowe led me back up the stairs to the attic. It glowed from the labyrinth of candles she had lit. She'd also made a little makeshift bed out of pillows and fluffy comforters; the bloody mattress was still drying. I lay out on the pillows. Harlowe fluffed out another blanket and draped it over my legs, as if we were in Pentecostal Church and I was being consumed by the Holy Ghost. Harlowe acted as a conduit between me and whatever period spirits she was summoning.

"You control the energy in your body. Never forget that, Juliet. Put your hands where it hurts the most."

I placed my hands right above my hips on my lower abdomen. Harlowe placed her hands over mine without touching them.

"Envision your ovaries as a color and tell me what you see," Harlowe said, in absolute concentration.

I closed my eyes and forced myself to believe. Well, at least she's not asking me to clap her to life like Tinkerbell in that old Mary Martin *Peter Pan* movie. Eyes closed, I saw nothing and felt acutely aware of the absurdity of my situation. A surge of pain pierced through my stubbornness, and I concentrated on the current within me. A vision of my inflamed ovaries popped into my head. I took in a nervous breath. Harlowe squeezed my hands, encouraging me to flow with it.

"I see them, but they're scratched. They're scratched, glowing red. This is so weird, Harlowe," I answered, surprised that I had the words to express what I saw.

"Weird is the only way to live," she said, her faith solid. "I can feel the redness from you with just my hands. You're going to have to concentrate your energy flow into your ovaries and change that color. They need to be visualized at peace, which will manifest itself in a different color. When you see them that color, you will have experienced your first healing."

At some point, Harlowe left the room. She left her strength with me. I used it to concentrate.

Sweat beaded on my forehead as my body released its inhibitions and got to work. My ovaries went from police siren red to soft, velvety purple. The purple subsided into a swimming-pool-blue. Blue. Calm. Cool. Smooth. I shifted that blue calm to smooth over my shame about Lainie not saying she missed me back. Her lack of response burned at my heart like arctic winds on exposed skin. It was part of all this. The blood on the bed and this ache in my body. I was low on love and iron. And instead of her giving me a boost, she'd kicked me and I'd apologized to her. I kept breathing until the pain subsided all over. The colors in my body kept me calm. The blue worked on all my aches. I lay in that meditative, pain-free blue sky space and lost track of time. Ava was going to bug out when I told her about this healing shit. (Oh, and she was gonna flip about the Lainie stuff too.)

I heard Harlowe welcome Maxine home. Their voices floated up the stairs as I lay on the mattress. I took a few puffs from

Saturn and blew out smoke into the air. Harlowe and Maxine were murmuring, giggling, all of it came up the stairs and mingled with the weed smoke.

Harlowe's bedroom door shut fast. The sounds of two people working up a love sweat wafted up from below. My body ached for that type of touch and connection. To make love out loud in your own home with the woman you loved was what life goals were built around, right? The thought of pressing sweet and totally hot librarian Kira against a stack of books made me bite my bottom lip. Hard. Then we were kissing against the copy machine and daydreams had to be exempt from cheating, right?

Meditation and masturbation are the only ways to relieve cramps. I made an executive decision and spent the next hour testing out the second half of Harlowe's sacred period ritual. Lainie didn't even cross my mind.

CHAPTER TWELVE

BANANA REPUBLICS AND CYCLES OF THE MOON

"Read everything you can push into your skull. Read your mother's diary. Read Assata Shakur. Read everything Gloria Steinem and bell hooks write. Read all of the poems your friends leave in your locker. Read books about your body written by people who have bodies like yours. Read everything that supports your growth as a vibrant, rebel girl human. Read because you're tired of secrets."

Raging Flower: Empowering Your Pussy by Empowering Your Mind, Harlowe Brisbane

I WOKE UP from my nap hours later, fingers sticky with dream shame. The library was out of the question today. If I bumped into Kira, it'd be all over my face that it was her and not Lainie that I thought about in the freshest way. I mean, dreams and fantasies are private and almost anything goes but still, I'd know. And if somehow Kira even picked up on any of my weird oh-my-god-please-don't-look-at-me vibe, I'd literally die.

No way in carajo was I chancing that. But also, my body, my orgasms, my fantasies. So I didn't feel too bad either. And obviously I smelled my fingers 'cuz that's what people do in real life and I'm not ashamed to admit it. Everything was fresh. Thanks for asking.

I pulled the covers over my head. Wrapped in the bright warmth of high afternoon sun and a fluffy white comforter, I ran my hands over my body. Checked on the beauty marks that dotted my collarbone and cleavage. Breasts swollen still but less tender than before. Hands down to pockets in hips, protectors of ovaries, I held them there. I wrapped my arms around myself and smiled.

"Hello, body," I whispered.

A cough, sputter, and rumble outside let me know that Harlowe had just left. I slow rolled out of bed and peered out the window. No black pickup truck either, so no Maxine. I had the entire house to myself. That never happened at home. Glory be.

I made coffee in my underwear: black booty shorts and a full-support red sports bra. But not one of those ugly ones, like one of the really cute ones that has mesh along the tops of the cups.

Anyway.

I plopped on Harlowe's couch with my café con soy leche

and went through my bag. Pulled out my purple notebook and saw *A People's History of the United States* at the bottom. I grabbed it too. Ugh, Phen gave me that book. Harlowe and I hadn't spoken about him since he left. I still felt bad about all that drama with him. If he had just been real and not judgmental, maybe we coulda figured out mom stuff together.

I turned the book over. It promised to be better and more thorough than anything I learned in history class. I compromised. No library day equaled committing myself to a thick history book. At some point, I was gonna have to combine everything I learned in this internship into a paper of some sort. I'd pull Phen's book into it all and beef up my bibliography section.

Reading something written by a white man in Harlowe's house was like breaking an unspoken rule of living in your feminism: no man-thoughts ever. But also, the book didn't have that annoying white-men-are-so-important-blah-blah vibe. This dude Howard Zinn was like "Hey you, wake up, look what really happened! The government's been lying!"

A People's History highlighted so many ways the US had always been involved in acts of terrorism and brutality. I chewed my thumbnail reading and linking shit to our current post-9/11 United States where color-coded levels of alleged threats of terrorism blasted from every television. I wondered if Latin America had something like that when the United Fruit Company ransacked them in the name of bananas and coffee and other natural resources. Fuck, just when you thought the US couldn't be any more brutal.

My parents raised me to believe that I should be proud to live in the land of the free. But what the heck did any of that mean if it came at the cost of other people's countries and lives? So, like, I'm free but your whole entire life has been gutted and everyone you know is either dead or indebted to some gringo corporation?

I read the passages on Latin America a few times over. I knew nothing about that region. As an educated Latina, shouldn't I have known something? Our democratic nation took over other people's lands, drained them of all the beautiful things native to their soil, and then enslaved the populations living there to harvest it all. I mean, that's what happened here in the U.S. White colonists committed genocide against Native people, snatched land, and created a whole entire violent-ass system of slavery by stealing people from Africa to make America a profitable and safe place for whites to live.

I just didn't know we did that everywhere else too. That's the fuckery they glossed over in Mr. McGregor's AP history class.

The underbelly of America creeped me out; the sociopathic patriarchy was still some old devil who never got put down.

I wrote down the terms that stuck out: *United Fruit Company, Guatemala, US interest, Good Neighbor Policy, banana republic.* The book mentioned banana republics but didn't define them. *What the hell is a banana republic?* Besides Lainie's favorite store, of course.

I cringed thinking of all the times she made me go to that bougie boring-ass store. The staff never spoke to me and nothing there ever fit my thick ass. I looked through index of *A People's History* and didn't find anything else specific to banana republics. I hopped up from the couch and scoured a beat-up dictionary on Harlowe's bookshelf for answers.

banana republic: a pejorative term that refers to a politically unstable country limited to primary productions (e.g. bananas) ruled by a small self-elected elite

What the unholy fuck? Gross. See, white people were just hella flagrant with their imperialist takeover shit. So since they needed special clothes to take over tropical countries, they decided to open up cute little stores called Banana Republics? Wow.

I flipped open my phone. No new messages or missed calls. Of course not. All of a sudden there had to be a "real" reason to call her. That shift threw me off, like why was she allowed to up and make that decision? And what's a real reason anyway? Isn't "I want to hear your voice" enough?

Still, though, this banana republic shit was important. This was the type of stuff we talked about in school. I had to call her; if she picked up, we'd get right into our rhythm of intellectual debates and nerd flirting. I paced in circles while it rang. She picked up. Milagro!

"Hi, babe," she said, her voice free of excitement.

I didn't let that bother me. Nope.

"Lanes, do you know what a *banana republic* is?" I asked, twirling my baby hairs into a frenzy.

"Yeah, it's the only place I can get khakis that fit right."

"No, Lainie, you can't shop there anymore. It's like named after some fucked-up shit the United States government did to Latin America for their bananas and control over them and shady stuff."

"Yeah, don't you think I know what a banana republic is? I'm surprised you didn't," she said. She sounded amused.

"Wait, this is like a thing people know? You knew this?! This is messed up, Lainie. Like, some store is profiting off a name that comes from fucking over people in Latin America. Isn't this the kind of thing we should be protesting? Or boycotting? Or one of those things you're probably doing at Democratic lesbian camp?"

"Juliet, calm down. It's just the name of the store, like the Gap. Awesome khakis again and the name doesn't mean anything nowadays anyway. Relax."

"You're just like them," I said, in a low voice.

"What?" she asked. The sharp edge in her voice with that one question was like if her whole body snapped to attention and focused on me.

"You knew and you didn't care," I said. "You're complicit—"

"Stop," she interrupted. "I didn't name the store that! Really, Juliet? I told you to call with something real and instead you call with accusations. We can't have a nice conversation these days, huh?"

"Conversations involve calls, something you seem to have forgotten how to do," I snapped, lungs losing air. "I've called and texted you. You haven't reached for me at all. I'm surprised we're even on the phone now." I strode back and forth across the living room. "I thought you'd get hype over this corporate-funded, materialistic joke on an entire region of the globe, but you're totally good with it."

"Yup, just call me Lainie the Invader of Latin America. Jesus Christ, Juliet," she said. Lainie sucked her teeth and sighed. The chatter of friendly voices on the other side reminded me that we were living in two different worlds.

"If the name fits," I said. I sucked a puff of air out of my thick plastic inhaler.

Lainie pounced before my lungs could even expand.

"Take it back," she demanded. "You know what?" she continued. "You have no idea how much pressure I'm under. You're off with Harlowe Brisbane, the Pussy Lady. I doubt she's got your time scheduled within an inch of your life." Lainie spoke sharp, her voice pointed. "I'm not doing this with you right now."

I heard the chime of an AOL instant message from her end of the phone and then Lainie hung up. That was it. That's all we said to each other. The albuterol-filled inhaler made me jittery. I couldn't relax. *Am I crazy? Did I just Harlowe out on her? She just fucking hung up on me.*

The front door creaked open and I jumped, still in my underwear.

"Hello, sweet Juliet," crooned Harlowe. "I brought us delicious things for dinner from my friend's communist farm."

She carried a bunch of reusable grocery bags. I rushed to

the door to give her a hand; she hugged me close, bags still in hand. We carried the bags into the kitchen. I threw on a tank top, hopped up on the counter, and watched her unpack all the groceries. The Joan of Arc wall clock chimed the hour.

"How was your day?" Harlowe asked.

"I yelled at my girlfriend for shopping at Banana Republic."

"It's funny that you have a girlfriend who shops at Banana Republic."

"Why?"

"Well, do you shop there?"

"No."

"Why not?"

"Because it's bougie."

"Exactly."

"Fair, but see the thing is, I really just wanted to ask her why she hasn't made more effort to call me and talk to me. I wanted to tell her that I miss her, but instead I bitched about imperialism and the United Fruit Company and khakis and shit, and then she hung up on me."

"She hung up on you?" Harlowe's eyes widened, amused, annoyed for me, it seemed. "Juliet, that is bullshit. Like, one, it's just rude, like absolutely rude to hang up on someone. Unless you were being abusive toward her, but I don't think you were, were you?"

"No, I don't think so. I called her complicit, though, like in league with white supremacy and foreign takeovers."

"Ooof. I mean, from the beginning the whole Banana

Republic thing would have been a deal breaker for me, but why do you care now?"

Why did I care?

"I didn't know about all that evil stuff before." I held up *A People's History*. "Phen gave me this book, in the most douche-y way, but still. I started reading it and now I care, you know? And I want Lainie to care and man, these cramps are the worst."

Harlowe patted my knee and handed me a bag of granola. She pulled peppers, mushrooms, and carrots from the reusable bag. The chop-chop of vegetables being split open on the counter filled the kitchen. I didn't move from my spot on the counter. My mom would have already been love-yelling at me to get off and help, but Harlowe wasn't my mom. Harlowe was something else. I watched her slice peppers and carrots into slivers. She heated up flatbreads on an iron skillet and moved them to a plate. She filled small bowls with hummus and mango chutney.

"She knew that the name Banana Republic actually meant something, you know. It's a tongue-in-cheek fuck-you to countries that have been exploited for their natural resources, and I just can't believe I didn't know and she did. And, like, I think I feel cheap. I've stood in that store with her a million times and have always felt my skin crawling. None of the clothes were made to fit me. None of the people shopping in there look like me. The few times I've been in there by myself, I've been followed around the store by employees. Everyone is white, skinny, and rich, and oblivious to the fact that I'm a person. I thought all those feelings were in my head, figments of my imagination, but maybe they're not. Maybe there's something ingrained in a store like that that's made me feel that way. It's bigger than the store too, right? Everything is like that in this world. It's heavy."

"Heavy as a huge set of beautiful ovaries. Get a little hysterical, Juliet. I mean, that's why vibrators were invented, right? Ask the questions that make you feel like your heart is blasting out of your chest. Society, government, white supremacist power structures, blatant hatred of women, and a whole slew of other institutions are all working together to make it so that you gotta dig to find out even a shred of truth. They don't want you to dig. That's how this world is set up. People don't even want to tell you that your vagina is called a vagina, you know? Why would someone spell out the violent and racist history of their business? Capitalism, baby."

"And what's funny is that Phen bought me this book," I said. "As harsh as he was, he still offered me another place to start digging. Your book was first but still, you know?"

Harlowe looked at me with those big watery blue eyes. "Yes, Phen's a glorious one," she replied.

"Are you sad that he left?" I asked.

"No way," she said. "He made the best choice for himself. I'm proud, actually."

"Word." I nodded. I took a bite and wished him well.

As we ate, Harlowe told me about her communist friends with the farm who were also doulas and played in a hillbilly funk band. The one named Jug also played the jug. I shared in-depth details about the daydream-inducing encounter with Kira the smoking-hot librarian and all the foxy dykes at Blend and how they wanted her to do a reading there. I told her that I wasn't exactly sure what white allies were and asked her about the Octavia Butler workshop and if Maxine was coming home tonight.

"Maxine has her own place over on Northeast Alberta, but tonight is a Zaira night." Harlowe shrugged.

"Wait, what's a Zaira night? Like, are they doing another workshop?" I asked. Jealousy crept in quick; I wanted to be there too.

"No, not another workshop. Zaira is Maxine's secondary partner," Harlowe said.

Escandalo. Tres Mujeres, Una Relación. Portland.

My mouth dropped open. "You're the primary and Zaira's the secondary. That's for real? Y'all have Maxine on different nights? This is how the poly thing works?" I asked, eyes wide. I needed to get myself together.

"Yes and no. Maxine shares her time as she sees fit with whomever she wants. This is how the 'poly thing' works for us. Zaira and I aren't romantic partners, but we've known each other for a long time. There's a mutual respect. Plus, she's one of the most vibrant and beautiful women I've ever met. I'm happy that they found love together too."

Harlowe's face was golden, even in the dark. And what she

said was the gayest, most beautiful love poetry. If Harlowe could be in love with Maxine while Maxine and Zaira loved on each other, then I could definitely have a crush on Kira the librarian and Maxine and still love Lainie, even after all this Banana Republic business.

Harlowe's mind seemed like it was somewhere else. She rolled a cigarette and set it down by her thigh, unsmoked. I ate more food and grabbed two Sierra Nevadas from the fridge.

Harlowe placed a calendar on my lap. It was almost as wide as my chubby brown thighs. "It's based on the cycles of the moon. I track my period with it, and I think it'll be integral in helping us keep track of the women we're researching."

A bright yellow moon, fluid in its watercolor-based design, stretched across the front of the calendar.

"You want me to track their periods?"

Harlowe laughed. Her laugh could also be mistaken for a cackle, a joyous cackle. She flipped through the calendar.

"No, I mean, yes. If somehow you can. Oh my goddess, that would be brilliant!" Harlowe cackle-laughed again. "But I was thinking we could mark their birthdays and their astrological signs and not only track their accomplishments but maybe connect them in some greater spiritual, lunar warrior kind of way. That'd be rad, right?"

"Yeah, totally," I said, flipping through the calendar. There was a giant red *P* marked on today's date and yesterday's date. The giant *P* was marked for every day of the week we were in.

Harlowe tapped today's date with her finger. "That's me, right there, alpha period. Always right on time. Always connected to Lady Moon."

"You think it matters if we track their birthdays, like you really believe in that astrological stuff?"

Harlowe took a sip of beer. "There's a lot of wisdom in the world that's been discarded because it comes from traditions created by women, indigenous peoples, and other non-white-dude customs. So, hell yeah, I believe in this stuff."

"Word, I'm down. You're right."

I grabbed the calendar, added my birthday, and placed a giant *P* in the following week. She lit her cigarette. We sat shoulder to shoulder and discussed what I'd uncovered about Sophia and wondered about what kind of majestic, surreal period the feminine representation of the wisdom of God would have. Harlowe and I talked late into the night.

Before bed, I checked my phone. No new messages from Lainie. I stopped myself from texting her, from calling her, from heaving out a weepy apology into her voice mails. I turned the phone off, took some deep breaths. Ten in, ten to hold, and ten to release. I needed sleep and time to think.

CHAPTER THIRTEEN

I DIDN'T COME TO KILL ANYONE,
I CAME HERE TO DIE

"I SHOULDN'T EVEN be on the phone with you right now," I whispered.

"*Pero* like, why not?" asked my cousin Ava, in the Puerto Rican accent she could slap on or turn off as the situation necessitated.

"Because, I'm in the library, yo." I hid between two aisles of books. This was my third day in a row at the library. Funny how a fight with your girlfriend can push your focus into hyperdrive.

"Ay, Juliet, no one in the library really cares," Ava said. "And I'm telling you the book you need on Lolita Lebrón is called *The Ladies' Gallery*. It was written by her granddaughter and I'm mad you don't know who she is and some white lady had to tell you about your ancestors."

"Listen, we grew up together and I never heard you talking about no Lolita Lebrón. How was I supposed to know? It's not like she's related to us, and Harlowe didn't tell me anything. I found this name in her pile of names, so, like, be easy."

Ava half-sighed. "Juju, if you were some clueless blanquita, I'd have so much disdain for you right now. But since you're my blood, I'll forgive you. Lolita Lebrón was only the illest Puerto Rican freedom fighter nacionalista. She, like, tried to blow up Congress in the fifties."

"Word? How do you know about her and I don't?"

"Nena, I'm on my ethnic studies grind. That's why you should come visit me. I'm out of school until August. Come sit on this balcony with me, smoke some trees, take the boat out, discuss the global impact of colonization and the merits of deviant sexuality."

"So many merits. All of that sounds good, Ava, but I can't take time off from this internship. I gotta stay in Portland 'til it's done. But girl, if I could, I would."

"Aight, but I miss you, and if you hit any more roadblocks with the ladies on those magic scraps of paper, you call me, okay? Call me anyway. I love you."

"Love you too. Oh and, yo, I have so much period stuff to talk to you about," I said, a little too loudly in the middle of the library.

"Period stuff?" Ava asked. "You know I fucking love period stuff."

"Word, we'll talk soon."

Ava made me smile big. She was cool, so damn cool, and her

heart was open to me. Our relationship was solid in that cousins kind of way. If I ever needed her, I know she'd be there, but we were missing that regular closeness. When did she get so with it? How was she able to just drop colonization into conversation like that? I fucking loved her. Any other time and I'd be on the first plane to Miami. But I felt needed here; Harlowe needed me. My purpose was so clear. I mean, not like it hadn't always been clear. Mom and Dad have asked only three things from me: get good grades, do as they say, and have faith in the Lord. I've always done those three things. Studying hard, receiving A's, and being obedient to them and God have been my way of thanking them and respecting their work ethic. As their first-born daughter, I never had much say in the matter. Get good grades or else! Worship God or go to hell. Do as we say or suffer the consequences. What the consequence would be, I was too scared to ever find out. But this internship gave me a different purpose. I chose this. I reached out to Harlowe. I asked. I wanted. I received.

Still, the idea of going to visit Ava and Titi Penny tempted me. Ava, the rebel, the brown goddess, the beautiful one, the one who received full scholarships to all the colleges she applied to, the one who wore black lipstick and fishnet stockings to temple. And Titi Penny, my secret favorite titi, encouraged her and allowed all of it while still maintaining this standard of excellence that both of them subscribed to. I'd spent many nights listening to both trains rumbling by and my parents' Christian music while wishing I was Titi Penny's daughter, that Ava and I were sisters, that I was somewhere else.

But this wasn't the right time to go on a trip to Miami. I was already somewhere beautiful and weird. I had a mission and nothing was going to distract me. Nothing.

Kira was at the information desk. I made a mental note about her working the Saturday morning shift. She signed me up for a library card and helped me find the library's sole copy of *The Ladies' Gallery*. I sat in a cubicle, fully immersed, swallowing images of a strong Puerto Rican woman and her fight for liberation all told through the eyes of her granddaughter. I felt like a granddaughter too. Seated at the foot of a rocking chair, taking in a story of the life someone's grandmother once lived. The weight of Lebrón's legacy rested heavy, tumor-like, on the life of her granddaughter. In fact, right from the beginning, Irene Vilar admitted that she'd tried to kill herself and was in a mental institution. Man, if my grandma tried to overthrow the government and then landed in prison for like ever, I'd have some really deep issues to deal with too. That type of pain has gotta get passed on, right?

But I took pride in Lolita Lebrón's bold moves; nobody stopped her from walking into the US House of Representatives and busting shots in the name of Puerto Rican nationalism. It was 1954 and the US government was treating Puerto Rico like its own private island: gouging it for sugar, using its shores for military purposes, and passing laws that made it illegal to display Puerto Rican flags or to fight for Puerto Rico's independence from the United States.

Apparently, the US didn't ask the people of Puerto Rico if they wanted to be a protectorate or not; they didn't ask the people anything. They just swooped in and took control after the Spanish American War. Lolita wasn't having any of it. She was a nacionalista on the island and when she moved to the US in the late 1930s, she saw how her people were being discriminated against and how they were pushed into obscene poverty. Lolita Lebrón took an order from Pedro Albizu Campos, leader of the Puerto Rican Nationalist Party, and made sure it succeeded. She led the coup d'état into the House of Representatives. She fired the first shots. She shouted, ¡Viva Puerto Rico *Libre*!

My United States did this to Puerto Rico? The country I pledged allegiance to all through school, this country where allegedly anyone could just pull themselves up out of poverty and make something of themselves; this country decimated an entire island? And I thought banana republics were the worst of it. How could I not know this history? How could I walk around my block with a boricua bandanna wrapped around my head or march down Fifth Avenue next to the Goya float in the Puerto Rican Day Parade but not have even one clue that people were imprisoned and killed because they rallied against the US occupation of Puerto Rico?

How did I know about Walter Mercado and Jennifer Lopez but know nothing of Lolita Lebrón? We watched *West Side Story* every Thanksgiving, rooted for the Sharks, and cried for Maria's heartbreak and grieved with her. Our identity as Puerto Ricans was tied into a movie where both lead actors were white. My parents didn't tell me that either. I had to find out on AMC that Natalie Wood was white, and I cried like a bitch that day. I felt robbed of something, as if a lie had been woven into the narrative of my Nuyorican identity. Why was a musical more important to have on a loop in our home but not an act of bravery in the name of a free Puerto Rico? Maybe America just swallowed all of us, including our histories, and spat out whatever it wanted us to remember in the form of something flashy, cinematic, and full of catchy songs. And the rest of us, without that firsthand knowledge of civil unrest and political acts of disobedience, just inhaled what they gave us.

I read and took notes on Lolita Lebrón's life, not paying any attention to the people milling about the library. I didn't even think about Kira. I wrote and read until my knuckles ached. The questions in my head didn't give me any sort of break. Did my parents know about her? They had to, right? Why didn't they ever tell me? Why was everyone on some don't-tell-Juliet-about-life shit? I would have traded everything I knew about Abraham fucking Lincoln or Jesus turning water into wine for one afternoon of Lolita with my mom and dad. How could they leave this stuff out? What kind of Puerto Ricans did they want me and Lil' Melvin to be?

A part of me wanted to get on the phone with my parents,

stomp around the library, and interrogate them. But that's what I did with Lainie and it all blew up in my face. It'd been two whole days since our Banana Republic fiasco and we still hadn't talked. To go through all that unnecessary drama with my parents seemed stupid. Besides, the absolute last thing I wanted to do was make things more awkward, to feel even more distance between us. I'd rather sit tight in emotional purgatory than dive right into the fiery pits of hell and question my parents' motives behind our upbringing. Maybe I was just punking out. Either way, I wasn't making any sudden movements in their direction. I counted to ten in my head and continued reading.

When they arrested Lolita Lebrón after her attack on the House of Representatives, she's quoted as saying, "¡Yo no vine a matar a nadie, yo vine a morir por Puerto Rico!" Even with my limited ability to read Spanish, I got it. "I didn't come here to kill anyone, I came here to die for Puerto Rico!" I wrote her words down in my purple composition notebook and wondered how they'd look tattooed across my chest. What did it feel like to be so committed to something that you'd die for it? I didn't feel that way that about anything. Not about being gay or trying to become a feminist, nothing. Maybe that was the difference between me and Ava or me and Lainie or me and everyone else. Did everyone else have that type of purpose in their lives?

A note from above fell into the pages of *The Ladies' Gallery*. I looked up in time to watch Kira turn the corner walking past with a pushcart.

Hi, I have cookies. Meet me on the front steps in 10? —K

I read Kira's note a few times. A flush of heat passed through my body. Cookies. She had cookies, and she was going to share them with me. I jumped up, threw the book on Lolita in my bag, and checked my fly to make sure my pants were zipped—nothing embarrassing was allowed to happen. I hadn't had a damn cookie since I left the Bronx and landed in healthy vegan Portland. I walked toward the front, saw the steps through the window, got nervous, and dodged left into the bathroom.

Overthinking. So much overthinking.

My breasts started to sweat, the skin above my lip started to sweat. Oh God. Was meeting a girl for cookies a date? Did I have to inform Lainie? Welp, couldn't do that right now anyway. No, it was fine. If Lainie was going to be all "present" in her internship life, then I had the right to do the same.

Also, damn, like, someone who wasn't Harlowe or Maxine was being mad sweet to me. Had I already taken too long? I checked my watch. Eight minutes left. Maybe it was just a totally normal, friendlike cookie-sharing situation and in that case, I was just wasting valuable cookie-eating time. Deep breaths.

The mirror reflected someone stressed out, too chubby in some parts, hair too frizzy around the edges. I hadn't done my eyebrows in two weeks. The cute librarian wanted to hang out with *me*? I wiped the sweat off my breasts and neck. I splashed some water on my face, slicked back my baby hairs. I could do this. I could eat cookies with Kira. I pushed the door to the bathroom open and made my way to the front. She sat on the top step. Next to her was a tin box overflowing with chocolate-chip cookies. My fucking favorite. She waved me over. Two halves of one cookie in her hand, she offered me one. I accepted and sat beside her. We ate in silence, glancing at each other, and tried to hide shy smiles. Her black boots came up to her knees. I stared at the gold buckles that crossed them at the ankles. In two bites, Kira's half was gone. She broke another cookie in half and offered it to me.

"I bake things. Cookies mostly. It's weird, but I can't trust people who don't eat sweets." The edges of her lips curled against her teeth when she spoke. Bottom lip pierced. I wanted to kiss her.

"Me neither. I don't trust people who can't share, so thank you," I replied, trying not to die of nerves. Eye contact was officially happening between us. I shifted a little closer to the tin box.

"You're welcome," Kira said, wiping cookie crumbs off her lips, accidentally smudging her plum lipstick. "I walked past you twice, and it's okay that you didn't notice, but it made me wonder what you were reading because, like, I've been reading all day and it hasn't stopped me from noticing you."

The amount of butterflies flapping inside me was immeasurable. Like, hella immeasurable.

"The Ladies' Gallery. It's a memoir about a woman named Lolita Lebrón. Long story short, she shot up Congress in the fifties, all in the name of Puerto Rican nationalism. I've spent

most of the afternoon wondering why my parents never told me about her. Then a sweet girl dropped a note on my lap, and I almost hid in the bathroom forever because she offered me cookies."

"I'm glad you made it out of the bathroom. And to be fair, I had three heart attacks before I dropped the note. I want to know more about your research and the woman who blew up Congress. And about you."

"More about me?" I asked.

"Yes, you. But my break's almost up," Kira said. She slid her long black hair over her shoulder in one slow movement. "Maybe I could give you a lift later or walk you somewhere?" She stood up. So did I. We were inches apart; no room to run. She smiled at me, a dimple in one cheek the size of a dime. Something I could press a finger into or my lips against.

"Um, sure, either. A lift home or you could walk me across the street to the bus stop."

Could she tell that I was about to geek out? That if she reached for me, I'd let her get it right here on these steps?

"I'll meet you here after closing. Glad you liked the cookies," she said. Kira picked up her tin and headed inside. She disappeared through the entrance doors. I still had half a cookie in my hand and plenty of time to hyperventilate before the library closed.

I don't remember walking back inside. All I remember is how warm I felt, how it'd been a while since someone noticed me the way Kira did. In the Bronx, I was used to men catcalling me on the street or cornering me in the bodega. Unwanted attention pushed upon me or demanded of me. And at school, I pursued Lainie. I put the effort into being sweet and finding ways to talk to her. But Kira, this girl from the library, she sought me out. She thought I was cute. She wanted to get to know me better. Kira. I wrote her name in the margin of my notebook. The cookies were damn good too. I'd go on another cookie date with her any day of the week.

Back in the library, I attempted to pull myself together. I still had work to do. I couldn't find any other books on Lolita Lebrón. I even asked Kira to help and we didn't find any. But we did find some books about Puerto Rico during her time as an activist, before the attack on Congress. In those books, the focus was on the men leading the revolution. Anything about Lebrón was at most a paragraph and often just a footnote. She wasn't alone in her ambush of Congress. There were men with her. Nothing about her or the attack was as substantial or as interesting as *The Ladies' Gallery*. The research kept me busy for a few more hours. It made me forget my nerves about Kira and my anguish over the silence between Lainie and me.

"Attention, the Multnomah County Central Library will be closing in fifteen minutes."

I made my copies and checked out my books. I almost walked right out of the library and then remembered Kira's offer to take me home. I made a hard U-turn and found myself back in the bathroom. Again, wild baby hairs and a nervous me. It was fine. It was just going to be a walk to the bus stop.

I splashed cold water on my face and used wet hands to pat down stray baby hairs again. Pulled my black curls into a pony-tail. The look: Severe. Slick. Cool. Unfazed. I pulled out black eyeliner, smudged a dark line along my eyelids, the slate-gray light of the bathroom not helping a bit. Then mascara, fluffed-out long lashes, looking less *Little House on the Prairie* and more *Mi Vida Loca*. I used Apple Blast lip gloss on my lips and took a look at myself. Better. Fresh-faced, I stared hard into the static of the bathroom mirror, trying to imagine her wanting to kiss me. I looked again and saw myself and it was okay. I'd kiss me.

The air outside was cool on my face. People spilled out of the library alone or with their children. The sky cracked into pieces of neon orange and soft pinks. Two teenagers made out on the street corner. So jealous. They were leaning against a mailbox. The bus I normally took flew by the stop. I waved, like, *Later, suckers, I got a date with a librarian.*

I sat on the front steps of the library and waited for Kira. The flurry of people exiting the building slowed. The soft pinks pulsed into blood-orange hues, the sky moved west and rolled clouds with it. Still no Kira. From down the block, a motorcycle engine revved, sounded like a street bike of some sort, maybe a Kawasaki or a Honda.

That sound reminded me of my next-door neighbor, Big B. He rode with the Ruff Ryders bike crew and fixed motorcycles for a living. The sounds of engines revving and tires being spun out for hard turns and endos filled my summer nights. I won-dered what he was up to tonight. So lost in missing the Bronx,

I didn't notice the bike until it pulled up right in front of me. It wasn't a street bike, though. It was an old Harley, something you'd see in a movie from the '70s or something. The rider wore tight blue jeans and a black hoodie under a black leather jacket. The black boots looked hella familiar.

"Hi, hope you weren't waiting long," a voice said. She took off her helmet.

I stepped closer to her, mouth agape. This was definitely happening to me. Hot chick on a motorcycle. My mouth went dry, other parts of me not so much.

"Still up for a ride home?" Kira smiled at me, holding her helmet on her hip.

"I would love one," I said. My brain was fuzzy. I felt all hot and twitchy. How were words even coming out of my mouth?

I told her Harlowe's address and pulled the straps of my book bag tight against my back.

Kira only had one helmet and she made me wear it. Chivalry was not dead in Portland. I wrapped my arms tight around her waist and breathed in the leather of her jacket. She zipped through the downtown area, a comet hurtling through the darkness of the galaxy. The vrooms and squeals of her bike as she accelerated and made turns thrilled me, made my thighs ache in that good way. I needed this noise to refuel. She felt like home, like the hum of a hundred street bikes and the neighbor who was more like a brother to me. Eyes closed, I imagined Kira zooming up the Bronx River Parkway and ducking under the elevated train on White Plains Road.

"You doing okay?" she asked, stopped at a red light.

"I'm amazing."

She put her hand over mine for a moment. Dinosaur-sized butterflies fluttered in my stomach. She smelled like citrus and leather. I was so into it. The whole scene made me feel like I wasn't myself. I was on the back of a vintage Harley, riding down the middle of a street I didn't know with a beautiful biker librarian. I was free of self-doubt. No question of whether I deserved this or if this was even my life. No one was yelling at me or trying to make me feel inferior. No one was telling me this was just a phase or that I needed to be better about knowing my history. I wasn't worried about my mom or my girlfriend or anything.

I held onto Kira's waist as she accelerated through the intersection. She weaved in and around the streets, down quiet back roads. Her path to Harlowe's didn't follow the bus route. It might have been a little longer, but I didn't care. She could have taken me on a road trip and I would have been just fine. Every time we stopped at a red light or a stop sign, she put her hands over mine. Each time made me weak, like for the first time ever I was swooning in real life.

Kira stopped her bike in front of Harlowe's house. I didn't move. I felt her hands on mine again. I thanked her in a rush, pressed the helmet into her arms wishing it was my body, and headed up the front porch steps. She was waiting for me to get inside the house. Again with the chivalry, who was this girl? I couldn't let her leave. No way. Not when I felt all these damn butterflies and everything. I spun on my heels quick, bounced back down the front steps, and hugged her. Her leather-clad arms pulled me close; she felt strong. We took a minute to look at each other. Our lips were so close together. If I had licked mine, I would have touched hers. I couldn't even breathe.

"You know that this means we have to go for another ride soon," Kira said, her green eyes staring into mine.

"Word," I said and nodded, trying not to kiss her even though that was all I wanted to do. *Word? That's the best I could do?*

Kira smiled. "Got a pen?"

Unable to formulate words, I pulled a Sharpie out of my bag and handed it to her. She wrote her number on my forearm.

"Call me whenever," she said, meeting my gaze. My body temperature increased by about ten degrees.

And then she kissed my cheek, revved her engine, and rode off.

This girl could ride. I watched her until she was a speck of magic dust in the distance. Deep breaths calmed my hands but didn't ease the fluttering in my chest. I could still smell her hair and her leather jacket.

A small package awaited me on Harlowe's front porch. The return address was Lainie's home address, not the one for her internship. I picked it up, still breathless from being that close to Kira. The package felt out of place in my hands, like it didn't belong in this moment. Lainie didn't belong in this afterglow that someone else created. She'd never kissed me on the cheek like that. Kira's kiss was thoughtful and gentle and why did Lainie have to arrive on this doorstep at this moment anyway?

I sat on the porch with her package on my lap and caught myself. I'd been craving Lainie's attention this whole time and here it was. Why did it have to come right after such a terrible fight? And such a delirious and beautiful ride with Kira? Both worlds were pulling at me, the Juliet I was when I left and the one I was hoping to be.

I had someone else's kiss on my cheek and I liked it. I had Lainie's love in my hands and in my heart. But something was different, I'd called her complicit. I accused Lainie of supporting all the systems we were fighting together. And here I was holding a piece of her affection and care for me, when I still hadn't sent her the mixtape I made. I walked into the quiet darkness of Harlowe's home full of feelings.

Maybe all I really needed was a love letter and a dyke feminist power babe mixtape from Lainie. I took a deep breath. It would be okay. It had to be, right?

Dear Juliet,

There are five crumpled pieces of paper on my desk. I'm hoping this won't be the sixth. I need to get through this. You deserve it.

I know I've been a little cold and distant. I've dodged you, my parents, other friends. All that matters is this internship and our politicians and their campaigns. Nothing and no one else matters.

That's a lie. Sarah matters. Sarah is a girl from Texas that I met at the White House. Wait, let me start over. Can I start over?

Before I tell you about Sarah, you have to know that my heart's been yours since the second you walked into Dr. Jean's women's studies class. I loved you from that moment, Juliet.

You need to know that I ignored Sarah at first.

You need to know that I tried to fight my feelings for her.

You need to know that I never for a second thought that this feminist, power-lesbian mixtape would become a breakup CD.

I love you, Juliet, but I haven't been honest with you.

I'm in love with Sarah. She's the one I want my parents to meet, like as my official first girlfriend.

I think she's my forever person.

I never meant to hurt you, Juliet. Never ever. I'm so sorry. I hope we can still be friends.

See you in September,
Lainie

CHAPTER FOURTEEN

OPERATION: WALLOW IN MY SADNESS FOREVER

"To love another woman is to streak naked across the sky, swallow the sun in one bite, and live aflame. To love another woman is to look at yourself in the mirror and determine that you are worthy of the galaxy and its fury. To love another woman is to love yourself more than you love her."

Raging Flower: Empowering Your Pussy by Empowering Your Mind, Harlowe Brisbane

MY FIRST BREAKUP. I drowned in pictures of her, in the replays of our last night together, and in every note of that fucking awful mixtape she made me and the one I never got a chance to send to her. Lainie was in love with another girl. Sarah.

Sarah. Sarah. She'd tried to fight her feelings, so shit was strong between them. All I saw in my head was what I imagined Sarah to be. Probably white, straight hair, blond, perfectly feminine. Everything I wasn't. Everything I'd ever hated about myself came out of my pores. Sarah was going to meet Lainie's parents as her girlfriend, no wait, excuse me: her forever person. I wasn't good enough. Thick-bodied, bespectacled, cautious, overtly Puerto Rican and brown-skinned, book-nerd, daydreamer. Were all these elements the sum of why Lainie refused to bring me home for real? Why she fucked me in the dark and in the back of her mom's car but never brought me to the table as more than a school friend? Why she had a fucking new girlfriend named Sarah take my place?

For three full days, I hid in Harlowe's home, under blankets in the attic. No library. No showering. Cell phone off. My stomach ejected anything I tried to put into it. So I stopped trying. I didn't have an appetite anyway. I cried during the day while Harlowe and Maxine moved about the house as usual. They checked in on me, asked if I needed anything, and left when I couldn't be around anyone. I cried at night when it was just me and the attic and all my thoughts. My Discman spun her mix CD and then mine and then hers again. When I wasn't crying or trying not to dry heave, I wrote and rewrote response letters to Lainie. I crumpled them. I tore them to bits. In my dreams, I lit them on fire.

I didn't have a girlfriend anymore. Nothing was going to

change that. And by putting her parents' address on the breakup package, Lainie blocked me from responding. She made sure I couldn't invade her magical little safe-haven-Democratic-bullshit internship. She made sure that no part of me could drop in on her and her forever person. Every time I thought of that phrase, I gagged a little and wanted to punch them both. *Forever person.* I wanted to scream at Lainie and tell her to go fuck herself and ask her how she even dared to include that cutesy hyperbolic shit in a breakup letter to me. What a self-important, miserable, cheating-ass human being. How could she do me like that?

I called Ava and cried, like straight-up wept into the phone when she said hello. She let me cry. Ava listened to all the sniffling and the wheezing and the cry/yelling I had in me. She didn't even make any cracks about me deserving this because Lainie was white and no one told me to date a white girl. She didn't do any of that. Ava listened to me as I read Lainie's letter to her and the track list to the breakup mixtape. She offered good advice; she called it "self-care." Ava told me that it was important to cry it out so that all the emotions didn't creep up on me later and with more intensity. She made me promise to eat more food and take a shower if I could. We hung up only when I swore I'd take care of myself and call her again.

I smoked a little weed to try and clear the nausea out of my belly. I thought about calling Mom but couldn't bring myself to do it. I didn't need someone who wouldn't understand why I was crying over a girl. The sun rose through the split in the curtain. I wasn't sure what day of the week it was. It was another day of crying, not eating, and writing awful letters I was never going to send to Lainie. I fell asleep out of sheer exhaustion and dreamed of drowning in a river. The dream wouldn't let me go. I slept until I hit mud and rocks, until the argument happening in real life shook me awake.

"Maxine, I want to make sure this conversation is grounded in respect and understanding," Harlowe's voice echoed up the attic stairs. "I'm not insecure about your love for Zaira; what makes me uncomfortable is how often you've been seeing her instead of spending time with me. We have specific nights for a reason."

"I know, I want to apologize for disrespecting you, Harlowe. I've been debating the best way to tell you that my feelings for Zaira are bubbling to an irrepressible point. Our relationship is evolving into the type of revolutionary love I need to continue thriving."

My eyes snapped open. Still wrapped in blankets, I crept toward the steps to listen. "So you're not 'thriving' with me?" Harlowe asked with an edge. "Wonderful. And instead of being upfront about how you're wilting into nothing with me, you spend our nights with her thriving all over each other."

"I can recall a few moments when the same has happened to you with less connection to the other person," Maxine snapped.

"Do not bring up Samara." Harlowe's voice grew even more

shrill. "I've already apologized for Samara. It's not fair for you to throw her in my face."

"I wasn't. I was merely reminding us both that we've been in situations where our passion for others has clouded our judgments."

"Max, you don't have to remind me of anything. And this conversation is about your fuck-up, not mine."

I sat with my hand over my mouth. Their argument provided a temporary break from the personal agony of Operation: Wallow in My Sadness Forever. The way they argued was so civilized and yet wrenching. Like they weren't going for blood, they were aiming at each other's souls.

"Nothing about my love with Zaira is a fuck-up. Not one single thing. The fuck-up was in carrying on with you when we both knew it wasn't working."

I clutched my heart. Damn.

They must have moved their conversation into another part of the house, because all I heard next were their footsteps below and their bedroom door closing. A new wave of heartache washed over me. I didn't want Harlowe and Maxine to fight or break up. It hurt my heart; I needed them to be an example of long-lasting adult lesbian love. Or something.

It was 5:00 p.m. Wednesday. Same clothes. Same mattress. I stared up at the ceiling. I cried, alone; wished I was home. What would Lil' Melvin be up to? I missed him never leaving my side when I was home from school. I wondered if he was okay. I remembered the brown paper bag Lil' Melvin gave me at the airport. I opened it. My eyes welled up again. I missed his chunky butt.

Inside the bag were two packages of TWIX bars, a Yu-Gi-Oh! Beaver Warrior playing card, and a note. The description on the Beaver Warrior card read, *What this creature lacks in size it makes up for in defense when battling on the prairie.* Beaver Warrior. Just the name alone made me laugh. My baby brother had made his first gay joke and it was perfect. I opened his note:

Sister,

I'm 100 percent sure I'm pyrokinetic. Also, I'm about 78 percent positive that I'm a homosexual like you.
The Force is strong with us.

*M

Whoa. I read his note three more times, unable at first to absorb its message. Lil' Melvin was gay too. We were both gay. And what the hell was a pyrokinetic? I ate those TWIX bars like I'd never eaten chocolate before. Lil' Melvin's admission of gayness left me feeling excited but also uncertain. How would I be able to help him through any of it? I put the letter back in its envelope and cried a little bit more. The amount of things that I could handle in a day had been reached.

I crawled back into bed. Thoughts of Lainie making out with

Sarah filled my brain. Sleep took me away, helped me hide from all the emotions I didn't know how to handle. Before drifting off, I thought about all the promises I'd made to Ava about showering and self-care.

Tomorrow. I would do all those things tomorrow. I slept all night long without dreaming.

HARLOWE SHOOK ME awake. The act wasn't aggressive. Her hands felt secure on my shoulders. She asked me to sit up. She opened windows and let the easy pastel sunlight into the room.

"Happy Thursday, Juliet. Today you will not lie in bed. Today we will take care of each other," she said. Harlowe handed me a stack of pancakes. "They're vegan."

I hadn't eaten anything substantial in the last few days. My stomach grumbled, hard. The pancakes smelled delicious. Whether they were made with hopes and dreams alone, they were glorious. Harlowe sat across from me. We ate together. I realized that Kira's phone number was still legible across my forearm; Sharpie ink was no joke. Harlowe saw it too.

"You've had an intense couple of days. I'm in a good place in my twenty-eight-day cycle and have so much room in my spirit to hear you. Not talking about a breakup can totally lead to a yeast infection," she said.

"A breakup yeast infection to add to my breakup CD. This could be the best week ever," I replied.

"I can cure yeasties, but it's better to let out the feelings before they throw off your pH balance, Juliet."

The last thing I wanted to deal with was a yeast infection. I pulled Lainie's letter out from under my pillow. There was nowhere else to start. It was one page long. I handed it over to Harlowe and felt how light it was. That crushed me even more. Was I not worth an Aaliyah-style four-page letter? Writing on both sides, pen pressed so hard against paper that the letter would feel textured and crumpled with pain? Was I not worth severity? Harlowe read her note and muttered an "Oh fuck."

"What?" I asked.

"'I'm in love with Sarah. She's the one I want my parents to meet, like as my official first girlfriend. I think she's my forever person,'" Harlowe read. Her brow furrowed as she rolled her eyes. "Adding that to a breakup letter is cruel. *Forever person*, jeez."

"I know, right?" I exclaimed and then started to cry, again.

I covered my face, embarrassed to cry so recklessly in front of Harlowe. Harlowe hugged me, pushed her forehead into mine. We met eyes.

"It's going to be okay. All you have to do today is finish these pancakes and maybe take a shower," she said.

I laughed against her shoulder. "Okay, I think I can do both of those things."

I did what she said. Showering brought life into my lungs,

running my hands over my body cleared away some of the sadness on my skin. I thought about my ovaries and how envisioning them different colors made the pain go away. The power and the ability to change the spiritual chemistry inside myself energized me. I focused on the color violet; it felt warm and healing. As I showered and dressed, I thought of the color violet. I didn't cry. I didn't think of Lainie. I chose faded black jeans, my hot-pink *BX Girl* T-shirt, and left my hair loose, gelled, and curly. I wiped off the dirt from my Jordans until they gleamed. I put on some lip gloss, eyeliner, and I was ready. Awake. Not crying.

I found Harlowe outside rummaging around in her truck.

"Look at you, all sorts of fresh and clean," she said. A stack of papers and envelopes sat on the hood. "I have a meeting today. And all of this is bills and fan mail. Maybe you can help with some of it? I'm about eight months behind on replies, and I like to respond to everyone and send out as many *Raging Flower* stickers as I can."

"Works for me," I replied. I reached out for the fan mail.

From the glove compartment, Harlowe retrieved a light purple bandanna and handed it to me. "In case of tears or snot," she said.

Violet. The bandanna was violet.

"Can I say one more thing about this breakup?" I asked.

"Of course, you can, sweet human," Harlowe replied. She sat next to me on the porch and ripped open old mail.

"She hasn't even called me. It's been days. Maybe that means I should call her, but I refuse. It feels like a setup. Is she waiting for me to call all freaked out and crying? Does she have some speech lined up? I don't know. I hope she does. I hope that just like I'm here feeling all fucked up, that she's there wondering why I haven't responded. I refuse to give her that. I'm not going to let her hear me cry or feel the weight of my rage and sadness. If she thinks about me at all this summer, I'd rather it be with a question mark pressing down on her rib cage." I wiped away unwanted tears and snot with Harlowe's violet bandanna.

"And if she thinks about you all summer, she might just see what a foolish mistake she's made and come running back with another mixtape. Or maybe for the rest of her life, you'll be the one that got away and, goddess, that'd be sweet," Harlowe added.

That felt right to me. The idea of being Lainie's biggest regret soothed my soul. Harlowe and I worked together. She went through her bills, and I muddled through her fan mail. It didn't disappoint. I read the best ones aloud.

Colleen—Denver, CO

Dearest Harlowe, Sweet Goddess of the Birth Canal,

*I've tracked my menstrual cycle in accordance with
Mother Moon. Celestial strength fills my every step. Thank*

you for connecting me to the inner chambers of my vulva
and its link to the cosmos. Please come over for ginger tea if
you're ever in the Denver area.

Tidings and waves,
Colleen

PS: I might legally change my name to Aysun, which means
moon water. Do you think that's too much?

•

KC—Olympia, WA

Yo, Harlowe—

I stopped cutting, which is fucking rad and super good for
my spiritual growth. To celebrate my first year cut-free, I got
this wicked Raging Flower tat. I broke up with my girlfriend
because she wouldn't read your book, which obviously means
that we were so not fucking meant to be.

In Solidarity, fellow pussy-loving dyke warrior,
KC

I showed the photo to Harlowe. It was a Polaroid of a brown-skinned Filipina, shaved head, holding up her denim pant leg to reveal a massive tattoo of the cover of *Raging Flower*. Her free hand was giving the middle finger.

Harlowe,

My seven-year-old daughter now tells people she "has a pussy and is proud of it." Just wanted to share!

XOXO,

Angela and Adele

Raging Flower stickers were giant sunflowers with the word p*ssy in hot pink written across the middle. I stuck them in all the self-addressed stamped envelopes from fans.

Samara, a friend of Harlowe's, stopped by to discuss the reading at Powell's. Their conversation faded in and out of my attention. One minute it was about how eating different seeds affected menstruation and then it was about some composting debacle at their friends' communist farm. It went on forever. I didn't even notice that Samara had her arm around Harlowe's shoulder until Maxine strolled up the walkway.

Harlowe disentangled herself from Samara. She rushed up to give Maxine a hug. Samara said hello and good-bye in an overly cheerful, awkward sort of way and walked off. Maxine hugged Harlowe but not body to body. It was one of those Christian side hugs. The energy was off and the not-speaking thing made my arms break out in goose bumps. Harlowe and Maxine went inside. They spoke in low rumbles. I kept my ass on the porch and worked through her fan mail. Their drama reminded me of my drama. My guts twisted up from missing Lainie and I still had Kira's number on my forearm and wasn't sure what I was going to do about any of it. So I let the day pass me by and found comfort in sleep.

CHAPTER FIFTEEN

OPERATION: STILL WALLOWING IN MY SADNESS

". . . and in the middle of it all: all of the self-empowerment, all of the radical womanhood, all of the community-building. You will still feel wrecked. Allow yourself to be wrecked. Know that it is finite."

Raging Flower: Empowering Your Pussy by Empowering Your Mind, Harlowe Brisbane

I WOKE UP the next morning with my phone in my hand. Checked my call history and Ava was the last person I'd spoken to. She'd ended last night's phone call by telling me "of course she knew that shit!" and that I better "emotionally drop that uppity gringa" and focus on myself and of course, to dip out early and come visit her. But the phone didn't wake me, the smell of breakfast did. It smelled like home on a Saturday morning and for one half-second, I forgot I was in Portland.

Maxine stood in the kitchen dressed in a denim shirt with cutoff sleeves, a faded yellow apron wrapped around her waist. She poured sliced potatoes into a hot pan. News radio hummed over the crackling. Maxine was so dreamy. I wished I'd gelled back my hair or put on cleaner, cuter shorts.

Maxine offered me coffee with cinnamon and cane sugar. It was thick and strong, the type of coffee that wakes up your whole body. Then she scrambled eggs and set them aside. The dish wouldn't be ready for a while. Tortilla Española took time, something about it tasting better if the person cooking wasn't in a rush. That's all she said. I wanted to know all the things: Were she and Harlowe still together? Why was Maxine even still here? But, out of respect, I didn't press for a story and I wasn't given one. We drank our coffee in silence. It'd been a while since I'd had any time with Maxine and it felt real good to be with her.

Harlowe burst in through the front door. Banshee-like, as usual.

"None of the lezzies were working at Anarchy Books today," Harlowe said, sighing, as she dropped two used books onto the table, "so I just spent the last two hours with bearded man hipsters, one of them wearing a *This Is What a Feminist Looks Like* T-shirt by the way, and we discussed why it's important to purge the soul of male authors and focus solely on women writers. And by discussed, I mean I spoke and they listened."

"I'm already exhausted," Maxine said as she poured the eggs into the potatoes. "I don't know how you're able to entertain fools."

"Someone has to push these guys. In my goddess heart, I'm doing their daughters, girlfriends, mothers, lady coworkers, any women they know a favor," Harlowe said, as she looked at both of us, "like I'm helping them become better men."

Harlowe grabbed a flyer from the back pocket of her denim shorts. "And I picked this up for you," she said, and handed it to Maxine. "Think of all the learning you could do at this panel!"

Black Womanists United Against Bush.
Discussion topics: 9/11 Cover-ups,
Capitalist-Based Fear Mongering,
Anti-Blackness, and Islamophobia.

"All the learning I could do?" Maxine asked, flipping the flyer over.

"I know it's for Womanists only. I obviously can't go, but you can and you should, and maybe Juliet can go with you? Does a closed space mean Puerto Ricans can't go either? I don't know."

Maxine sighed. "Harlowe, just because you see something that is targeted toward Black people doesn't mean that you need to bring it home to me and encourage me to learn Black people things with other Black people, okay? And if Islamophobia is one of the topics, it won't be just for Black women."

I rose to leave, but they both stopped me. They said it was

fine, that these conversations weren't a secret. They were discussing something major, but no one had to leave. In fact, a third party might be useful if they needed a mediator. I sipped from my cup of coffee and listened to them. Harlowe swiveled her head around and looked right at me.

"What do you think, Juliet?" Harlowe asked. "Shouldn't it be okay for a white dyke to bring their partner of color information about events related to their race or ethnicity?"

"Now, hold on just a minute," Maxine said. "Are you going to write me and Juliet checks for our analyses on race? 'Cuz our labor isn't free."

My eyes went wide, and I laughed. Maxine made the record scratch with that one. I loved it.

"Max! I'm just sharing information," Harlowe said. "I was there when Janae from Black Womanists United came in and set out the flyers."

Maxine nudged me and rolled her eyes. She turned around without responding to Harlowe and checked the potatoes and eggs.

Harlowe attempted to clarify but Maxine didn't budge. And in a quick flurry of dramatics, grabbing her candles and books, Harlowe left the kitchen. We heard her stomping up the stairs to the attic.

Max shook her head, mostly unbothered.

"Max," I started, "if I have questions about race and stuff, should I get my checkbook too?"

"Yes," she said. "Don't let me hear about you not paying Black women for their expertise."

I nodded and immediately got up, about to dash out of the kitchen when Maxine put her hand on my shoulders, laughing hard. "Sit down and eat some breakfast," she said. "I won't charge you yet."

Our conversation continued. Maxine's main points were that Harlowe shouldn't be concerned with her Blackness and that in essence Harlowe was committing microaggressions against Maxine. Maxine felt that Harlowe should be focused on educating her own self before she worried about Maxine's involvement in the Black community. It was all super complicated but, like, to me, also really simple: if Maxine didn't want it, Harlowe shouldn't do it. I added hot sauce to my potatoes.

"If Harlowe wasn't white, would it be okay? Like, if you were dating a brown round Latina and she brought home something from a Black feminist collective or whatever, would it be weird too?" I asked, and helped myself to a delicious bite.

Maxine took a deep, slow breath, crossed her muscled arms across her chest. "The thing is, Juliet, I've never appreciated someone else's unrequested guidance on my identity. I don't want their interpretation of who I am or where they think my politics should lie. My Blackness, my queerness, my theological inclinations, what I'm like at a family reunion, who I am in the classroom or in a relationship, all of that is mine," Maxine said, each word chosen, thoughtful. "And if Harlowe had asked, I would have told her that Janae called me two days ago to tell me about the event. Black people speed-dial, you know."

I laughed, nodding my head. We ate our breakfast in an easy silence. Right as I was scarfing down the last bite of eggs, my cell phone buzzed in my back pocket. It was my mom. I excused myself from the table and answered.

"Hi, Mom," I said. I shut the door behind me and sat on the porch steps.

"Hi, Mom, yourself. It's been days since you called me, nena. I'm over here worrying about you in the cornfields and you can't even call," she said, in one breath.

"Mom, I'm sorry. Things have just been . . . busy."

"Why do you sound tired? Are you sick?"

"No, Mom, I'm not sick, I just—"

"You just probably haven't been sleeping on a good schedule. Always up late like your father," she said. Her voice softened. She paused.

The distance between us was palpable. She cleared her throat.

"You know I love you, right?"

I teared up. I smudged some of the chalk writing on Harlowe's steps with my fingers to give my hands something to do and my eyes somewhere to focus.

"Yeah, of course. I love you too," I said. "Mom?"

"Yes, Juliet?"

"Oh, Mom." My voice cracked. All the anguish of the breakup built up in my throat. Her voice erased my reserve.

"Juliet, what's wrong? What happened? Talk to me."

"Lainie broke up with me, Mom," I said. I didn't trust my voice to remain steady.

"Oh," she said.

"She sent a letter, a stupid breakup CD, and that was it. She didn't even call. I didn't do anything to her. She fell in love with someone else, Mom. How could she?"

"Well, nena, these things happen. Best to just move on, move forward. Give it to the Lord."

"The Lord, Mom? I can't just give this to the Lord. Or move on. Mom, come on." Wrecked, all of me was wrecked. I hated all the birds chirping around me. I wanted metal train tracks and car alarms.

"Juliet, you have to calm down. It will be fine. Listen, I know it will be better soon," she said. "You know how I know?"

I didn't answer.

"I know because just yesterday I bumped into Awilda from my old job. We were both at the bus stop. And guess what? She asked about you and told me that her son, Eduardo, is home from school and will be here the week you get back. We're all going to have dinner together. You and Eduardo would make such a good match."

"Mom, I don't think that's the thing that's gonna make this better," I said, biting my lip, angry, annoyed.

"Juliet, Eduardo is a good man," Mom said, in that reverent voice she often used to talk about other good men.

"No, Mom. Eduardo is gross. And, Mom, I don't care. I can't believe that I'm here crying about Lainie and you're trying to set me up with Awilda's gross son, with anyone's son for that matter."

"Nena, you never gave men a chance. That's why your heart is broken right now. That love with Lainie wasn't real, not like the love between a man and a woman is. . . ."

"I gotta go, Mom. Like right now, I have to go."

"Juliet, I love you. I just want you to be the person we raised you to be."

"I'm never going to be that person, Mom. I gotta go. I can't do this with you."

We said hushed, strained good-byes, and hung up at the same time. I stretched out on Harlowe's porch and stared up at the sky. At least Mom said she loved me. Tears slipped out of the corners of my eyes. The neighborhood and the sky around me were still, calm. They were the absolute opposite of the tectonic plates of grief and confusion that shifted inside me. Did I have to be the one who guided my mom toward understanding all this gay stuff? I just got onboard with it myself and still didn't have it all settled. And fucking Lainie. Literally that's all I had for her, just a bunch of swears and questions and the suffocating shock of being cheated on and dumped like I was nothing.

I lay on the porch for a while. I'd spent the last few days lying around Harlowe's house in a daze. The summer was about to pass me by. Harlowe's big reading at Powell's was next week. I still had an entire box of women to research. But I couldn't move, couldn't get unstuck. Something had to give and give quickly.

CHAPTER SIXTEEN

I WISH SHE WOULD

POST-BREAKUP AND STILL alive, my desire to get lost in research kicked into overdrive. Having come to the realization that I wasn't going to marry power dyke, young Democrat Lainie Verona, I focused on the work. I wanted to show Harlowe that I took the internship seriously. I didn't come all the way to Portland to flop around her house consumed with melancholy like a character on *Dawson's Creek*. I was there to research amazing women, assist Harlowe with her speaking events, and become her best friend forever. Well, definitely the first two, and hopefully the last one.

I spent every one of the next five days at the library. Scraps of paper spilled out of my pockets and my notebook. The other librarians recognized me and offered their help. Kira helped too. She made no mention of me not calling her. I didn't bumble around trying to explain why I hadn't. I worried it would make me sound self-absorbed and pathetic. "Hi, sweet human that I shared cookies with on the front steps of this very library. My girlfriend and I just broke up and I want to eat a bucket of nails and I cried so much that I couldn't call you. Still wanna hang out?" Yeah, nope. We worked around each other. The rhythm between us was secure, open. I hoped we'd ride together again. Maybe there'd be a soft kiss along the way. I left it up to the universe.

Like before, I started with a few scraps of paper at a time. Harlowe didn't want an entire biography on every woman. She needed the basics and if possible, a little extra. I wanted to have enough information for Harlowe that she'd be able to build up a strong foundation for her next book. Thorough, not overwhelming: that was my approach. The names I had with me were as follows:

Crumpled blue paper: *Del Martin*

Stained napkin: *Boudicca*

Georgia O'Keeffe stationery: *Fu Hao*

I stared at the piece of blue paper. Harlowe's left-handed scrawl swerved toward the bottom of the page. Del Martin. I'd never met a woman named Del. I hoped she was a dyke. I didn't want to assume that at first but why not? Why assume she wasn't? I knew Del had to be a woman, at least. Perhaps Del was also an activist? Or maybe a softball player?

I sat in my favorite computer cubicle near the window. Wrote some notes down, took my inquiry to Lycos.com. I searched for Del Martin.

Del Martin: Born May 5, 1921. Cofounder of the Daughters of Bilitis (DOB) in 1955, a social organization for homosexual women that evolved into a feminist group. They published *The Ladder* in 1956, the first lesbian print news publication. The Daughters of Bilitis disbanded after the Stonewall riots due to differences in newly emerging lesbian politics.

Differences in newly emerging lesbian politics? I guess even back then women dealt with high levels of lesbian drama. The word *Bilitis* struck me as something one could be afflicted by, like gastritis or tonsillitis. *Lesbian, Bilitis, dyke*—why didn't words for gay women ever sound beautiful? I printed out the paragraph on Del Martin while looking up *Bilitis*.

What I found next was that *Bilitis* was the name given to a fictional lesbian contemporary of Sappho by the French poet Pierre Louÿs in his 1894 work *The Songs of Bilitis*.

So, Bilitis was Sappho's butch girlfriend. I wondered if the Daughters of Bilitis were all white women. Would I have been a member of the DOB? I collected my information and moved forward.

I raced through the next two names. Boudicca and Fu Hao were both warriors who protected their people from invasions. Boudicca was queen of the British Iceni tribe and led revolts against the Roman Empire. Fu Hao was a military general and high priestess during the Shang dynasty. Basically, they were like Titi Wepa and Titi Mellie but, like, from way back in the day. I filled my purple notebook with battle dates and names of countries that didn't exist anymore. I'd review them in the same way that I'd reviewed *The Ladies' Gallery* but at home, with Harlowe's moon cycle calendar and all my highlighters.

I found more books about all the women before the library closed. Kira wasn't around. I'd written her number in the margin of my notebook before it wore off my forearm. I stared at it. As I exited the library, I decided that I would call Kira later and invite her to Harlowe's reading. Like a date or something. I pulled the hood up on my black *Righteous Babe* hoodie. If she said no, I'd die a thousand more deaths on Harlowe's porch and find another library.

Instead of waiting for the bus, I decided to walk. I was more comfortable with the route and finally had a general idea of where Harlowe lived. Dusk cooled the air around me. I let the night envelop my skin and my frame. I envisioned different scenarios of how to ask Kira out. I straight-up dorked it out, had imaginary conversations with her, and role-played how it would all go down.

My phone buzzed in my back pocket. For a moment, I thought the universe had delivered Kira to me, but when I pulled out the phone, I froze: Lainie. I still hadn't deleted her from my contacts. I stared at the phone as it vibrated in my hand. Lainie. I wasn't prepared to talk to her. I'd assumed I could avoid her until

September. But why the hell was she calling me now when she hadn't returned any of my calls pre-breakup? I pressed the IGNORE button. Fuck her. Fuck her breakup CD and her letter that was mainly about some other girl. Sarah. Fuck you too, Sarah. My phone vibrated again. Voice mail: Lainie. Jeezus. A voice mail.

"I've got, like, twenty seconds to explain to you that I think I made a mistake. Juliet, baby, I fucked up. The CD, the letter, even mentioning Sarah. Terrible. I'm terrible. It's all a mess. Please call me. Let's fix this."

As the message ended, I heard Lainie tell someone she'd be right out. I wondered if she made the call to me while she was with Sarah. I listened to her message a few times while standing in the middle of the Steel Bridge. I missed the way her lips pressed forward when she said the *J* in my name. *Juliet.* She missed me. She thought she made a mistake . . .

People made mistakes sometimes, right?

I didn't know what to do. I couldn't call her. I was afraid. What if she was with Sarah? I'd be so pissed. It'd ruin everything. I'd curse her out. I'd curse her out if she was alone too. Even though I didn't really curse people out like that. I didn't do fighting in the streets, mad loud, airing out all the business type of fighting, but damn if that's not how I felt. Lainie deserved it and more. I wished I had that type of free-spirited strength that goes with calling people out on the ways they've wronged you, loud enough and public enough for the world to feel it too. For me, everything was internal. I had all the what-if words and fuck-yous in my heart, but they didn't ever come out.

I couldn't call her because if none of that happened, if it was sweetness—like when she slipped love letters under my dorm room door—then I'd crumble. I'd be vulnerable. I'd give in to her.

I feared that the most. I'd waited for her to call me when things were good and she didn't reach out. Lainie could wait to hear from me. She could sit with herself and wonder what I was up to and who I was with. I didn't want to jump for her and make a brand-new decision on our relationship based on her remorse.

AT HARLOWE'S, I paced around the attic for about half an hour practicing what I'd say to Kira over the phone. I wasn't cool enough to call and say, "Hey, girl, come to this cool feminist reading with me." Was I? Did I need to apologize for not calling after she drove me home that night or just pretend like all that had happened during a rift in the space-time continuum and didn't need to be accounted for? My boobs started to sweat. A first, second, and third text message came from Lainie during that time and I ignored them all.

I dialed Kira's number praying it'd go to voice mail. She picked up right away. "Hello?" she asked.

"Hi, um, Kira? This is Juliet, the girl from the library. You gave me a ride home once. . . ."

"Hi, Juliet. I was wondering if you'd ever call."

"Yeah, I just . . . things kinda like . . ."

"Don't worry about it. When's your birthday?"

"My birthday?"

"Yeah, you know, so I can astrologically check you out."

"Oh, okay, cool. September sixth, nineteen eighty-three."

"Virgo. I fucking love Virgos. We're not a match at all. Geminis and Virgos are pretty much guaranteed to blow stuff up lovewise. But you're super cute so, I mean, hi, let's keep talking. You called me."

She made me laugh.

"Yes, I did," I said. "I was wondering if you'd want to go with me to Harlowe Brisbane's reading at Powell's tomorrow night. I know it's last minute but . . ."

"But I'm already going with friends, which means you'll get to meet them all and it'll be totally fine. Maybe you want to come out for stargazing with us afterward?"

"Stargazing?" I asked. Her hippie cute astrology thing caught me off guard and I liked it.

"Yeah, like lie out along the bluffs and watch the sky move, trace the constellations," she said.

"Yes, I'm down," I replied. "Sweet, see you tomorrow night."

She hung up with a soft click. My cheeks were on fire. I flopped on the mattress with a huge grin on my face. Kira worked that conversation like no one I'd ever talked to before. I thought I had game. Nope. I had a belly full of nerves and an array of nerdy pickup lines that never made it out of my head. Kira just moved with the flow of the conversation. She asked me to hang out with her friends too, like, ugh, I didn't even know I needed that until she said it. Lainie texted again. I didn't answer. Thoughts of Kira, her lips, and the two of us on her bike filled my daydreams.

They pulled me out of this tense emotional place with Lainie. Everything was going to be okay. Right?

CHAPTER SEVENTEEN

A READING FROM THE BOOK OF WHITE LADY FEMINISM

"Blood is literal. Blood is spiritual. Blood connects through birth, through chaos, and through intimacy. Embrace the stories of your sisters. Listen with hearts open and offer affirmations. Never assume their struggle. Never consume their truths. Do not let the assimilationist nature of the patriarchy infiltrate the sacred bonds of blood."

Raging Flower: Empowering Your Pussy by Empowering Your Mind, Harlowe Brisbane

THE NEXT AFTERNOON, Harlowe, Maxine, and I focused on preparations for Harlowe's reading. Powell's already had boxes of books. I was put in charge of the merchandise. There were *Raging Flower* stickers, limited-edition *Raging Flower* period pads, *Raging Flower* patches, and three different types of T-shirts. Everything needed to be loaded into the pickup truck.

Harlowe moved around the house, from the attic to the living room and back. She read excerpts from *Raging Flower* out loud. As she wove her way through the hall and over the couch, she moved random items out of place. I stopped to watch her. This was something I hadn't seen her do. She was bugging. Or maybe just Harlowe being Harlowe. Maxine stood by me. Together we watched her move.

"That's how you know she's nervous," Maxine said.

We moved from the house to the porch. Maxine helped me label and load boxes of merchandise into the pickup. The neighborhood fluttered around us. An elderly lesbian couple walked their massive wolf-dog. People stopped as they strolled to say hello. Everyone who stopped received a solid hug and the most sincere inquiry about their well-being. We moved slow and talked to everyone. Neither one of us wanted to be in the middle of Harlowe's whirlwind of preparation and anxiety. With all the merch packed up and ready, we took Maxine's matte-black pickup to Powell's. There was only an hour left 'til showtime.

"Tonight is Harlowe's night to do what she does best. Rage against the patriarchy and talk to women about how we're all spiritually bonded," Maxine said.

"Do you think we're all spiritually bonded?" I asked. She and Zaira seemed to be.

"Oh, Juliet, I think a lot of things. Like how it's hard for me to feel any sort of bond to white people in general and yet here I am with Harlowe."

"Sure must bring up a lot of feelings, especially when she challenges you on stuff like with that whole flyer thing," I said.

"I didn't mention this before, but I'm on that nine-eleven panel," Maxine replied. "Black Womanists United reached out to me for my theological perspective. I've been working with a colleague from Iran to present connections between US anti-Blackness and Islamophobia."

"Maxine, that's deep. That hits me right in the chest. Is it a secret that you were working on this?"

"Not a secret, just complicated. Zaira's the head of the BWU. We've been friends forever and now we're spending more time together, figuring out the panel, and getting closer in other ways. Working with her is exhilarating. . . ."

"Are you and Harlowe gonna break up?" I asked, biting my bottom lip.

"An easy answer to that would be lovely. Tonight's not for that though. Nope. It's all about *Raging Flower* and Harlowe Brisbane, the feminist phenomenon," Maxine said. She stood up and stretched, shifting our conversation elsewhere. "I wish we'd be able to get as big a crowd for this nine-eleven talk as Harlowe's going to get for her reading. It's interesting to see what other white feminists really care about, you know?"

I didn't know. I was curious about Maxine's upcoming talk. I wanted to know more about her relationship with Zaira. Maxine's not-secret filled the space between us. It bonded us.

Maxine guided the conversation and asked me about 9/11, how I was affected and what I understood of the current political climate. In a rush of thoughts, I shared my feelings. The term *anti-Blackness* was new to me; so was the concept of Islamophobia. We were coming up on the two-year anniversary of 9/11 and the news still made it seem like bombs and terrorists hid around every corner. The attack in New York took my uncle Louis and my neighbor Jameka Watkins. She worked at Windows on the World and Uncle Louis had been a firefighter with the FDNY for fifteen years. Titi Wepa spent months at Ground Zero as a first-responder. Her uniform, covered in dust and ashes, hung untouched in her closet.

By the time we pulled up to Powell's, we'd swapped 9/11 stories and moved on to breakups and casual date-type things with librarians. I spilled my guts left and right. We dropped off the boxes of merch with Samara. Maxine and Samara exchanged polite words, but there weren't any hugs or smiles between them. I wondered what kind of beef they had or if I was so used to Portland people hugging each other with their entire spiritual selves that anything less affectionate seemed off.

The space for the reading was huge. There were about a hundred empty seats and a podium set up for Harlowe. My stomach fluttered; I was excited. The rush of geeky nerves I had when I first read *Raging Flower* flooded my body. This shit was gonna be cool, and I got to be a part of it.

Harlowe arrived about a half hour after we did. She was ushered into a room in the back. People started trickling in and soon

Powell's was packed with humans. At last count, about seventy-five weirdos sat and waited for Harlowe Brisbane to preach her pussy magic. People continued to file in through the door and make their way to the reading area. Some of them posed for pictures with the cutout of her in the walkway. I slipped out and found Harlowe in her holding room, pacing. Her frailty endeared her to me more. Like look, even one of the people I admire most in the whole world gets scared sometimes.

"I should have warned you, Juliet. I'm the queen of stage fright. The universe sure loves to humble me," she said, fidgeting. "In my guts, Juliet, I know it's going to be fine, but then I get freaked out and I feel like that 'crazy lady' all over again. The one that fifty publishers denied, the one that some bloggers have called 'a raging feminazi,' and I doubt myself. Maybe everyone is just here to watch the spectacle, to say, 'I saw the Pussy Lady. What a crazy bitch she is.' Maybe they're not in it for the struggle, to take down the patriarchy, to be my blood sisters. Maybe they're all just here to laugh and point."

She slid down the wall to the floor.

I sat down next to her. "Well, then, fuck them. Right?"

"Right, fuck them," Harlowe said. She laughed. "You're good, you know? It's been good having you here. I've got so much love for you, Juliet."

"I love you too. But you've got shit to do," I said. "There's a room full of probably the coolest lesbians ever, some of them are even breastfeeding their babies, and tons of other hippie-ass people waiting for you to speak. So, get it together, okay?"

She laughed. Her hands shook slightly from jitters. We found the bathroom. Harlowe splashed cold water on her face, took a few deep breaths. She smoothed down her cowlick. The Pussy Lady was ready. We moved to the reading area and waited in the back. I scanned the crowd and saw Kira with her friends. She waved me over, smiling.

"If that's the hot librarian, you better go," Harlowe said, nudging my back.

"I'll bill you for the white lady pep talk," I said, tapping her on the shoulder.

I ran over and sat next to Kira. Samara stepped up to the microphone. She introduced Harlowe to much applause; someone even let out a Xena warrior call. It had begun.

Harlowe stood at the front of the room, mic curved toward her mouth. She waited for the room to quiet down and then asked for a moment of silence to honor survivors of sexual violence. The energy among us all heaved inward like a brick to the chest. All eyes were on Harlowe. She stepped away from the microphone, bowed her head. For two minutes, we were still. The woman next to me wept, black mascara running down her face. She wasn't the only one. She asked us if we'd been terrorized because of our bodies. Had we ever been made to feel abnormal or unwanted because our flesh and bones were different? In what ways had the world and our families abandoned and betrayed us?

She promised that her questions weren't intended to invade our personal lives. Harlowe had me.

I remembered the time Dominic Pusco felt me up at Murray's ice-skating rink. He'd pushed his hands down my pants and told me to keep them warm and to stay quiet. Ketchup stained the edges of his mouth; he smelled like french fries and sweat. But I'd wanted to be his Valentine, so I didn't stop him and I kept my mouth shut.

Harlowe asked that we release the burden of those memories into this shared space. She asked us to find strength in the energy of our sisters and trust that together we could heal.

Harlowe offered her vulnerability to the room without question. She opened with the chapter about Teddy, her mother's boyfriend, the one who jerked off outside the bathroom whenever she showered, the one who tried to do the same thing while she slept. Harlowe told us about the night she snapped a picture of him in her bedroom. The flash freaked him out. She had just turned sixteen and told him she'd chop it off next time if he did it again. Other men wouldn't be so easily intimidated; Harlowe spared no details of later instances of sexual violence.

But it wasn't sexual violence that encouraged her to reclaim her body and investigate her vagina. Harlowe smoothed down her cowlick.

"I'm not going to connect sexual trauma with feminism," she said. "That's not my deal. The whole damaged-woman-becomes-a-lesbian-and-a-feminist trope doesn't work for me. The patriarchy, aka the He-Man Woman Haters Club, created it because they don't want us to be taken seriously. They don't want us to have access to the divine knowledge our bodies possess. They fear our power. So no, we aren't damaged. We have suffered from the brutality of an inherently violent system that favors maleness over womanhood. We've been victimized, but that doesn't make us all victims. We're not the outcomes of what men have done to us. I refuse to be reduced to that.

"My curiosity about my body and my spiritual power exists because it is mine. My womanhood awed me. The women in my life made me drop to my knees in revelry. And many of us move in this world with the beauty and courage to write our stories on the backs of napkins and at the edges of our sanity so that others may find strength in our words and know that our lives belong to us, not a husband or a father. We build countries, slay dragons. I will always be awed by women who are strong enough to walk down the damn street. I'm here because of all of you. I wrote this book because of my undying love for my sisters. I've chosen to learn everything I can about our bodies, our brilliant but often-erased ansisters, and our divine goddess spirituality so that I can share it and so we can all learn from one another. May we come together, own our power, and breathe a little freer."

That section of *Raging Flower* was my favorite. Hearing her read it made my heart burst open. In that moment, I loved Harlowe Brisbane. Loved her like family. Loved her in that for-real forever way. I felt bold and ready to write down my own story. Brave and full of stupid cute butterflies, I reached for Kira's hand and held it. She shifted closer to me, keeping my hands in hers.

Harlowe read about the time she grabbed a flashlight and a mirror, smoked a lot of weed, and explored her pussy. She was twenty-three and had never looked at her vulva. She spent an entire evening spreading the folds of her flesh, noting the color and density of hair. She liked it so much she did it again on her period. And that was her catalyst into pussy obsession.

The entire room laughed. A collective orgasm teased out of us by Harlowe Brisbane. Harlowe moved past the personal and read sections that built the foundation of the cultlike worship that followed her. She asked us to reflect on the first woman we'd entered into community with. It's assumed that mothers are the first, but in this world nothing is promised, not even a mother's love. So who was that first woman? Who were our blood sisters? Could we count them on our hands? See their faces in our daydreams? Did we honor our bodies, our spiritual selves, and harness our energies to envision a future centered around us? We were creatures in sync with the moon, after all. *Raging Flower* live reinforced the dedication of my discipleship.

The final section Harlowe read was a reminder that the fight never ends. Every day that we existed on this planet the forces of white men in power were aimed at policing women's bodies and subjugating our identities to make us feel lesser than, to control us through physical and economic annihilation. These acts of violence were experienced by trans women and women of color at higher rates. Harlowe urged her fellow white women to remember this and to never forget the vast amount of privilege they experience because of whiteness. It is the duty of white women to stand in solidarity with queer, trans, women of color, listen to their needs and make sure that feminism and sisterhood brings all of our voices together.

Pussy power forever!

Another round of wild applause erupted for Harlowe. She asked if anyone had any questions. Most of the questions were from wide-eyed fan girls.

"Oh, Harlowe, I love you. How did you get the idea to write *Raging Flower*?"

"Hi, Harlowe, I was wondering if you had any suggestions for new writers?"

"Hi, so I love that you use the word *pussy* so much in *Raging Flower*. Was it weird at first?"

Zaira and Maxine were seated next to each other. I'd missed Zaira's arrival but was so excited to see her. She stood up to ask a question and was handed the mic.

"Harlowe, do you think that tacking on a message of unity and solidarity for queer and trans women of color at the end of *Raging Flower* was powerful enough to make a difference? As if a few sentences could bridge the disparity among women who experience oppression due to their multiple intersectionalities and women who don't have to navigate those intersectionalities? Do you think that this message is enough to rally non-white women to your particular brand of feminism? To be your blood sisters?"

The room stayed silent. All eyes on Zaira. Regal. Poised in a gold dress cinched at the waist with a silver belt. Zaira's intensity and grace manifested through her every pore. I stared at her, mesmerized.

Harlowe cleared her throat.

"I believe in my heart that we can all be blood sisters. *Raging Flower* isn't perfect by any means, but I believe it's a good start. It was for me. It's the beginning of my journey into a more politicized, woman-centric consciousness, and I wanted to share that. Do I think that queer and trans women of color will read my work and feel like they see themselves in my words? Not necessarily, but some will and do. I mean, I know someone right now sitting in this room who is a testament to this, someone who isn't white, who grew up in the ghetto, someone who is lesbian and Latina and fought for her whole life to make it out of the Bronx alive and to get an education. She grew up in poverty and without any privilege. No support from her family, especially after coming out, and that person is here today. That person is Juliet Milagros Palante, my assistant and friend, who came all the way from the Bronx to be here with me and to learn how to be a better feminist, and all of that is because of *Raging Flower*, because anyone can see themselves in that work. Juliet is the proof. Juliet, can you stand up for everyone, please?"

Zaira looked over at me, her eyes wide, apologetic. People turned their heads in every direction to see who Harlowe was referring to. What did that poor child raised in the violent ghetto look like? Was that who I was to Harlowe?

A slight wheeze burned through my lungs. Air. I needed air.

I dropped Kira's hand, cracked my knuckles. She touched my thigh, and I jumped up. God, I couldn't look at her. Not in the middle of this. Head down, I avoided the wide eyes and nodding heads. A few of the women in the audience pointed at me with philanthropy in their eyes. They agreed with Harlowe and didn't even know me! I whipped my body around and into the aisle, gagging on shame and embarrassment. The floor blurred beneath me. Tears spilled down my cheeks. My face was hard as a cement block. I didn't have any words. All I heard was Harlowe calling my name and the door slamming shut behind me.

I don't remember when I started running, but the whoosh of fresh air that ran over my skin and into my lungs was a godsend. I ran all the way from Powell's to the Steel Bridge. Okay, that's a lie. I ran, like, four blocks, lost my breath, and used my inhaler. I walked the rest of the way. The streetlamps glowed white and orange. I wasn't afraid to be alone or to be out in the dark, but the quiet felt strange. I still wasn't used to it. If I'd had Zaira's number, I would have called her. When she referred to someone as sister, she seemed the type to mean it. I didn't know if Maxine would understand or if she'd be mad that I left Harlowe's event. And Harlowe, I'd left her there without a goodbye. Guilt like hot wax spread through my insides. Her words repeated themselves in my head. *Fought her whole life to make it out of the Bronx alive.* Yeah, the Bronx was tough, but that wasn't my life. Had I misled Harlowe? Or had she really just used me to make a point?

I had no people in Portland. No Titi Wepa. No Mom and

Dad. No Ava. No Lainie. Maxine called three times. I picked up on number three. They left after I did. She and Zaira were concerned. They wanted to come find me and process. Maxine's gentle voice, deep with love, made me feel cared for. And yet, I told her that I felt too messed up to process, that I just needed to be outside for a while. She understood and asked me to touch base with her when I was somewhere safe. Word. Done. Zaira's voice in the background told me to stay strong, young sister.

A full moon held court over the Willamette. The sky rippled with stars. I prayed for guidance and clarity, released my intentions into the night. I prayed for those things because I couldn't handle the rage that flared up inside. Harlowe said things about me that weren't true. I thought she got it. I thought she was someone who understood me the way I understood her. She called me "the proof," as if my existence could be summed up as the answer to any and every question about race and representation in *Raging Flower*. Had I handed myself over to her by being here? Was my presence permission? I felt foolish for loving Harlowe so hard and for thinking that we were blood sisters. I wanted to disappear.

Ava called while I paced the bridge. I picked up and she was off and talking at her usual, high-speed pace.

"I had a dream 'bout you, loca. The number three was mad prominent in it. In the dream, you had wings and were falling from the sky. And two angels tried to save you. I was the third one and my outfit was really dope. And anyway, I caught you, long story short. So I had to call you, obviously, for good luck. And this is the third and final time I'm gonna ask you to come see me."

"Let's book the flight right now, Ava."

"What? Like, right now, right now?"

"Yes, like, I'll give you my card number over the phone, right now," I said.

"Damn, girl, are you okay?"

"Shit is weird. Mad fucking weird and I don't want to get into it. I just want to see you," I pleaded. I was crying again and didn't care if she heard me.

"I'm booking you a flight for tomorrow. My dream shit is so real, loca. Where are you again? Titi Mari said Iowa or some shit."

Titi Mari was my mom. She'd been in touch with my mom. "Portland, Ava, I'm in Portland, Oregon; look for flights out of PDX."

She didn't press me for any other info. Ava and I booked a 6:45 a.m. flight 'cuz it was the cheapest and would get me to Miami with time to enjoy the rest of Friday. She even chipped in to cover the cost. Ava told me she'd pick me up at the airport. I'd spend the weekend with her, Titi Penny, and Uncle Len. It'd been a few years since our summers together, running around the beaches of Miami as kids. Ava told me she loved me. Primas for life.

Kira texted me. She wanted to come find me and offered to give me a ride anywhere. I told her where I was, and then for a while, it was quiet; just me and the moon.

Harlowe called my cell phone. I almost picked up, but I realized I had nothing to say to her. Everything was a lump in my throat. Harlowe left a voice mail. I didn't listen to it. Avoid. Avoid. Somebody would let her know I was okay. She'd be fine. Harlowe had gotten all of my energy before her reading. I was in full-on self-preservation mode.

I heard Kira's motorcycle before I saw it. She pulled up, handed me a helmet, and I hopped on. We zipped up Burnside and dipped through different side streets until I didn't know where we were. I kept my arms around her hips, nestled into her back. Kira pulled up to her house and invited me inside. She promised to take me stargazing another night. She made a quick salad and boxed mac and cheese. It was the most normal thing I'd eaten in Portland. Kira listened to me as I tried to piece together complicated feelings and not cry. Was Harlowe racist? Was I oversensitive? Did my being from the Bronx scream so loud of poverty and violence that my actual story didn't matter? What did it mean for me as a person and a wannabe feminist that I looked up to Harlowe? Was I proof that her feminism was for everyone?

I stopped after admitting that I loved Harlowe and that made me an even bigger fool. How could I love some fake-ass, kinda racist (?), clueless person like Harlowe?

Kira said she had wondered about Harlowe for a while after reading *Raging Flower*. She wondered if Harlowe was the ally that most people praised her to be. That what Harlowe said about me solidified her impression that Harlowe was like every other white lady feminist she'd ever met.

"People are fucked up like that sometimes, Juliet, especially white people. I'm white and Korean and even some of my friends will assume I'm good at math or know martial arts just because of how I look. Those assumptions live inside people and they do their best to dodge them and intellectualize around them, but they're still there. They also don't see me as politicized or as someone who experiences microaggressions. It sucks. We deserve better. You deserve better," Kira said. She kissed my cheek.

I leaned into her. I asked her if I could take a shower. Kira showed me to the bathroom. I turned on the hot water, slipped off my clothes, and stood under the stream with my eyes shut.

After a few minutes, she knocked on the door and told me she was leaving me a towel.

"You can come in, if you want," I said. The second the words came out, I couldn't believe I had said them.

"Okay," she replied. It was quiet for a minute, then the curtain was pulled back. Beautiful, naked Kira moved into the shower with me. She pressed me against the cool tiles and kissed me. The weight of the evening slid off my skin as the hot water washed over us. She soaped up my chest, belly, and back. Her hands were firm. She kneaded my back muscles and kissed along my shoulder blades. I let her hands roam my flesh and explore the curves of my body. I didn't think about anything else but kissing her, all of her. She slid her hands along my thighs.

"You feel really good to me. Are you good?" she asked. "We don't have to do anything you don't want to do. I just want to check in."

"I don't know what I want to do. I like this. I like kissing you and feeling you. But I don't want to use you," I replied. I gazed at the droplets of water along her eyelashes.

"I'm here. I know what it's like when you need to be kissed and touched. I don't feel used. We can take it slow and stop whenever," she said.

Kira turned off the shower and led me to her bedroom. Both of us wrapped in towels, bodies warm and wet, we flopped onto her bed. I followed her lead. Where she touched and pressed her lips, I did the same. She kept her hands on my thighs while she kissed my belly. Kira slid up my body. Her mouth a whisper away from mine. She made me wait for a kiss. Eye contact the whole time made me feel grown in my own body: sexy mami in full bloom. When our lips finally touched, I was hers. My body had never felt so desired and alive. We moved in rhythm with each other. And when I felt her inside me, I wrapped my hips tight around her waist and gave her everything. I fell asleep with my head on her chest.

In the soft early hours of the morning, after all the gentle kisses and assurances that everything would be okay, she dropped me off at Harlowe's. Maxine was the only one home.

She said Harlowe was so upset that I'd left that she'd run off to her favorite meditation temple. Maxine didn't seem worried about Harlowe. She hugged me and said she understood why I had to take off for a bit. There was too much to say and not enough time to process. I packed fast and left my copy of *Raging Flower* on the bed.

Maxine took me to the airport.

And I was gone. On a plane to Miami.

PART THREE

BIENVENIDOS A MIAMI. THE WORLD IS YOURS

CHAPTER EIGHTEEN

QUEER ABCs AND 123s

AVA MET ME at the luggage carousel. She wore black leather leggings, a ripped black T-shirt with the word *Bruja* written across in red letters, and studded knee-high silver boots. We stared at each other for a moment and then Ava wrapped her arms around me. We hugged tight enough to make up for the three years that had passed between our last visit. She smelled like Gucci Rush and all the summer nights we'd shared together as kids. She released me just a stretch, enough to look me in the eyes and see my tears. Ava hugged me again.

"Come on, prima, let's get you home," she said, as she grabbed my suitcase and my hand.

Ava drove a black Mustang she nicknamed the Bullet. It was half sweet-sixteen gift and half two years of saved income from working at Hot Topic. Ava blasted Snoop Dogg and Selena with the windows rolled down as we roared down State Road 953 to

Coral Gables. The rearview mirror trembled with the bass. Ava and I rapped and sang along to all the songs on her *Como La Doggystyle* CD, a mix she made for me.

The hot sun felt good on my skin. It blazed, an endless blue sky and golden-yellow sun rays for miles. We pulled up to Ava's giant house; it sprawled out in every direction. The front door burst open and out came Titi Penny in all her foxy Titi glory. Her dyed hair, a combination of auburn, blond, and brown, was styled in loose banana curls. Titi Penny ran to me and covered me in red-lipstick kisses. She hugged me so tight, I felt weightless.

"Ay, Juliet, it's been too long. Que bella. You look more and more like Mariana every time I see you," Titi Penny said. She placed her hand over her heart.

Wrapping her arm around my shoulder, Titi Penny led me into the house. Ava grabbed my bag, not because she wanted to but because Titi Penny would have asked her to do it anyway.

"I spoke to your mother this morning. She didn't know you were coming." She ushered me into the kitchen. The marble island sparkled, a set of ceramic canisters lined the middle in size order. "She was very upset that you didn't tell her. Nena, call your mother. Let her know you're okay. I'll make you a plate."

That's how I found myself sweating to death on Titi Penny's lanai argue-talking with my mother for almost an hour. No, I hadn't told her I was taking a trip to Miami. Yes, I realized that my internship with Harlowe counted as credits for graduation.

No, I didn't waste my grant money on unnecessary travel. Yes, I was listening. (But no, I wasn't gonna watch my tone.) I didn't even bother mentioning anything about Harlowe's reading. She wouldn't have gotten it. She didn't understand. She knew what was best for me. I was disrespectful. I had better change up my attitude. I didn't understand a mother's love and need to protect. It was all fine. I should call her back when I found my respect. I sighed at her, not even meaning to. The pause in her breath let me know she caught it. Our phone call ended with her telling me she loved me. She hung up before I said it back. That swallowed "I love you too" burned all the way down my throat.

Titi Penny and Ava breezed into the room with plates of arroz con gandules, tostones sprinkled with salt, and grilled chicken topped with cilantro and avocado. A crystal pitcher filled with iced sangria accompanied the food. Titi pressed a heaping plate into my hands.

"Hey," she said, her free hand on my cheek. "She's talking to you. She loves you. You did good. Respira, mamita."

I leaned into Titi Penny's forehead with mine.

"I've missed you, Titi," I said.

"Good," she said. "Now don't let your food get cold."

Ava pulled me into the spot right next to her on Titi's wicker loveseat. (Gotta love that Florida furniture.)

"So, what did Harlowe fucking Brisbane do to you?" Ava asked, kicking off her boots.

I laughed, raised my plate off my lap. Ava put her legs over mine. Titi Penny sat curled up in the chair next to us. And I told them everything. I started with the most mortifying: coming out to everyone at my good-bye dinner. We even laughed a little bit about Titi Wepa until I passed around that picture of Mom and me at Battery Park. Titi Penny held it in her hand, studying it.

"She didn't mention the picture," Titi Penny said, shaking her head. "That sister of mine is something else."

"What *did* she say to you?" I asked, ignoring Ava's hard poke to the thigh.

Titi Penny looked over at me, eyebrow raised. "What's between sisters stays between sisters. Talk to your mother, Juliet."

I dipped a piece of tostone in ketchup. Ava switched gears to the breakup with Lainie. They both knew I'd been broken up with because Mom told them, but they hadn't gotten the memo about the breakup CD. That revelation brought out some choice words: *puta gringa* and *malcriada* to name a few. Once again, I pulled out the infamous letter. They both read it, sucking their teeth. Ava took this moment to ask if Lainie and I had ever banged in my mom's house and if we dated because I "had a thing for white girls." You know, the important stuff.

I briefed them on Harlowe, Maxine, polyamory, and the new words I'd learned but still wasn't sure what they meant. Ava tapped my head at that last one. "Nena, I'm gonna learn you some queer shit before you go home," she said, as she refilled all our glasses with sangria.

I told them about Kira, her motorcycle, and how she scooped me from the bridge. And before I could say anything else, I blushed so hard and couldn't look at either of them.

"So you caught feelings for the librarian. Continue," Ava said.

When I got to the part about being heartbroken over Harlowe, Ava stopped me. On her third glass of sangria, she gestured with her hands.

"Wait, what? How could she break your heart? Did you fall in love with the Pussy Lady? ¿Dímelo qué?"

"No, it wasn't like I wanted to date her. I fell into some kind of love with her though, like when you look up to someone and want to be like them and feel like they're family. That kind of love. Ava, when she talks about feminism and faeries and all that shit something inside of her lights up, glows even. No one on this earth is like her, yo. How could I not love her?"

"Girl, c'mon, you could have realized that she was some hippie-ass, holier-than-thou white lady preaching her bullshit universal feminism to everyone. Is there no backlash on Harlowe Brisbane in Portland? 'Cuz around here we give no fucks about that book," Ava said.

"It's not that easy. She wasn't like that, really, not until the night of the reading. You don't even know her. And since when do you know anything about being gay and being a feminist? Last time we chilled all you could talk about was Limp Bizkit and cheetah-print tights."

"Enough," Titi Penny said. "You two clear the dishes and the food. Leave the sangria." We did as we were told. Ava and I brought the dishes to the kitchen, both of us quiet. I continued my Portland story, giving them the extended director's cut of Harlowe's reading at Powell's. It was so fresh and I was still confused. I recounted Harlowe's version of my life to both of them. Ava sucked her teeth again but said nothing. Titi Penny laughed, amused but not in league with Harlowe.

"So you're some poor little ghetto girl stuck in the Bronx, huh? Wow, some feminist," she said. "And so after stereotyping my beautiful niece, this lady hasn't checked in on you beyond one phone call, didn't take you to the airport, and now you're here with us?"

"Yes, Titi Penny."

"Well, a whole lot of life has come your way this summer. You came out, experienced your first breakup, learned about veganism. All the big things."

Titi Penny's smile revealed the same gap Ava had between her front teeth. "Are you teasing me, Titi?"

"Yes and no. I'm glad you're here. We have three days to love you good," Titi Penny said, "and discuss the importance of naming racism when it comes for you unexpectedly in the form of a mentor, a lover, or someone who exists in the gray areas. But for now, maybe you two go upstairs, unpack, and reconnect."

Ava laughed. She put her arm around my shoulders and led me to her bedroom on the second floor. Her domain covered the entire back section of the house. She had movie posters of *Mi Vida Loca* and *Kids* on her wall next to magazine covers of Rosario Dawson. She'd pinned protest fliers and bulletins for LGBTQ outreach programs to the wall. She pulled me out onto the balcony and lit a Black & Mild. Together we watched the sunset. Ava bumped her hip into mine.

"I didn't mean to upset you, prima. You know I love you," Ava said. "I'm still figuring out my shit too, and the circles I run in are mad with it. Like, no time for white supremacy or second-wave white feminism. But it's not fair for me to judge you, you know?"

I was surprised by her apology and curious about everything she was learning. "No worries. Let's just start over. Tell me all the things," I replied.

"I'm still figuring stuff out," she said. "Like, I'm not gay, but I'm totally in love with a girl named Luz Ángel. And most of the time, I'm basically attracted to everyone and lots of times no one at all. So what does that make me? Queer? I'm trying that out for now."

"Whoa, Ava, I had no idea," I said. I reached out for the last inch of her cigarillo and said, "I wanna know all about Luz Ángel."

"Oh my God," Ava said, as she slid open the door to the balcony. "Where do I even start?"

Ava jumped on her king-size bed and spread out. "Luz Ángel is a brown-skinned fucking babe, queen of my heart. She doesn't even know it. She's so busy running Tempest, the queer and transgender people of color group on campus. Every time she speaks, I'm just done. I sit in on Tempest meetings basically hoping she notices me while learning about how to organize against and fight oppression."

"So, like, exactly how I started dating Lainie by signing up for a women's studies class?"

"Yeah, but a little more radical," Ava replied.

"I don't know how anyone could *not* notice you, Ava. You're fucking gorgeous, and I've been jealous of you for having all the looks ever since we were little kids," I exclaimed. I put out the cigarillo.

"Oh stop, you're gorgeous too. And you got all the tetas in this family," Ava said, as she poked the side of my breast.

We lay side by side on her big, comfy bed like we did when we were kids. I snuggled into her pillow and put my legs over hers.

"You know how you said you were going to 'school me on some queer shit' earlier?" I asked. "I'm gonna hold you to that. I've literally been writing things down all summer. Things like PGPs and what should I say when someone asks me how I identify. And honestly, I don't know much about trans stuff, either. Everyone else seems to know all the things but all I know is that I'm not straight."

"Damn, mama. We've got a lot to talk about then," Ava said. She cracked her knuckles. "Lemme go get the rest of that sangria."

For the next few hours, we lay out on her bed, sipping sangria. Ava answered my questions. Ava didn't like the term preferred gender pronouns.

"Whatever pronouns a person chooses, if they choose any at all, are their right. Not a fucking preference," she said.

I clasped my hands over my belly, mulling over what Ava had said. Before this summer, I'd never considered there was anything beyond *he* or *she*. Or that folks could experience a multitude of genders within their person, like what?! That sounded amazing. Beautiful. Wild like the universe.

"Why not just ask someone straight up if they're trans?" I asked.

"Girl, how rude do you plan to be in this life?" she questioned, stretching out on her big-ass bed. "Your one job is to just accept what a person feels comfortable sharing about themselves. No one owes you info on their gender, body parts, or sexuality."

Mind blown. I twirled rogue baby hairs between my fingers, thinking all this through. I definitely wasn't running around declaring what types of genitals I had to folks. But I figured it went without saying, like my large breasts and thick hips were all the indicators the outside world needed.

"But, like, I'm out here assuming girls have vaginas and I like vaginas a lot. And if I was in the process of hooking up with a girl and she didn't have a vagina, I would feel a type of way, I think," I admitted, face in my hands.

Ava sighed and it sounded like she was tired of the world for a second.

"It's not you, you know," she said, "We're socialized into this madness. One step at a time, Juliet. Would you shame that girl?"

"What?" I asked. "Shame her? No, I'd feel awkward as hell. I don't know what it is to be transgender, but I do know what it's like to be treated like shit for the type of body you have and I wouldn't wanna do that to anyone in the world, you know."

"Well, maybe there's hope for you yet," Ava said. "Love all the vaginas you want, prima, just remember they're attached to people. Okay? And it's the people that matter most."

I rolled over and looked at her. Ava broke these huge ideas down into small chunks because I needed level-one-style education.

She talked about people I'd never heard of like Sylvia Rivera and Marsha P. Johnson. They were transgender women of color and helped start the Stonewall riots. I didn't even know that Stonewall was a fucking riot. I thought it was just that bar that had Lesbo-a-Go-Go parties on Tuesday nights in the city. I stared up at the ceiling mesmerized. I wished I'd decided to spend my summer with Ava. Maybe I wasn't such a freak, feminist, alien dyke after all. I was part of this deep-ass legacy and history of people fighting to be free.

Ava nudged me. "It's okay not to know things, prima. I'm always here for you. Anything you ever need or want to know or do, call me. Okay?" she said. The expression on her face was serious, like, as if we were about to make a pact.

"Okay, I will," I said.

We pinkie-swore and drank more sangria. After my lesson on basic gay stuff, Ava moved on to gushing about Luz Ángel some more. I told her about my night with Kira. We traded secrets about the girls we liked until we both stopped talking and fell out.

CHAPTER NINETEEN

LOVE IN THE TIME OF A BRONX TALE

I WOKE UP in the clothes I'd traveled in, crawled out of Ava's bed at 6:00 a.m., and took a shower in her private bathroom. Clean and in fresh underwear, I went right back to sleep next to her. I didn't wake up again until noon. Ava snored, mouth open, a black satin mask over her eyes. She got all the pretty in this family. Even in her sleep, Ava was the type of beautiful that made it hard for people to concentrate.

I licked my finger and stuck it in her ear. She swatted my hand, then my face. She threatened me with imminent death. I threatened her with gas that I'd held in since last night. She ripped off her face mask, eyes wide. I laughed until I couldn't breathe.

She offered me use of her computer. I had a thousand spam e-mails and one e-mail from Harlowe.

Juliet,

Many apologies. I'd like to pick you up from the airport. It's how we first met. Let's start over? I'm flawed. I've been wracked, praying to the goddesses for guidance. I fucked up. I said things that weren't true. My white privilege spewed out, all over, onto you. I'm really fucking sorry about that.

I hope your family loves you good. And I hope you come back and that we can work this out.

But if you don't feel comfortable around me anymore, I understand. We'll make different arrangements.

Love,

The fucked-up white lady that's trying to live an anti-racist, pro-woman, feminist life that loves you something fierce.

I wrote her back without hesitation.

Harlowe,

I'm still figuring out why I had to leave. I'll be back Monday morning.

Starting over is always good.

Juliet, the kid just trying to live right

I read Harlowe's e-mail to Ava. Teeth were sucked. Eyes rolled hard. Ava had no time for Harlowe. She wrote me a list of all the other books I needed to read about feminism that weren't written by Harlowe Brisbane. I laughed and promised to read them all. But even after everything that went down at Powell's with Harlowe, I still had to ask: What was so bad about *Raging Flower*? Ava said Harlowe didn't make queer and/or trans women of color a priority in her work; that Harlowe assumed that we could all connect through sisterhood, as if sisterhood looked the same for everyone. Ava spoke while she brushed her teeth, applied dark eye makeup, and checked out her body in the floor-length mirror.

"This is kinda like what we talked about last night, right?" I asked, watching her get ready.

"Yeah, mama," she replied. "I can't fuck with Harlowe because all she does is equate being a woman to bleeding and charting moon cycles. Like, I'm so not with that."

I ran the water in her tub and started soaping up my legs. "Okay, but, like, don't those things count too?" I asked, shifting my hip on the edge of the bathtub. "Our moms and grandmas have this woman thing going on and it has a lot to do with bodies, and babies, and periods."

"Don't I know it," Ava said, plucking brows in the mirror.

"So then why does it feel like you're trying to separate them?" I asked, lathering up my legs.

Ava turned, like stopped in mid-pluck, and looked at me.

"Because that's how you unlearn the fuckshit," she said. "We are so much more than Harlowe can even comprehend. Her consistent linking of genitals to gender as an absolute is violent as hell. It's a closed fist instead of open arms, you know? And besides," she added, staring at herself unflinching in the mirror, "womanhood is radical enough for anyone who dares to claim it."

"Damn, cuz, you're making my brain explode all over again," I replied, eyes wide.

I shaved my legs sitting along the edge of Ava's tub. The thick coarse hairs disappeared with each swipe of my razor. I bit my bottom lip, thinking. I hadn't thought anything of Harlowe's pussy worship before. In fact, it was the opposite. I was here because of her words about my body parts and my womanhood. So was I also somehow being violent too? Could it be both? The water from the faucet trickled over my ankles and washed the hairs from my razor.

"So Mom and Grandma have their experiences of being women and we can honor that, like all the breasts, babies, and marriage stuff. But it's not our job to be like, 'Oh, in order to be a woman, everyone has to have all these things checked off the list' or something like that," I mused, my face a little scrunched up, trying to get it all out right. My cheeks felt hot.

"That. Hold on to that thought right there and stick with it," she said, admiring her brow work.

"I will," I said. "And like, I want to be able to get it like you do. I don't want people to feel hurt by me 'cuz I don't understand something. I think that's why I still have so much room for Harlowe. I really believe that she's trying to create safe spaces for all women."

"Was Harlowe trying to create that safe space before or after she sold you out to her crowd of believers?" Ava asked. She turned all the way around and sat next to me along the edge of the tub.

I sighed. "That's fucked up, cuz."

"Juliet, I'm asking because I love you, and I want to keep challenging you, babe. What are you basing your ideas of womanhood on? You gotta question everything, especially who you give your love and respect to. This is about perspective, you know? Like, where do you stand?"

I didn't have an answer for her. Or for myself.

WE CHILLED ALL damn day. Lounged by the pool in bathing suits, sipped iced tea and ate pastelitos filled with cheese and spicy ground beef. Titi Penny took every opportunity to kiss my cheeks and tell me that nothing Harlowe said was true. She lay out next to me. I wondered what her life was like when she was my age. When did people become titis in a void, without visible teeth marks from their histories on their skin? When did they become women who sent Christmas gifts in the mail and had conversations with your mom about your gayness? Looking at Titi Penny, I remembered what Mom had told me.

"Titi, can I ask you something personal?"

"Of course, nena, ask me anything," she replied.

"How do you identify?"

Ava coughed and spun around in her lounge chair. Titi Penny peered over at me. "What do you mean?" she asked. Her voice soft, a slow smile spread across her lips.

"Yeah. What do you mean?" Ava asked, as she stared straight at me.

"Okay, you promise not to get mad?" I asked.

"Juliet . . ."

"Mom told me that I was going through a phase just like you did. She said that you had a lady friend once but now you're married to Uncle Lenny and so my gayness isn't permanent either."

Titi Penny laughed. Ava's jaw hit the floor.

"Juliet, your mother never understood three things about me. She couldn't grasp why I was an activist and worked with the Young Lords. She didn't understand how I could love a woman, let alone Magdalena—our super's daughter—and last but not least, she was dumbfounded when I decided to marry a skinny Jewish guy named Leonard Friedman. And yet, she never turned her back on me, Juliet."

"You were in love with a woman!?" Ava asked. "And you never told me about her? I bet she was smoking hot too. Magdalena. Mom! What's with the secrets?"

"Yes, I was in love with a woman named Magdalena, okay? I was eighteen and she was gorgeous. She taught me how to dance bachata and rat my hair. Don't ask. We were lovers for almost the whole summer."

"Lovers, Mom? That word is so . . ."

"Oh, stop. *Lovers* is a fine word, Ava. It didn't last long. She cheated on me with some guy and was pregnant by September. I didn't say a word about her to your mom after that, Juliet. And well, less than a year later I was seeing Uncle Lenny anyway."

"So it *was* just a phase?" I asked.

Titi Penny paused. "I don't know. Things were different then. I didn't have a name for my feelings, I just let myself fall in love with her. And then, I was deep into organizing with the Lords for a better and safer Bronx when I met Lenny. He was a socialist and I fell for him hard. We fit immediately. I didn't feel confused about my sexuality or who I was. I've always just been Penny and that was enough for me."

I turned over and laid my head in her lap.

"Mom, oh my god. Are we both bi? Holy shit. We're. Both. Bi," Ava shouted, giddy as hell.

Titi Penny got quiet for a minute and then let out a full-body laugh that made Ava and me glow.

"Yes, *bi*. Of course. That tiny word feels so good. Do us *bis* get a parade too?"

"We better," Ava said, wrapping her arms around Titi Penny. "If not, we'll make out own."

They hugged, crying all soft with big smiles on their faces. After a minute, Titi Penny pulled me into their embrace.

"And as for you, Juliet . . ." Titi Penny started. "You are your own person. If liking girls is a phase, so what? If it's your whole life, who cares? You're destined to evolve and understand yourself in ways you never imagined before. And you've got our blood running through your beautiful veins, so no matter what, you've been blessed with the spirit of women who know how to love."

The three of us talked all afternoon. Titi Penny also told me that she and my mom spoke on the phone almost every day since I left for Portland. She said that my mom had read a bunch of books, including *Raging Flower*. Titi Penny urged me to be gentle. Mom was trying to understand me in her own way. I needed to reach out more. Titi Penny told me to trust my mother's love. I'd try harder. If Mom was trying, I'd try too.

Uncle Len made it home that night an hour before sunset. Together, we sat and ate Shabbat dinner. He blessed the meal. Baruch atah Adonai. I bowed my head. It felt good to pray, to remember to give thanks and feel connected to something beyond the confusion of being human.

Ava hyped me up after dinner. Convinced that I needed community, she decided to take me to a Clipper Queerz party. Part dance party, part self-care, sliding-scale haircut extravaganza, Clipper Queerz parties were hot and underground as fuck. The CQ crew threw events for queer and trans people of color only; no white allies, be they lover, family, or otherwise. Mixed race and biracial people were welcomed, of course, and no one did any ethnic policing. The CQ crew expected its people to honor their no-white-folks rule, and anyone who tried to circumvent it lost their respect and invitation to the next party. Shit sounded mad secretive and exclusive, like gay Masons or some shit. I was intrigued but hella skeptical.

"I don't know, Ava. Don't you feel weird going to a party where a young, political, good-hearted white person, like your dad when he was younger, wouldn't be able to attend?" I asked her this as she layered my eyelids with black and silver eyeshadow.

"No, I don't feel weird. You are just looking to make all the room for white people, aren't you?" Ava asked. She turned around to look at me.

I sat on her bed, ashamed to look her in the eye. I shrugged. "No, that's not what I'm trying to do."

"Listen, babe, it's okay. Look, the Clipper Queerz parties are for familia to fucking chill and not worry about the clueless gringa from their job saying some racist shit about Cubans or Black people or anyone. And it's less about there being no white people and more of a night for us to breathe easier. Okay? None of the lez parties are doing this. It's electric, prima."

I needed to breathe easier. Ava reached for my hand. I gave it to her. She slid me off the bed and pulled me back into the bathroom. We looked at our reflections in the mirror. We shared the same lips, heart-shaped and full. Ava had grown out of her chubby cheeks, though. She pinched my chin and turned my gaze to her.

"Let's get ready together, okay?"

I nodded. As Ava did my makeup, she told me about her friends in the CQ circle. She dropped secrets in between facts. She got all hyperbolic about Luz Ángel, who also organized the parties, and it was so cute. Ava wasn't sure if she could keep her feelings for Luz Ángel to herself. But she was terrified of letting them out.

"Love wrecks you. It devastates everything," she said.

Ava was convinced that Luz Ángel's voice could make millions march. She believed that being part of someone's cause or fight was just as solid as declaring love. And she was in it thick over her; Ava called it that no-justice-no-peace kind of love. I wondered about love. Would I ever feel that kind of love? I fell in something for Harlowe, maybe it was hate-love? No, I didn't hate Harlowe. Her words hurt because I loved her, but what did it mean? Did love make me run from Harlowe to Miami or did I get here because I loved myself enough to fly away?

CHAPTER TWENTY

UNDERCUTS AND TRANSFORMATION

THE MUSIC WAS good and loud when we pulled up in Ava's Mustang. We walked along the side of the house and Ava pushed open the fence gate. The Clipper Queerz party stretched out before us in all its radical glory. Lit from the bottom, the in-ground pool shimmered. To the right was the DJ setup and along the back were the barber's chairs. A person in a bright pink bikini ran over to us and pulled Ava into a full body hug.

"Florencio!" Ava shrieked, a huge smile on her face. "You're soaking wet, dammit. Hey, turn around, I want you to meet my cousin Juliet."

Florencio spun in my direction. "Well, hello. I've never met a Juliet before. I'm Florencio and my pronouns are she and they."

"Hi, I'm Juliet," I said. Florencio's use of she pronouns surprised me, but I remembered Ava telling me not to be a rude-ass bitch, so I just went with it.

Florencio eyed me for a moment. "Are you a hugger? 'Cuz I'm a hugger."

I nodded and Florencio hugged me good. She kissed both of my cheeks.

"Darlings, I hate to leave, but the pool is calling me. I do hope you both find your way in," she said. "Oh and, just so you know, Luz Ángel's here." Florencio hip-bumped Ava before darting off to the water.

"I'm not going to make it," Ava said. She audibly swooned.

"It'll be fine, prima," I replied.

The atmosphere at the Clipper Queerz party boomed; it was vibrant and open. Ava and I walked over to the cooler and grabbed some beers. Shitty, cheap, and totally perfect American beers.

Ava introduced me to twins, Alonzo and Necia. "It's good luck, I swear," Necia said. She reached for my hand. "Rub my head. Make a wish."

"There's no such thing as good luck, Necia. It's all about what the universe wants," Alonzo replied.

I rubbed both of their heads. Their short Mohawks matched. They looked like brother and sister, but since neither of them said anything about pronouns I didn't say anything either. They were Necia and Alonzo.

I took a long swig of beer. More folks filtered in and out of our small circle near the coolers.

Ava did her best to introduce me, but her eyes were on the one person who seemed to never be close enough. Luz Ángel moved around the perimeter of the pool, talking and laughing with everyone else. It made sense that Ava felt like Luz Ángel didn't know she was alive. Maybe my cousin wouldn't find her no-justice-no-peace love with this girl.

Florencio wiggled in between me and Ava to grab a beer. Her body was covered in water droplets. She looked like a glistening mermaid queen.

"Are you going to get a cut?" Florencio asked.

My eyes widened and I looked down for a second. I felt a little nervous. "Never. My hair's too long. I couldn't ever cut it," I said.

Another swig of beer. Florencio clinked bottles with me.

"If there was ever a place to do something you'd never do, it's here," she said. "Shit, at the last party, I left with someone's name tattooed on my ankle. To this day, I swear, I don't know who it was. But when I meet whoever Valentina is, we're going to kiki like it's nineteen ninety-nine."

Florencio showed off her ankle tat and I laughed. I felt freer than I had all summer. Ava pulled an ultra-slim cigarette from Florencio's gold case. She made her way to the edge of the pool. I didn't follow. It seemed like she needed a moment to herself. Besides, I wasn't alone; people flowed in and around me all night. Everyone had big ideas to share. They dropped phrases like *radical politics, gender essentialism,* and *government-sanctioned inequality* in between conversations about silver lipstick and the importance of self-care. Each cluster of humans wanted to take on the world and reimagine it. In the background, along with the bass thumping, was the sound of clippers buzzing.

The music faded. Luz Ángel stood in front of her table with a microphone in hand. She waited for the party to hush on its own. All eyes were on her and her red thigh-high boots. I moved closer. She cleared her throat.

"Mi gente, this is the third Clipper Queerz party and I'm honored to still be organizing and partying with my CQ familia."

The crowd cheered Luz Ángel on.

"We're here to chill, get sick haircuts, and dance. But let's not forget our fallen camaradas who've been brutalized by police and lovers or left for dead in the street. My fellow trans women, I will not forget you! We will not forget your names. We will not forget being discarded by our families, being homeless and used and taunted. Bullied, murdered, oppressed for being brown, Black, Asian, for being queers, faggots, dykes, genderless renegades, trans warriors, for all our glory. We are not like those fake, fancy gays from *Queer as Folk* or *Will and Fucking Grace*! And we will never be them. We will never assimilate. Basura! The capitalist system that favors whiteness and wealth over all has denied us the right to live well, to be well, and to love. We won't let them win. We will riot and party and honor our ancestors, and no one can stop us. Glory be to la madre, Sylvia Rivera; la Virgen de Guadalupe; and la reina, Selena Quintanilla-Pérez. And to you, my people, my Clipper Queerz, Luz Ángel loves you, if no one else does."

The CQ crew cheered and hollered for Luz Ángel.

Ava squeezed my arm. "Do you see how incredible she is, Juliet? I'm done. Absolutely fucking done," she said.

I thought Ava was going to cry. She had that wide-eyed, moody daydreaming look on her face. I leaned in, pressed our foreheads together.

"If you're aching for radical queer love with her, prima, go and get it," I said. "Do it now so I can watch and remember it for you later when you try and tell the story and don't do it any justice."

Ava put her palms to my cheeks, like when we were kids. "I'm so glad you're here, Juliet," she said. Ava drank the rest of her beer and walked off in the direction of Luz Ángel.

I grabbed another beer and drifted over to the haircuts. The CQ barbers were dreamboats, all of them. They trimmed sideburns, etched lines into skin, and listened to everyone's requests: buzzcuts, bald fades, and undercuts. One of the barbers in particular was wicked with a flat razor. Their bright pastel-blue lipstick caught my attention. They looked up and we locked eyes. I blushed but didn't break eye contact. Neither did they. There was no attitude or bravado in their demeanor. None of that I'm-a-harder-dyke-than-you shit that I got when Lainie and I would sneak into Gallagher's, the only dyke bar in Baltimore. Blue-Lipped Barber looked sweet, all short and stocky, alcapurria brown, and muscular in their vintage *Purple Rain* Prince T-shirt.

I was about to walk over to them when a gorgeous human sashayed right onto their barber's chair. Blue Lips' attention shifted to them. Whatever passed between us floated off into the night.

It's not like I was going to cut my hair, anyway. Never. I'd promised myself that I'd never be one of those manly lesbians. I watched Blue Lips work from afar.

I surveyed the party in awe. I felt like I was in some futuristic music video. It made me think of the science fiction story I'd written in the Octavia Butler workshop "Starlight Mamitas: Three Chords of Rebellion." I still hadn't submitted it to Zaira's anthology. I didn't know if I would, but the party connected to that world. A world where three Latina sisters would start a heavy metal revolution. Clipper Queerz was a revolution too. I hadn't met one person at the party that fit into the regular, straight, normal version of what society wanted them . . . wanted *us* to be. Gender-wise alone, it was as if the spectrum of the galaxy, with all its manifestations of human beings, beautifully imploded and all the people here were imbued with its majesty.

Luz Ángel emerged from the pool. Glorious hair flowed down her back, and for a million reasons I saw why my cousin loved her. She walked over in my direction, staring right at me. I didn't have time to weird out and run off. Her direct eye contact made me feel at once shy and important.

"I don't think we've met yet," she said. "I'm Luz Ángel and you're Juliet, Ava's cousin. The really cute cousin who's been standing alone in a corner for way too long."

"What? No, I mean, yes. But, like . . ." I stammered, losing my train of thought.

"But, like, nothing. Everyone here is family and that means you too," Luz Ángel said. She put her arm around my shoulder. "Is this okay?"

"Yes, totally, thanks for asking. You're sweet," I replied, leaning into her. "We should find Ava."

"Oh my God, I need a break from your cousin."

I tensed up. "What? Why?"

"Because she's just too fucking gorgeous for me to handle, okay? I've literally been running from her all night and obviously, I'm telling you because I'm a drama queen and my crush on your cousin is out of control. And I fucking love it." Luz Ángel pulled me closer. "Let's do a lap."

We walked through the party like homecoming royalty. Folks were dancing, doing flips into the pool, and taking time to reinvent themselves. The haircut line ebbed and flowed with the music. Necia handed out Jello-O shots to me and Luz Ángel. Mine was bright blue. I'd never done one before. The three of us clinked Dixie cups and swallowed. Necia flittered off to hand out the rest of them. Ava was surrounded by a small group of folks, immersed in an intense conversation. Luz Ángel attempted to lead us in the other direction. I stopped and turned to her.

"Oh no way, Doña Let's-Lead-the-Revolution. You're not avoiding Ava any more tonight," I said. "Come on."

We edged in around the circle. Florencio had the floor.

"In my heart, I believe we need to rethink masculinity, Ava, not dismantle it," she said.

"I hear you, but it's super damaging and violent. Why not just be rid of the whole thing?" Ava asked.

"Because, well, at least to me, masculinity is forever linked to the feminine and to all other forms of gender expression. It's only damaging and violent because we've elevated it above everything else. Society allows masculine people, specifically white men, to exert tremendous power without consequence, and that's where the trauma comes in. It's not masculinity in and of itself," Florencio said. "But, to be perfectly honest, I'd rather spend my energy exploring and elevating divine feminine energy."

I stood there with Luz Ángel's arm still around my shoulder and took in what Florencio said. Instead of feeling blocked and confused like I'd been in Portland, something clicked and I got it. I got what they were saying. It connected to *Raging Flower* and Harlowe. It connected to all my issues with Lainie and my mom. I'd been so busy trying to be what they wanted me to be that I wasn't exploring and elevating my own divine feminine energy. I went from Luz Ángel to Ava and wrapped my arms around her waist.

"Thank you for bringing me here, prima," I whispered to her.

"Oh, babygirl, you're welcome," she said.

"I'm gonna wander and you're gonna be cute with Luz Ángel. Okay? Like, just do it. Trust me."

I looked her in the eyes. Ava pushed her forehead into mine

and nodded. I walked off and when I turned around, Ava had moved closer to Luz Ángel. They were almost touching. I made my way to the haircuts and stood by Blue Lips. I watched them use a flat razor to etch lines in someone's newly shaved head. I ran my hand through my curls. I had my mother's hair. Thick, black, and prone to sweating out a relaxer and frizzing up in the summer. Blue Lips dusted off their customer and used a hand-held mirror to show off the cut and the line work in the back.

Pleased, the person hugged them and offered to grab them a drink. "You gonna get a cut?" Blue Lips asked.

"I'm afraid of looking like a dyke," I said.

"Are you a dyke?"

"I think so."

"Then no matter what you do with your hair, you're gonna look like a dyke," Blue Lips said. They smiled at me and patted the chair.

"I hadn't thought about it like that," I replied. I sat my ass down on their chair and took a deep breath. "Okay, let's do this. I haven't gotten a haircut beyond a trim since I was in fifth grade."

Blue Lips walked around me, inspected my hair for a minute. "How about a little undercut?" they asked. Blue Lips touched behind my ears. "I can shave off the back from here to here and leave all the long hair on top."

"I don't know you, but I'm going to trust your skills. Do whatever you think will look good. I'm Juliet. And to be honest, I've been calling you Blue Lips in my head all night."

They laughed. "I like that. You can call me Blue Lips, Juliet."

J.Lo's "Jenny from the Block" dropped over the speakers. It was a sign from the Boogie Down goddesses. I said a quick prayer to la Virgen. "Okay, undercut me."

Blue Lips undid my ponytail and brushed out my curls. They used a thick comb to divide my hair into sections. A small crowd gathered. Four sets of eyes watched Blue Lips do their thing. I think people were caught on how long my hair was and wanted to see if I was gonna shave it all off. Blue Lips clipped hair on top of my head and then peered into my face with their sweet brown eyes.

"You ready?" they asked. It wasn't an out, it was an act of confirmation.

Was I ready? I nodded yes and then said yes and then I shut my eyes. Blue Lips snipped off about a foot of hair. They held it in front of me. I misted up. My hair. My beautiful long hair. I shut my eyes and pulled myself together. Blue Lips put their clippers to my sideburns and buzzed the entire underside of my head. They used a sharp razor to make the edges crisp. They asked if I wanted some lines and a cut in my eyebrow. I nodded yes, not really sure what any of it meant. Blue Lips carved three lines into the left side of my head and a line in my eyebrow. I liked the feel of their hands on my head, the pressure of the clippers, the hum of them and the care put into the cut. The energy focused on me was the good kind, the kind that didn't expect anything back.

Blue Lips clicked off the clippers. They used a neck duster

to brush off my neck, swabbed a cotton ball of alcohol along the edges of the cut. The slight burn felt good. For the first time ever, I felt a warm breeze against my scalp.

"All done," Blue Lips said. They held a mirror to my face.

"Holy shit," I said. "Thank you!"

I could see my head. I looked fierce, fucking gay as hell, queer even. Shit, maybe I was queer too. Whatever I was or however I decided to identify, the cut was rad. A few tears fell down my cheeks.

"Oh shit, it's okay, Juliet. Transformation is a huge deal," Blue Lips said. They put a firm, gentle hand on my shoulder. I laughed, still crying.

"I'm fine. This is just a really beautiful night, party, everything. I'm okay."

From behind, I heard Ava gasp. And then she screamed like a Puerto Rican—a scream that's more of a yell, a gasp, and a get-out-of-here all in one word: *Ay!*

"Ay, Juliet, that hair, ay, it looks so good. Oh my God, you badass bitch. I love it. Your mom is gonna freak out!" Ava exclaimed. "It's perfect. Girl, you found your look. Hot fucking damn."

I couldn't stop running my hands over the bottom half of my head. Other people asked to touch it too and I let them. Like an altar call, all the Clipper Queerz laid hands on me. I got up, ready for everything. I was ready to go back to Portland and figure shit out with Harlowe. Ready to do me. I moved closer to the music and danced with Luz Ángel and Ava. When a slow jam came on, I backed away and let them get close. They held each other by the hips. I was hot, sweaty, and a little itchy. The pool glowed turquoise. I stepped away and walked over to the edge. A hand reached out for mine and held it. It was Florencio. She let go, took a little leap, and jumped into the pool.

"You coming?" she asked.

I laughed, stripped down to my underwear, and jumped right in after her. And when Luz Ángel and Ava wandered off behind the pool, holding hands, no one but me even noticed. And when Blue Lips found me in the water and reached for me, I didn't run away. And when they kissed me, I kissed back.

THE SKY RIPPLED with gold streaks. They pierced through the deep indigo and welcomed the sunrise. Ava and I made our way out of the party. Once in the car, I called Lainie, not drunk, not high, just exhausted and peaceful. I left this message on her voice mail:

"Lainie, it's me, Juliet. Listen, I want you to know that it's all okay. Really and truly okay. You didn't make any mistakes. I don't think we can really make mistakes because I just had the best night ever and if we hadn't broken up, I don't think it woulda been this incredible. You did what you needed to do and it's fine. I'm okay. We're all okay. We are beautiful. And you need nights like the one I had, a night to be free and surrounded by queer family. And so, I know it's taken me a while to call you, but I needed to think. Thinking is good, you know? Honestly, it's better for both of us that we don't talk right now. But I know we will later; I know that when I see you at school, I'm going to hug you and I'm going to love you without being in love with you. I want to know you forever, Lainie, and this is how we get there."

PART FOUR

HERE WE GO AGAIN. PORTLAND OR BUST

CHAPTER TWENTY-ONE

WHEN ALL ELSE FAILS, TAKE A FUCKING NAP

ON THE SUNDAY plane ride from Miami to Portland, I imagined my reunion with Harlowe. I saw Harlowe wanting to dissect what went down at Powell's and find out exactly where things went wrong. We'd cry about how she'd stereotyped my life story and how it was all connected to her racism. I'd tearfully admit to thinking that I was in love with her. We'd hash it out with Maxine and Zaira too, maybe over tofu and organic beer. We'd all talk about how we need to communicate better and how fighting racism together would make us all winners and better lovers. Maybe we'd all contribute to a mixtape. Melodrama at its highest level. Performance art for hippie lesbians. I got carried away, but I felt super hopeful.

Harlowe met me in the exact same spot at PDX. Just the sight of her made me light up; I couldn't help it. She was the woman who wrote the book that opened my eyes to my body and the world. All those love feelings flooded over me. Harlowe shouted my name when she saw me. She gushed over my "rad dyke haircut" and ran her hands all over my head. It felt weird to not be asked, but I was too excited to see her face to make a thing out of it. She hugged me like we were family, tight and without reserve. We took pictures of our feet next to each other on the PDX carpet with all the crazy lines and patterns. It was all laughs and normal questions; nothing unusual. Maybe everything was just fine.

The car ride to her house was quieter than the one when I'd first arrived. Harlowe played the power feminist mixtape that I'd made for Lainie but never sent to her. She admitted that she listened to it while I'd been away. Said it helped when she missed me and built up her energies when she felt low. I told her to keep it. The universe wanted her to have it. She hadn't said a word about the reading at Powell's. That moment felt like it'd been a weird trip, a glitch in the smooth feminist internship matrix. The rush of certainty I'd felt in Miami about calling Harlowe out felt far away, like I'd left it in Ava's room. "Wide Open Spaces" by the Dixie Chicks played and it gave me a minute to think. Nothing I learned in Miami would go away; I wouldn't let it. Whether Harlowe and I spoke about what went down at the reading or not, I was stronger and the clarity I found would stick with me. I believed that deep in my spirit. I could feel weird and awkward but I wouldn't ever be lost.

Fucking Dixie Chicks, yo. I loved them. The song played until we reached Harlowe's.

All of Maxine's stuff—clothes, records, and pictures—were gone. Whatever imprint she'd left on the house had been erased. I felt it the second I walked in; I know that sounds weird, but it was hyper real. Have you ever just known that someone was gone? Without a call or anything?

That's what it felt like.

Harlowe put my bag by the staircase to the attic. She ushered me into the kitchen and proceeded to cook me a meal. That's when the words spilled out of her. Maxine moved all her belongings out of Harlowe's house the day after the reading at Powell's. They were no longer partners. Harlowe wept without pause. It'd been a long time coming and with everything that happened, Maxine saw no reason not to make the split official. They'd put up a good front for me, even had themselves convinced that it was all going to be okay, that Maxine wasn't falling hard for Zaira, that Harlowe's white privilege wasn't an issue for Maxine, and that they were just as in love now as they were when they met on a dance floor so many years ago. Harlowe admitted to being intimate with Samara behind Maxine's back. None of it was pretty. Harlowe disrespected their honesty clause physically, and Maxine had done it emotionally.

Zaira and Maxine remained partners, but Harlowe wasn't sure if they were primaries now or not. She was ashamed of herself but also angry that she'd been judged. Neither Maxine nor Zaira waited after the reading to talk to Harlowe. They both left without a word. Harlowe didn't think she'd be welcomed at any of Zaira's open POC writing groups anymore. No one had bothered to talk to her about it. Neither one of them asked for her side of the story. Harlowe wasn't sure if she could forgive them for that.

I was curious about how Harlowe's interpretation of events would be different from mine.

Zaira and Maxine knew that what Harlowe said about me was inappropriate and kinda fucked up. If they didn't want to talk to Harlowe, it had to be because they didn't want to waste the energy. That thought alone made me quiet. Damn. I wanted to talk to Maxine and Zaira. Harlowe stopped weeping and continued her story. At no point in her retelling did she ask me how I felt when it all went down. I didn't offer my perspective either. Before Miami, I would have blurted out all my opinions. But after being surrounded by a community of people who were committed to one another, to every political cry and hazy love daydream, I couldn't spill my guts to someone who wasn't asking for them.

Harlowe heated tortillas in a pan and burned them. The white rice she'd set to cook on the stove also met a fiery charcoal death. It was impossible for her to cook and tell emotional stories at the same time. The kitchen smelled of pegao and rotten eggs. I boiled cinnamon sticks and opened all the windows to counter the foulness. Harlowe cried again. I encouraged her to sit down and keep talking. She needed to let it all out. I threw away the burned stuff and started over. I made white rice, black beans, and mushrooms. I heated the last two tortillas without burning them. Harlowe thanked me, hugged me. We ate together.

"I've lost my love," she said. Harlowe wiped her eyes. "And I'm not good at apologies. I honestly didn't think I'd said anything wrong or mean about you. But I shouldn't have used you as an example. Zaira baited me and I countered. But even before all of that, my love thing with Maxine was in a rough spot. I'm good at ranting about the world. It's harder to be a participant in it. I've got some work to do if my spirit is ever going to clean. And I'd like to offer you a session of care."

"A session of care?"

"Yes, I traded my friend Lupe a one-on-one writing workshop for an hour of acupuncture. I got the acupuncture for you."

"I've never done acupuncture before. Does it hurt?"

"Nope. It's glorious."

Her apology mixed itself up in personal heartbreak and feelings of guilt about everything from the reading to not being honest with herself about Maxine. It was a lot to take in and still not what I needed. I didn't know how to just dive in and say what I wanted to say without feeling pushy. Ava's harsh but mad real sentiments about Harlowe banged around in my head. Funny how Harlowe was worshipped among one group of gay people and dismissed by another. How had I been so naive? How could anything as huge as feminism be universal?

I had one week left in Portland. Seven days. If I just kept my head down, my ass in the library, and focused solely on my internship, perhaps all of this would be fine and the complications would unravel themselves. Maybe I made things complicated when they didn't need to be. What did Harlowe owe me anyway? Nothing, right? Instead of unpacking my suitcase, I took a long, undisturbed nap.

CHAPTER TWENTY-TWO

POKE

HARLOWE REMINDED ME of her self-care trade: writing for acupuncture. A gift from her to me. I wanted to be thankful or
something, but what did I need acupuncture for anyway? Was
this some sort of hippie bribe? I asked myself these questions
and then felt hella guilty for questioning Harlowe's motives.
I hated feeling this way. It was much easier to be in groupie
love with her, to keep her on that Pussy Lady pedestal. But I
couldn't do that anymore either. I existed in this strange purgatory of love and doubt. Also, I woke up craving a thick and juicy
cheeseburger.

Was that the first sign of backsliding into the Dark Side?
Did Portland even serve cheeseburgers made from real meat?
If I agreed to have needles stuck in my body, maybe Harlowe
would find me a burger.

I didn't mention the burger to Harlowe. I chickened out

when I saw her eating tofu for breakfast. Harlowe started telling me all about her friend Lupe, the acupuncturist, and how they'd been friends for years. I sat at the table and made myself a cup of coffee. Lupe was married to Harlowe's other friend Ginger Raine, who was also a writer and pregnant with their first child. That caught my attention. I'd never met pregnant, domestic partnered lesbians before. Harlowe didn't even have to mention acupuncture again. I was excited and curious to meet her friends.

I asked Harlowe to stop somewhere so that I could bring her friends some flowers. Grandma Petalda always told us to bring something when you visit someone's house for the first time. It's an offering of respect and a gift to whatever spirits may live in the house. We picked some roses from her weed dealer's garden. Her dealer was a short, tattooed, super chubby woman named Planks. I tried to pay her for the flowers, but she wouldn't take any cash. Instead, she slipped a joint into my back pocket and told me to come over anytime. Damn, I loved Portland folks. We hopped in Harlowe's truck and were off.

Lupe appeared in the doorway holding a silver cane. She walked toward us, her black hair flowing down her back, majestically. She moved with a slow and steady limp. A tattoo of a hammer graced her right forearm. Her other forearm had a railroad spike tattooed down the middle. Lupe, the patron saint of badasses. I wondered if she was Latina or Native or both. I was almost mad at Harlowe for not bringing me to her sooner.

Harlowe got out of the truck and rushed over to Lupe. Big hugs all around. I followed and Lupe wrapped me up a hug too.

"Juliet," she said, "I've been super excited to meet you. We should go straight to my office so I can poke you, get the energy flowing."

Lupe's Chicana lilt killed me. I wanted her to talk forever just to hear it. I followed her inside and met the very pregnant Ginger Raine. I offered her the bouquet of orange and yellow roses. She knew right away they were from Planks's garden because that's how tight all the Portland dykes are. Or at least that's the joke Ginger made; I liked her immediately.

Lupe led me down a narrow staircase into the basement. A green shag carpet lay under a long table. A faded piece of parchment hung from the back of the hall door. The human body, spliced in half and divided into sections, stared at me. Bones, muscles, segments of spine: all the parts of the body were listed and connected to lines and black dots. Straight lines connected points to explanations. A dot under the right buttock connected to a line ending at *sciatica*. A dot in the middle of the back connected to *lumbago*. Next to the English words stood Chinese characters. I studied the acupuncture poster. I'd never thought of my body as cross sections of flesh to be diagrammed and poked. I wondered if that was what Lupe saw when she looked at me.

Lupe told me that acupuncture could cure anything as long as I was open to it. We sat across from each other on the couch and talked about my mental and physical health. Asthma and heartache were my main issues. I didn't know how much I could let out because she was Harlowe's friend. Could I tell her that I also felt hella weird around Harlowe and that I vacillated between loving her and wanting to demand an apology? Oh, and guilt, because from the beginning Harlowe and I have been as honest with each other as we could be. I mean, when did this internship get so skewed anyway?

I felt like Lupe was someone I could trust. I told her about the breakup with Lainie and then I switched gears. I thought about Lil' Melvin and his letter.

"My little brother says he's pyrokinetic. I'm not exactly sure what that means, but I know it's connected to fire. Do you know anything about whether or not a person can control fire with their bodies or their minds or is my little brother buggin'?"

Lupe stood up with her cane and walked over to the massive bookshelf that ran along the back of the room.

"Fire is inside all of us, camarada. Your brother isn't bugging. He probably just feels the pull," Lupe replied. Her hands ran along the volumes of books. "Fire is a virtue. It's connected to the heart and to joy. And the best thing about fire is its transformative qualities. If your brother feels connected to fire, then it could mean that he's ready for great change and he wants to be the one to do it."

Lupe pulled a slim book from the shelf and tossed it at me. She said that if he wanted to study how to utilize and shift energy, he'd be studying for a lifetime, which would be beautiful and powerful. But if my little brother wanted to indulge his curiosities, this book was about the practice of Qigong and it was a graphic novel. She told me to keep it.

"Accept it as a gift and an apology," Lupe said.

I flipped through the book. "Apology for what?" I asked.

"For not finding a way to get you here sooner or checking in on you," Lupe replied. She pulled out a box of fresh needles. "Harlowe doesn't have the best track record with interns. I mean, you're probably on that impossible hunt for unknown women. Ginger and I usually check in, but with the baby on the way, we got distracted. And we heard about the reading, so please keep the book."

I sat there numb. Once again, the words didn't come. My mind raced. Harlowe had other interns? She said I was the only one. Maybe I was misunderstanding Lupe. With everything else going on in my head, I shrugged it off.

"And Harlowe told us that you're Puerto Rican and from the Bronx, and I should have connected with a fellow Latina sooner," Lupe said. "But for now, let's focus. If you're comfortable, it'd be easier to work on you with your T-shirt off. If not, I can work around it. Whatever makes you feel more relaxed."

Lupe tapped the massage table and turned to her needles. I slipped off my shirt and lay down on the table. While I prepared for the acupuncture treatment, she stood over me and stuck slim, semi-frightening needles into different spots on my body.

"Deep breaths, Juliet," Lupe said, as her hands pushed needles into my back to ease the pressure in my lungs.

The sensation the needles produced was strange and exhilarating. At first, I was freaked out, thinking it was going to be mad painful. But they didn't cause any pain; it was more like small bubbles of tension that eventually subsided. Lupe finished pressing the needles into my skin and told me she'd be back for me. I inhaled and exhaled and got caught in a daydream. Water rushed all around and above me. I was stuck to the sandy bottom of the ocean.

My purple notebook hovered in the air, rippling in the light. It burned red and orange. Flames of Pentecost. Voices of everyone I loved and had met on this trip called to me. I couldn't understand them. The water flowed fast, but I wasn't afraid.

Lupe returned and pulled the needles out of my back. She offered me a glass of water and told me to move only when I was ready. I lay on the table for another ten minutes, too spent to stand. My whole body was relaxed. Damn, I still wanted a cheeseburger though. After a few more moments, I eased myself off the table and put on my shirt. There was a lightness in my body. My arms and legs moved easier somehow, like the way it feels to run in a dream. So weird, but good. So, so good.

I moved up the stairs toward the dining room with the same lightness.

"But you can't sit here and act like you didn't cause that child some harm," Maxine said.

Her voice filled the kitchen, paused me in mid-step. From where I stood, I could see all of them seated around the dining room table. With all their attention on Maxine, I sank to one knee and listened. My heartbeat quickened and set that weird vein in my temple throbbing. Why were they all here?

"Have you even checked in with her about any of it?" Maxine asked.

"We haven't talked about it yet," Harlowe said. "She just got back. I didn't want to push."

"Acknowledging that you harmed someone isn't a push, Harlowe," Maxine said.

"Look, I sent an e-mail and now she's getting acupuncture," Harlowe replied. She folded her arms across her chest.

"So you decided to smooth things over with acupuncture from Lupe, our friend, who also happens to share some very key identities with Juliet?"

Lupe coughed, trying to stifle a laugh. Like when your friend snaps your other friend so hard, but you want to stay mature with it so you don't break. That cough.

"I don't like what you're implying, Max."

"You know how valuable community is," Maxine said, standing up. She put her hands on the table, palms down. "Offering Juliet access to Lupe provides her with connection to another lesbian Latina and gets you off the hook."

"What a reach," Harlowe replied. She went to light a smoke, looked at Ginger Raine, and thought better of it. "Okay, I'm the big bad white lady. Look how awful I am, trying to get someone acupuncture." Harlowe sighed hard. "She's fine, by the way. Juliet is just fine. Jeezus," Harlowe exclaimed.

I popped up from the floor quick, a spring released.

"How would you even know?" I asked.

All eyes flipped to me. A few beads of sweat dripped down my forehead. My body flashed hot, panic hot. "You never asked and that's cool or whatever, but don't act like you know how I'm feeling."

My insides tightened. Everyone was still looking at me.

"But also, I feel like this is more about you and Maxine, maybe, so . . . like . . . thanks for the acupuncture. But . . ."

"But hey, it seems like I'm the one making everyone uncomfortable," Harlowe said. She stood up in between me and the table. "So I'm just going to go."

Harlowe grabbed her cigarettes and peaced out the front door without another word.

CHAPTER TWENTY-THREE

THE SUN, THE SKY, AND THE MOON

FOR THE NEXT few hours, the rest of us took a break from Harlowe Brisbane. Essays and sketches lay in messy bunches on the dining room table, each one a submission for Zaira's anthology. We sorted them into HELL YES, MAYBE, and nope piles. Armed with a hot-pink highlighter and black gel pen, I focused on other people's stories. I hadn't decided whether I'd be submitting mine. In my hands were stories about everything from post-apocalyptic merpeople to elderly cyborgs looking for love. And with almost everyone queer and of color, the stories read like Miami.

I wondered what Ava would say about Harlowe leaving.

What if I talked to myself like Ava talked to me?

Maxine curled her fingers into Zaira's. They met eyes for a moment.

Their shared look rushed over my skin, like a hot and gentle August breeze. I imagined them charging out of Portland and starting movements across the U.S., leaving Harlowe in their dust and gathering all the baby gays along the way. But like how did anyone know when to shut someone out for real? Was it always going to be issues of race that wigged people like Harlowe the fuck out? I wanted to believe in the creation of an unbreakable multiracial community of women. But could we all really have one another's backs?

The dining room felt cramped all of a sudden. I needed some air. I asked them where the nearest post office was. Lupe gave me directions that involved making a left at the house with a statue of Medusa on the porch and continuing forward until I hit the vegan waffle truck. With the Qigong book under my arm, I took off. The walk felt good. Gave me time to think about how complex all these older dyke relationships were. It went beyond just sex and romance and that's the stuff I wanted to know more about.

Like what TV show or movie could I watch to learn about race and friendship among lesbians in the Pacific Northwest? None. Right? Like, but here it was all happening around me and there was no *Cosmo* quiz to take on how to know whether to ditch your possibly racist, possibly ex-mentor, older white lesbian friend, you know?

But I wanted to believe that we were all love renegades and that we didn't have to discard one another. People break hearts and love disappears. The vegan waffle truck stood before me in all its glory.

I made it to the post office and mailed Lil' Melvin the book with a note.

Brother,

You are everything you believe yourself to be. A healer gave me this book for you. She said fire is transformation. So burn deep, brother.

Love you to the moon and back,

Juliet

I cried a little as I watched the mail person weigh the package. I missed Melvin's chubby little face covered in chocolate from those damn TWIX bars. I missed his easy laugh. I missed being little and safe at home like him. I wanted Lil' Melvin to burn so fucking bright that his fire would scorch the earth.

I walked alone until I came upon a restaurant that smelled like cheeseburgers. I stopped inside, sat by myself at a table for the first time ever, and ordered a bacon double cheeseburger with french fries and a Coke. It was glorious.

Post–burger and fries, I went for a walk and realized that I hadn't talked to my mom since our less than stellar conversation in Miami. I had to call her back. I could handle it. If she brought up Eduardo and me dating men, I'd just roll with it. Titi

Penny said she was trying to love me the best way she knew how. I had to trust them both. I sat on a bench and dialed the house number. Mom picked up on the first ring.

"Nena, are you back in Portland?" she asked.

"Yes, Mom," I replied, shocked to all hell that she'd remembered where I was, finally.

"Titi Penny said that you were wonderful. I'm thinking we should plan a big family trip to her place next summer, what do you think?"

"That sounds perfect, Mom. Titi Penny told me that you were reading *Raging Flower*."

"Oye, that Titi Penny talks too much, doesn't she?"

"Mom, I think that's so good. It means a lot to me that you're reading it."

"Listen, nena, I don't know what you're going through, but I want to try. I don't want us to be a mom and a daughter who don't talk and all they do is fight. I cannot do that with you, my Juliet."

"I can't do that either, Mom," I said. I wiped my eyes with my sleeve.

"We won't let that happen to us," she said. Her voice softened. She sniffled.

"Mom, I mailed something to Lil' Melvin today. Will you keep an eye out for it and make sure he gets it?"

"Oh my gosh, of course. He's going to be so excited. He's been really into fire and dragons lately," she said. "But before you left it was falcons, so I just follow his lead."

I laughed. "Dragons are cool. We should get him a dragon for Christmas," I said.

"I'll talk to your father. Maybe he'll get a puppy instead," she said.

In the small pause, I heard her afternoon soap operas on in the background.

"Your time is almost done over there. Are things good with Harlowe?" Mom asked. "Are you all ready to come home?"

I was quiet for too long, unsure of how to answer. I looked up at the trees around me and wished Mom was sitting right next to me.

"Nena, talk to me," she said.

"Mom, I don't know if Harlowe is the person I expected. I don't know if it's because she's some random white lady or if it's because we're from different worlds. I just don't know," I said.

"White lady or not, her book inspired you so much. Don't deny yourself those feelings."

"I just thought she'd be different, Mom."

"But what did you think of yourself?" she asked. "What did you want to learn from this experience?"

"I wanted Harlowe and this internship to change everything."

"But how, Juliet? What did you want to be different?"

"The world," I said. "I wanted her to change my world."

It was Mom's turn to pause. The television noise died down on her end. She must have lowered it. We sat for a minute together, on opposite ends of the country, listening to each other breathe.

"Mi amor, only you can change your world," she said.

"I don't think I know how to do that." I sighed and looked up at the sky.

"Juliet, I gave you your first set of purple composition notebooks when you turned thirteen. Do you remember what I wrote in your card?"

"Remember? How could I forget? You said reading would make me brilliant, but writing would make me infinite."

"And that's the truth, así es," she said. Her mom voice was back.

"But, Mom . . ."

"But nothing. Let go of whatever expectations you had of this woman and her book and write your own. You must write. You will write. You are Juliet Milagros Palante. This world is yours to reinvent. Do you understand?"

"Yes, I understand," I replied. "Mom, we're good, right? This is the start of us being good, better than when I left?"

"Juliet, my love for you is the sun, the sky, and the moon. It's the air I breathe. It lives in everything I do. It's better than good. It's everlasting."

"Same, Mom. I love you too," I said, weeping on the bench. My sleeve was wet from wiping my nose and all my hot tears.

We said good-bye right after that. I imagined her going back to the couch and watching the rest of her novelas: *All My Children* and *General Hospital*. I'd be home with her soon enough and then back to school. But I wouldn't be here again, not like this. I wouldn't be Harlowe's intern again. I wouldn't be nineteen again. I sat on the bench for a long time, taking in the sunlight. The thought of being infinite swelled all around me. I could change the world. Right? Like, if Mom pressed infinity into my palms via purple notebook, then maybe I could push change into the world around me. But change it into what . . . ?

Man, moms are wild creatures. They got like this spidey sense about your whole entire self and it's all mixed up with their fears and preconceived notions. And then you're all like daydreaming about this other self, this super great, take-on-the-world self, and the purple notebook comes out. And there you are writing down your shit, not 'cuz your mom said so, but definitely 'cuz your mom blessed it so.

CHAPTER TWENTY-FOUR

BLUFFS

BACK AT HARLOWE'S, shit was QUIET, even for a Monday. She left acorn muffins on the stove for me with a note that talked about how nourishing our bodies was akin to celestial healing. Harlowe being hella Harlowe. Full from that cheeseburger, I had a valid excuse for not eating acorn anything.

She moved in the house like a ghost, felt but unseen. I didn't mind it. I didn't know what to say to her. And I think she was running, like here I was, some kid landing at her crib, and then her whole life gets all sorts of wrecked. Inside me there was this tight pit, like somehow I did this to her. I walked around reading and rereading *Raging Flower* hoping it would offer some types of truth like it always had.

But like a good first-born-daughter, A-student, I didn't give up on the research. And I had this weird idea that "Starlight Mamitas" and my weekend in Miami, learning about all the gender things, could come together in a really dope reflection paper for Dr. Jean and my women's studies class. Full of weirdo excitement, I took the same bus to Multnomah County Central Library, sat in my favorite work spot, and kept digging. All the librarians knew me now. We shared excitement over new scraps of paper with names of new women.

Kira and I snuck long, tender kisses in between bookshelves and hidden corners of basement stairwells. We went for longer rides on her motorcycle. She taught me how to make pizza dough in her kitchen and told me her favorite show as a kid was *Punky Brewster*. Kira mastered the art of packing picnics on a bike. She fed me sliced cantaloupe and read excerpts from *This Bridge Called My Back* by Gloria Anzaldúa to me. It was one of the books on Ava's list and Kira didn't know that and that was the best part. She was just fucking reading it on her own, you know?

I was freefalling into the best oblivion. Kira said she saw all my beautiful brown everything. You see my brown? What?

Full stop.

She was this wild burst of soft love and who knew it could be like this? Wait, I loved her. Damn, man, I did. Are you supposed to just up and tell people that when it happens? She didn't say it. So I just held it in my hands whenever I held hers.

As my time in Portland ticked away, Kira brought me home more often. She made me love full-body massages and taught me how to return the favor with a mix of coconut and lavender oil. She was so many things. Matter of fact, we were summertime love things. No questions asked. I'd run my fingers through her hair, even told her my middle name. Milagros. That happy ache became my regular and I was good with it, with her. Mostly, I was glad we both felt this good together. She still dropped notes onto my books, and there were cookies and letters pressed into skin via fingertips. I told her all about how we made pasteles at Christmastime with Abuela Petalda. My job was to put the acete on the banana leaf and even a little on the wax paper. She got the goods from me. Kira. My goodness.

We knew I was leaving. But still, this thing between us was real. Connection, goofy-ass smiles. Kira was all that. Real like velvet sunsets and all the ways you adore yourself when no one else is watching. Kira was the one who scooped me up from the Steel Bridge when everything with Harlowe went to shit. She understood my hot, angry tears and raged against universal feminism and the whitewashing of womanhood. She'd been the first person to wonder out loud if Harlowe was an ally or an antagonist. Kira, the librarian, the only-est motorcycle babe human, was now this vibrant force in my world and I wished I could bring her back with me.

We weren't dating, obviously. We didn't have one of those what-are-we-doing conversations. That shit wasn't necessary. She loved my body so good. She made me more chocolate-chip cookies, like even if she'd tried to have a conversation about the state of our relationship, I wouldn't have known what to say. All I knew was that I fell, thick inch by thick inch, into some kind of wonderful with her. On my second to last day, she pulled me into the Rare Books room and kissed me so deep and so honestly that it felt like she was telling me that she loved me too. But it was August and what does love mean at the end of a summer?

Kira took me to the bluffs in North Portland. We sat, cuddled up under a willow tree, smoked skinny joints, and watched the trains rumble by. The sky stretched out forever. She read to me from James Baldwin's *Giovanni's Room*.

"'You don't have a home until you leave it and then when you have left it, you can never go back,'" she said, her fingers curled in mine.

"That can't be true," I said. Ugh, gross, I cried a little bit.

"No, hey," Kira said. She put the book down.

"Who wouldn't want to go home?" I asked, looking up at her. I could be soft. She got it. Kira was right there with me.

"Juliet, it's not that you can't ever go home. The idea is that once you're able and confident enough in yourself to leave, the world changes you, and you're not the same person anymore ever again and that's the beautiful part," Kira replied.

I lay on her lap looking up at her, past her, and into the sky. "Yo, when I was growing up, we went to church all the time, and one time I met God," I said. I picked each word while she teased out strands of my hair. It was so much of what I imagined love would be like that I could barely breathe. It was like as alive as I felt all my acute senses were lost in this bright warm light. Jeezus, even describing it is so . . . intense.

Her skin against mine was electric. Hey, like I said, I was leaving.

She looked at me. "Everyone has a God story. What's yours?" she asked. She ran her fingers through my curls. Her arm reached across my belly.

"Hmmm." I took a long deep breath. "I was twelve and our church was having a youth prayer service. I didn't even want to go, but my parents made me. I sat there watching all the pastor's kids lose their shit and speak in tongues. They sure knew how to put on a show. At some point, I realized I was on my knees, on the chair, praying. I prayed until everything around me went quiet and turned golden. I swear, Kira, everyone disappeared."

"I believe you," Kira said, as she curled up into my arm.

"It was just me praying in another space until a stillness settled over my body. Peace and warmth like I'd never experienced washed over the room and I knew God was with me. I opened my eyes and all I saw was the golden light, but I knew it was God. And I could hear God speaking to me from inside my chest and I was all crying and stuff. It had to be God, right?

"And then I heard Pastor Diaz yelling at me and snapping his fingers. I opened my eyes and I was back in church. Pastor Diaz was inches from my face. He said I was praying wrong and that I should have been kneeling on the floor. I walked out of that church and never went back."

Kira shifted against me. I moved off her lap. We lay side by side. She held my hand. Her thighs were warm against mine. "What did it feel like afterward?" she asked.

"Free. I know in my heart God is real. No one can take that from me. And, like, I'm here with you. Feeling vibrant as hell and that moment in church with God was one of the best moments of my whole life and so is this, right now with you. This is everything. I guess I just needed you to know both of those things."

"Can I kiss you, Juliet?"

I nodded. Kira leaned over me and kissed me. Her lips never left mine. What kind of kisses were these? Kira and I swapped secrets and bottom-lip bites until the stars fell into formation in the sky. We wrapped up in her blanket. Her hands found their way under my bra, into my pants, and her lips kissed all the bare parts of my flesh. It wasn't my last night in Portland, but it was my last night with Kira. I didn't stop her when she touched between my thighs, past my pink boy shorts. The air was cool on my skin. I bit her neck to keep the sounds between us.

The ripples of all that tight beautiful everything washed over us, breathless. We counted the constellations and smoked the last joint. She dropped me off at Harlowe's after midnight. I promised myself not to ever forget that final kiss against her motorcycle or how she once again waited 'til I was inside before she rode off. I watched her from the window 'til her bike turned the corner. I wondered if I'd ever see her again.

CHAPTER TWENTY-FIVE

THE CLEANSING

BRIGHT HOT SUNLIGHT streamed into the attic. I woke up damp
with sweat and confused. Kira? Was I still in Miami? No, definitely in Portland. I hadn't felt heat this intense any other day
here. I stripped off the blankets, raised all the shades, and
basked in it. My last day in Portland was going to be hot as hell.
I had woken up ready.

Harlowe poked her head up from the staircase. Sweat matted
her temples. Her cheeks flushed ultra pink. She let me know
that Maxine and Zaira were on their way to pick me up for the
cleansing. Harlowe walked halfway down the stairs and then
came back up.

She lay down next to me in the sunspot. Harlowe reached for
my hand and held it. I was surprised by how cool her hand felt.

"Are you coming to the cleansing, or are you gonna keep
being weird about everything?" I asked.

"I owe you all the apologies. I haven't had the words I've needed," she said, her legs bent in toward mine, "but thank you for being brave and patient and for not losing faith in me."

Oh, Harlowe. I didn't believe that I'd been brave or patient, and I didn't know if I still had faith in her. She flailed a little on the floor, turning her face toward the sunlight. Guess she was going to keep being weird and evasive. Maxine and Zaira honked out front. Harlowe stayed up in the attic. I threw on shorts and a T-shirt over my bathing suit and was out the door in less than ten minutes. I wasn't privy to this who-gets-to-pick-up-the-kid convo, but I was happy I landed in their car. Harlowe hollered about meeting up with us on the road. So she was coming. Cool.

I sat on the passenger side with Maxine driving and Zaira curled up in the middle. We'd meet up with Lupe and Ginger Raine along the way, if she didn't give birth first. I wished Lupe was in the truck with us because then it'd be like my neighborhood where everyone has black or brown skin, and we ride for each other so hard and with so much love even when things are messed up and when times are tough. Least that's how it felt sometimes. In the Bronx, everyone lived so pressed up on each other, we barely had enough room to breathe, let alone separate. And everything I'd experienced in Miami showed me the power of being connected to queer people of color and the beauty of POC-only spaces.

This was part of that too, just with different words for community, right? All of a sudden I had a million questions to ask Zaira and Maxine.

What happened when I left? What had they thought about Harlowe's words at Powell's? How did they feel about connecting themselves to a white friend who was brilliant, loving, and problematic? I wanted and needed to know. And just as I was about to ask all of them, it was river cleansing story time. Maxine opened up and all this excited and joyful energy spilled out of her.

On the hottest day of the summer they'd all take a trip up to the Sandy River. They'd hike up to a certain spot and then ride the river down. Sometimes they'd invite friends or new lovers; all were welcome. They called it "the cleansing" because riding the river was like an annual baptism. Zaira spoke on connecting to water spirits the first time she rode down the river and about the way she wept when her first Octavia Butler writing group participated in the cleansing. I listened to all of it. I even got a little misty-eyed when they told me how excited they were to share this day with me and how proud they were to know me. I hadn't even done anything but exist. How could they be proud to know me when I'd run away? I didn't question them, I just took in their words and let them fill up the weird and uncomfortable spaces in my heart.

Finally, it was quiet. They'd both found memories to sit with while we drove. The vibe in the car was peaceful. I almost felt bad about disrupting it, but I knew I'd feel worse if I left without asking them all the things that burned in my heart.

So I asked. I brought up everything all in one breath. The silence that followed was deep. Maxine and Zaira both took a solid pause and then laughed. Zaira, in between Maxine and me, leaned on my shoulder. Her skin, soft like rose petals, brushed against mine.

"Oh, girl," she said, as she patted my thigh. "Everything you feel is valid. And your instincts are already questioning those who say they act in all our names."

Zaira stretched her arms out before her, as if reaching for better things to say about Harlowe.

"My issues with Harlowe run deep. She sees a society that enforces a patriarchal system of beliefs. This system imposes itself on her body and lifestyle. Therefore it's corrupt and must be destroyed, right?

"But what's missing from the fist in her fight is any sort of racial awareness. That erasure validates whiteness, frames narratives of people of color around poverty and violence, and propels her into perpetuating the very structures she's trying to dismantle. But I'm not here to make space for good white people. There've been times when I've needed to distance myself from Harlowe and people who love her."

Maxine cleared her throat. Zaira shifted her hips to look at me. She winked. Her knee-length coral-colored dress shimmered in the sunlight. Her dark brown eyes made me want to weep. Gorgeous. Deep. Honest.

"People you love fuck up," Zaira said, she touched my knee. "You weed out the assholes from the warriors. Pick up on folks who aren't soft spaces for your heart. Move with forgiveness but listen to your instincts when it comes to eradicating the unworthy from your spirit. Juliet, you're already on your path."

Maxine let out a rush of air. "Harlowe was family for me when my own wouldn't accept me being in the life," she said. "Hard to push her out when she's kept me alive many times over."

Maxine kept her eyes on the road. One hand on the wheel, the other held between both Zaira's hands. "And with you, Juliet," Maxine continued, "you look at her the way I used to, and it worries me. That adoration, that way we elevate folks and can't hold them accountable. We get so caught up in the easy glow of them that we forget to do the same for ourselves."

Her face grew serious. "No one held you back from standing up and telling that room of people at Powell's who you really were and what your story really was," she said. "No one. You chose to walk away. This isn't a judgment on that choice. This is me pointing it out. You did that. You let Harlowe's narrative be the air people breathed about you. This isn't about Harlowe or her whiteness; this is about choice. What choice will you make next time when someone says something like that about you? Will you walk away? Or demand your voice be heard? Will you speak your truth, Juliet? I mean, why did you even come here?"

I said nothing. Teardrops left little dark spots on my shorts. Maxine was so right, and I don't know how I missed it. I felt ashamed of myself. Embarrassed. How could I ever trust myself to make decisions if I didn't have that type of insight? I never opened my mouth to counter what Harlowe said. I froze and ran. Froze and ran.

All the women in my life were telling me the same thing. My story, my truth, my life, my voice, all of that had to be protected and put out into the world by me. No one else. No one could take that from me. I had to let go of my fear. I didn't know what I was afraid of. I wondered if I'd ever speak my truth.

Why had I come? I pulled out my notebook and answered Maxine's last question for myself. If the narrative was going to shift, it had to start with me.

Why Am I Here?

Feminism: To understand what it meant in real life, outside of textbooks and if I could ever call myself a feminist.

To get the hell out of the Bronx.

Lesbians: To chill with all the lesbians and see if there were different ways to be one, to make sure I was one, to find out if I was something else.

Harlowe: Because Raging Flower changed my life, and I had to know what it was like to live with and learn from the person who created it.

Pussy: Because before Raging Flower,
I didn't know there was power between
my thighs.

Politics: I had none. Never thought
anything was worth giving too much of
a shit about. That shit was changing. My
identity is political as hell, yo.

Womanhood: To pull it still humming
from my chest and inspect its
contents. To tear down the mural of me
commissioned by Mom, patriarchy, and
shame. Finesse a new one out of brown
girl sex, confessions in composition
notebooks, and poolside shapeups.

Me: Messy. Emotional. Book nerd
weirdo. Chubby brown human. A jumble
of awkward bits and glory, now full of
ancestors and stories. Needed to learn
self-love, like the real kind. Instead of
asking 'Can I live?' gotta demand to
thrive.

I read my list a few times over. Womanhood stood out. I chewed
it in my mouth like a piece of cheek. It was mine to puncture.

Knowing it would heal over allowed me to be merciless with womanhood. I had to crack it open and investigate the layers. It often manifested itself from other women in the forms of care-giving and tenderness, like Mom cooking arroz con maíz to send me off. But there were ways in which womanhood pinched. It was too tight white stockings on chubby thighs before church and questions about boyfriends I never wanted. It was Dominic Pusco's hands down my pants without consent and the disbe-lief and eye rolls and me thinking I did something to make it happen. It was Titi Penny falling in love with Magdalena and not hating herself for it. Complex, chaotic, beyond even biology. Like Ava said: womanhood was radical enough for anyone who dared claim it.

Reflections of my womanhood rolled over me each with its own expectations like all the times I stared in the mirror as a kid wishing I was pretty like Ava. Or like, just not "fat and ugly" like me. I closed my eyes and imagined myself on my knees offering myself to the glory of womanhood. I broke off the pieces of me that were brittle from getting hollered at and also threatened on the block. Shook forth the doubt that came from lungs afraid of change and brick-ass NYC winters. Offered all of it to the glory and asked for clay to rebuild.

I'd fold purpose, blue lipstick, and declarations of love pressed into kisses on bluffs, all of this into fresh womanhood. Just for me. Just mine. I could do that. That's the thing. If my life was going to change, it was on me: these hips, this brain, and this attitude. I looked over my list again.

Shit. It was honest.

I relaxed for a minute, eased my shoulders, enjoyed the ride.

Maxine blasted Donna Summer's "Love to Love You, Baby" and "Hot Stuff." The vibe in the car was good, like hella good. Maxine and Zaira had said their pieces and that was it. They didn't pressure me for any response. They went back to being humans in love, Zaira curled up next to Maxine. I had my list. We made it to the river having spent the last few minutes in the truck with the windows down and the radio up. The spirit of the cleansing took over. We were all ready to be reborn.

CHAPTER TWENTY-SIX

I WAS REBORN BY THE RIVER

THE SANDY RIVER terrified me. But I'd also never been to a river before. Sure, I'd been to Orchard Beach in the Bronx, but Orchard Beach was man-made and the only things rushing there were the Puerto Ricans to the handball courts. The Sandy was surrounded by real live nature. Mad trees everywhere. Trees so tall they looked like they touched the sky. Trees as wide as a subway car. Trees, yo. By the Sandy River, amid all those trees, I felt incredibly small, dust-speck-floating-around-in-the-universe small.

We piled out of the trucks and stood at a split path. One way led into the woods, the other was a paved path to the riverbank. I'd expected a ceremony of sorts, or at least a reading from the Gospel of Mother Earth. Ginger Raine and Lupe weren't going to hike this year. Nobody wanted Ginger Raine to give birth in the woods, not like that, not without a birthing tent or some mid-wives. Lupe and Ginger Raine held each other as they walked.

I watched them and sighed. The little lesbian family thing was still so new. We all pitched in to help carry things to the landing spot. Maxine dropped the folding chairs and cooler and looked around. The sun rays bounced off the water and bathed her in warm light.

"Wait, the river's right here," I said. "So why the hike through the woods?"

"Because it's fun. It works the body and it's part of the ritual," Maxine said. "But if you want to stay here with Lupe and Ginger Raine, feel free."

I sighed and shook my head with a smile. "Okay, I'm coming. I'm already here, why not go all the way?"

"Hmm, I'm going to set off on my own," Zaira said, her eyes focused beyond us.

I followed her gaze and saw Harlowe heading down the path to us. Maxine turned to follow her. Zaira put a gentle hand on her chest. "That means you too, handsome," she said.

Zaira moved up along the water toward another path leading up the bank. Maxine watched her go with the biggest smile on her face. Harlowe made it to us in time to see Maxine making her own way to the hiking trail. I shrugged and followed. Harlowe pulled up the rear.

The path was fenced in with dense foliage. Ten minutes into the hike and I couldn't see the way out of the forest. Everything was so green. I climbed over and around massive tree trunks with deep, gnarled roots that stretched out in every direction. The trail had a slight incline, and my thick thighs were no match for it. I was sweating and chafing about a quarter of the way in. Maxine and Zaira, swift on their feet and experienced with this trail, moved along without a break. The slower I went, the less of them I could see until they faded out of sight. Harlowe kept pace with me because she stopped often to pet nature. For real, she stopped to coo at ladybugs and hug trees.

My lungs wheezed slightly. I'd had excellent lung capacity for the last week since Lupe's acupuncture, but the exercise wore me down. I needed another session, but that wasn't going to happen in the middle of the forest. I needed to stop smoking cigarettes and maybe even weed. I prayed to Father Mother God that if I made it through this hike, I'd quit one (probably cigarettes, please, Father Mother God, don't make me quit weed).

The trail wasn't getting any easier. I scraped my knees and thighs against scraggly bushes. I could hear the water rushing but couldn't see it. When were we going to clear the damn path and get to the water? Why did people think nature was fun? I didn't understand. I kept on. Wheezing a little harder, I looked for my inhaler. I checked my bag, my shorts, and then I checked them again. No inhaler. I dumped the contents of my bag out onto the ground, amid dirt and bugs, and looked. No inhaler.

"Juliet, you should hug this tree with me," Harlowe said. Her arms pressed around a tree trunk, but it was too wide to wrap them completely around it. Harlowe the tree hugger, which was the term Titi Wepa used to belittle people who cared about the environment. "Stupid tree huggers," or her favorite, "punk-ass tree-hugging liberals."

"I'm good on hugging the tree," I said, a familiar tightness settled into my chest, the beginning of an asthma attack. "Right now, I wish I had a different body, one that could sprint up mountains and not keel over from lack of oxygen."

I paused for minute to catch my breath. I shut my eyes, retraced my steps, and remembered that I'd left my inhaler on the bed in the attic.

"Fuck, Harlowe, I don't have my inhaler," I said, freaked. My heart began to beat so fast. I didn't know what was happening inside, but I thought I might faint.

"It's okay, Juliet," Harlowe said as she walked over. "Just come and hug the tree."

"I'm not going to hug the damn tree, Harlowe," I replied. "I can't breathe."

"Trust me, Juliet," Harlowe continued. "Just hug the tree. It'll absorb your worry."

She looked like she belonged in an ad for a meditation retreat. I kinda wanted to scream. The serene smile on her face, the complete lack of awareness of all the other things happening around her. I wasn't in the mood for it. Asthma was serious and hugging some goddamn tree wasn't going to help me.

"I'm not hugging the tree!" I said. The rasp in my chest wouldn't ease up.

"Juliet," Harlowe called to me. "Pressing your body against the foundation of the forest will open your lungs. Come, hug the tree."

I stomped over to the massive tree and I kicked it. I stared at her, arms folded across my chest. Yes, I kicked the fucking tree. It's not like I hated trees. But damn, why did she think she knew what my body needed better than I did?

Harlowe looked at the tree, mouth wide open. She touched its bark and whispered an apology, then she turned to me.

"Do you feel better?" she asked.

"No, not really," I said. I sank to the ground and she sat next to me.

"What do you need, Juliet? Besides your inhaler, what can I do for you? Want some eucalyptus oil?" she asked. I rolled my eyes at her and let go.

"I was so fucking mad at you for saying all that stuff about me at the reading, that I was dodging bullets and grew up in the ghetto. I never made my life out to be rough like that. Ever. You just made up some shit so that you wouldn't look stupid in front of everyone. And I know you apologized, but that e-mail wasn't enough," I said. My voice was tight, breathing still a bit ragged. I refused to cry. "And I was so mad because the night before you went there, I felt like I loved you, Harlowe. Like I could love you forever, like we were family and sisters and deep-ass friends, you know? The second I felt that love, boom, you blasted me right out of the room. And I let you, and that's why I won't hug your tree, that's why I'm frustrated right now and probably why I can't breathe, okay?

"And you know what, Harlowe? That shit was racist. I thought you could really see me, beyond all of that," I said. "Like, just me, Juliet."

"Fuck," she whispered, looking down.

"And what was all that 'I'm the big bad white lady stuff' at Lupe and Ginger's house?" I asked, looking over at her.

"Ugh, I know," she said, sighing. "It was just splurting out my mouth and I couldn't stop it. That was misdirected shame and white guilt."

"I need you to say that it's everywhere. Say that even someone like you with all your beautiful words about womanhood and feminism and faeries everything . . ."

"Can still be a racist ass?" she asked, furrowing her brow.

"Yes, that even someone like you could still be a racist ass," I said.

"Juliet, I am a racist fucking moron and any white person living in this damn country, if any of us tell you otherwise, is a liar and not to be trusted. You can be white and poor and racist as hell and wear your Confederate flags, and there's rich white people who hide their racism behind homeowner's associations and luxury condo income requirements. And then there are hippie gentrifying, well-intentioned whites like me, and none of us are better than the other. But, like, just know that I really do love you and I'm sorry about all of it."

Our eyes met. Harlowe's eyes were big and wet. I looked away from her. Did her tears eclipse my pain?

"So that's it?" I asked. "You love me. You're sorry. And hey, white folks are racist. Hate to break it to you?"

The sudden rasp of my tight lungs filled my ears. I sucked in a slow breath, still not looking at Harlowe.

"That's not enough," I continued, holding the tree I'd just kicked. "And what sucks is that I know that you know that. Deep down you also know you get a pass. Maybe not from Maxine and Zaira, but from every white lady in that room. All of them just looked at me all sad. Like as if they were ready to 'discover' their own little lesbian Latina from whatever hood and make themselves a savior too."

The ache in my chest announced itself with a hard cough. I doubled over against my knees. I stayed there for a minute and put my hand out to stop Harlowe from reaching for me. I was fine. Fucking fine.

"You told those white girls in the bathroom to check their privilege. But what I wanna know is when you stopped checking your own?"

Harlowe's eyes were redder now. Cheeks even more tear-stained. We stared at each other from the furthest points of our intersections.

"This is a moment of reckoning. I love you, but I refuse to continue loving someone who won't be real about their shit and change up their actions to match."

The heat of the day hung in the air like a sweaty fog. Harlowe dug through her bag and pulled out a small glass bottle. She shook it up and looked at me.

"A little eucalyptus oil should ease the tightness in your chest," she said. "Can I dab some on you?"

I nodded, despite my pride. Her head hung low. She focused on the small bottle in her hand. She tapped the opening and a drop of oil landed on her fingertip. Harlowe put her fingers to my chest. I closed my eyes and breathed in the cool, menthol-esque vapors.

"I definitely need to change my shit up," she said. "You think I want to be the messy, racist white lady who rains bullshit down on women of color? It's awful. Oh goddess, here I go . . . ."

She rubbed some more oil on my wrists and on my neck. It reminded me of Vicks VapoRub. Whatever she rubbed on me started to work and the tension in my chest eased slightly.

"Feeling any better?" she asked, closing the bottle.

"I just ran off," I confided, shrugging, still feeling weird. "I didn't stick up for myself."

"You shouldn't have had to," she said. "You're not anyone's proof. My work should hold up on its own merits, on the integrity and care that I put into it. I think calling out racism in other white folks has made me feel like I'm above it and that . . . that's just a big old mess. I've messed up with you, Max, Zaira. I have my work cut out for me. I hope one day you'll forgive me."

Harlowe rested her hand on my shoulder. I looked at her. We both smelled like funk and eucalyptus oil.

"I thought I needed you to change my world," I replied slowly, and took a deep breath. "But what I really needed was a push, and I got one from *Raging Flower* and from the Bronx and Ava and my mom. And now it's on me. I gotta shout when I need to and ask more questions. And demand better of myself and everything around me."

I stood up and Harlowe dusted the dirt and bugs off my body. We nodded at each other. And then I turned around and hugged the tree. And it was good, like the-world-went-silent-for-a-minute good.

HARLOWE AND I continued to hike up through the forest. I breathed much better with her oil on me. After another fifteen minutes, we made it to the edge of the small cliff. The Sandy River roared below waiting for us. Maxine and Zaira had already made it down to the river. Ginger Raine and Lupe had set out blankets and lounged by the river at our camp. Harlowe and I descended the ridge and made it to the river's edge.

But it wasn't over. The main point of the entire excursion was to climb the river and ride it down. Yes, climb the river. I didn't know people could even climb rivers. One by one, everyone except Ginger Raine and Lupe, walked into the water, stopped at a certain spot in the middle, and waded upstream. Maxine and Zaira held hands until they reached that middle point. They were in their own world, moving at their own pace. Harlowe followed. And then there was me. I watched. I had no intention of following. I'd never been to a river before, it was like bearing witness to the spirit of Mother Earth. I was no match.

Ginger Raine reached for my hand and placed it on her swollen belly. The baby kicked against my hand.

"Never thought I'd have a baby," she said, "then one day, I

realized that I'd accomplished everything I set out to do. And I thought why not elevate my existence and create life. So I did and it's so fucking rad, Juliet."

I rubbed my hands along her belly and felt the tiny human inside her as it reached out for me.

"Fucking rad, indeed," I replied.

We sat there and watched the group move against the current. The water was smooth. It wasn't like grand rapids or anything, but still, the current was real. It was cool to watch three badass dykes on a mission. They waited for each other at a point parallel to one of the tallest trees along the bank. They each made it to the breakpoint and then one at a time, they flattened their bodies and rode the current back down. The water carried their bodies swiftly, churned them from side to side. They laughed, and yelped when they could, until they made it back to our camp. Maxine and Zaira emerged from the water, holding hands, droplets glistening on their skin.

I sat in between Lupe and Ginger Raine and their soon-to-be-born baby, then realized that not having my inhaler wasn't a good enough reason to sit on the sidelines and watch. I needed to let the eucalyptus oil work its magic and try to stay calm. The fear was making my lungs tighter and I refused to let it take me down.

Fuck fear.

I got up as Harlowe made it to shore, the last of the group. I walked past her to the middle point and did exactly as I had seen them do. The river water splashed over my knuckles and into my face. The sun's glorious heat warmed my back. It urged me onward. My body felt unusually strong. Muscles in my arms and thighs flexed and released as I crawled against the current. One step at a time.

I made it to the stop point, looked to my left, and saw the tree. I was nervous but ready. Now all I had to do was ride the river back down. I turned onto my back, rested my head on the water, and unstuck my heels from the riverbed. In an instant, I was off.

My body rocketed down the river like lightning through the clouds. Glory. Glory. Hallelujah.

Weightless. Fearless. The water rippled under me like a heartbeat. Faster and faster the current moved me, and for a second the fear I was trying to face grew even bigger. Panic started to set in. I popped my head up a little too high. My foot caught against some small rocks in the riverbed. I slipped under the water, the hazy sun blurred above me. I opened my mouth, water flooded in and out of my nostrils. My body flipped over and I was done.

I was somewhere else. Like, floated off in my head, the entire internship flashing through my brain. Harlowe taught me how to envision my body as an entity controlled by my mind and my heart. Lupe made me believe that Lil' Melvin, and maybe all of us, could control fire with our spirits. Zaira set my words free with Octavia Butler. Maxine pushed me to question myself and my actions. They showed me the power of choice. And that was just Portland. In Miami, I'd connected to my ancestors, to the glorious Titi Penny and Ava, my radical, gorgeous cousin who loved people something fierce. My love for Ava, mi prima, burned deep and she in turn showed me an infinite number of ways to love and be loved, to be queer and brown and give not one single fuck about what anyone thinks. And then there was my mom, who reminded me of my power through her love and protection and that I could live forever, if I just let go of my fear and lived my truth.

The river spun my body over and around. My lungs wheezed. I couldn't stop the current. I couldn't stop my body. I thought I was going to die. Fear had fucked up my flow. It had flipped me over. I let go of everything I was afraid of and concentrated on my body. I spun myself over, spat out the water in my mouth. Used my heels to steady myself and flew right on down with the current until it spat me out at its edge.

I lay there alone.

And in that moment, I finally knew what it was to just breathe.

EPILOGUE

AFTER THE CLEANSING, we shared a big meal at Ginger Raine and Lupe's house. I showed Zaira "Starlight Mamitas: Three Chords of Rebellion" and asked if she thought it was good enough to submit to her anthology. She made me type it up and hand it to her before I left. Zaira told me to keep adding to it, that it would grow and evolve into something incredible. That's when I *knew* it'd be part of my post-internship reflection paper. Maxine wanted me to keep in touch and to investigate myself and my intentions as thoroughly as I would anyone else's. Lupe told me to come back for acupuncture any time. And Ginger Raine didn't have time to tell me anything because as we were leaving, she went into labor.

Harlowe drove to the airport. We listened to the feminist, power-lesbian mixtape one last time. She hugged me and cried all over my neck. She would always be *the* Harlowe Brisbane to me. My copy of *Raging Flower* was safe in my backpack, but with it was the list of all the other books Ava insisted I read next.

AT JFK, THE entire Palante clan met me at the terminal. I hugged my mom so tight, tighter than ever while she criticized and complimented my undercut. We were going to be okay. I was going to write it all down like I promised. At home, alone in my room, with the sounds of the 2 and 5 trains rumbling in the distance, I started with a letter to myself.

Dear Juliet,

Repeat after me: You are a bruja. You are a warrior. You are a feminist.

You are a beautiful brown babe.

Surround yourself with other beautiful brown and black and indigenous and morena and Chicana, Native, Indian, mixed race, Asian, gringa, boriqua babes.

Let them uplift you.

Rage against the motherfucking machine.

Question everything anyone ever says to you or forces down your throat or makes you write a hundred times on the blackboard.

Question every man that opens his mouth and spews out

a law over your body and spirit. Question every single thing until you find the answer in a daydream.

Don't question yourself unless you hurt someone else.

When you hurt someone else, sit down, and think, and think, and think, and then make it right.

Apologize when you fuck up. Live forever.

Consult the ancestors while counting stars in the galaxy.

Hold wisdom under your tongue until it's absorbed into the bloodstream.

Do not be afraid.

Do not doubt yourself.

Do not hide.

Be proud of your inhaler, your cane, your back brace, your acne. Be proud of the things that the world uses to make you feel different. Love your fat, fucking glorious body.

Love your breasts, hips, and wide ass if you have them and if you don't, love the body you do have or the one you create for yourself.

Love the fact that you have ingrown hairs on the back of your thighs and your grandma's mustache on your lips.

Read all the books that make you whole.

Read all the books that pull you out of the present and into the future.

Read all the books about women who get tattoos, and break hearts, and rob banks, and start heavy metal bands.

Read every single one of them.

Kiss everyone.

Ask first.

Always ask first and then kiss the way stars burn in the sky. Trust your lungs.

Trust the Universe.

Trust your damn self.

Love hard, deep, without restraint or doubt.

Love everything that brushes past your skin and lives inside your soul.

Love yourself.

In La Virgen's name and in the name of Selena, Adiosa.

"I want the freedom to carve and chisel my own face . . . to fashion my own gods out of my entrails."

—Gloria Anzaldúa

ACKNOWLEDGMENTS

First and forever, I have to give love and honor to my parents, Martha and Charles Rivera. Mom always told me to write the wild stories down. And Dad taught me how to tell them out loud. Every day they encouraged me to finish this book no matter what. They instilled in me the unwavering belief that I am capable of achieving all things. They are my joy.

To my grandparents, may each one of you rest eternally in power. Thank you for this life.

Phil, aka Brother Princess, you're the greatest brother this world has ever known. You are my heart and the inspiration for Lil' Melvin.

Marcela Mejia, you've been my best friend for over twenty years. Your unwavering support and goofy friendship helped *Juliet* take flight. Love you, seester.

Jo Volpe, Devin Ross, Hilary Pecheone, Pouya Shahbazian,

Abbie Donoghue, Jordan Hill, Cassandra Baim and the entire team at New Leaf Literary & Media, thank you for championing this very autobiographical but totally fictional book about a young queer Puerto Rican babe from the Bronx. You've supported, protected, and celebrated me and *Juliet* at every turn. Jo, I thank the universe every day for you. Look at how far we've come!

Nancy Mercado! Thank you for believing in Juliet and bringing me into the Penguin Dial family. Love to everyone who made magic for Juliet: Vanessa DeJesús, Rima Weinberg, Kelley Brady, Ashley Branch, Cerise Steel, Venessa Carson, Carmela Iaria, Tabitha Dulla, Lauri Hornik, Emily Romero, Shanta Newlin, Rosie Ahmed, Jen Loja and Jocelyn Schmidt, and Marisa Russell.

Cristy C. Road, thank you for joining me and *Juliet* on this journey. You're a revolutionary artist and a living icon and the first cover was a dream come true.

Steffi Walthall, thank you for the joy and abundance bursting from this glorious cover.

Sol, your courage and bravery during 9/11 and while working for months at Ground Zero left an impression on me that will last a lifetime. You're the inspiration behind the character of Titi Wepa. For that and much more, I thank you.

Thank you to Inga Muscio for taking a chance on a persistent Latina baby dyke from the Bronx who wanted to learn everything about feminism. Thank you for sitting with me in your attic and talking to me about the mysteries of the universe and the power I held within my body.

Ariel Gore, you're the best! Thank you for publishing the original iteration of *Juliet Takes a Breath* in your anthology, *Portland Queer: Tales from the Rose City*. All my love and gratitude to you for editing the first version of this book while letting me crash in your minitrailer out in the New Mexico desert.

Much love to Titi Nereida and Uncle Carmelo for praying for me every single day, like since I was born.

Vanessa Martir, I'm a better writer because of you. Your mentorship and guidance keep me grounded and recklessly in love with this writing shit. Camaradas por siempre.

Phoenix Danger, your Brooklyn Phresh Cutz parties inspired the chapter "Undercuts and Transformations." May your glorious heart beat forever and nourish the universe.

Riese Bernard, thank you for giving all the f*cks about this book. Autostraddle saved my life.

Marisol Smalls, you loved Juliet before I did. Thank you always.

Thank you to the Reverend Kelly Brown-Douglas for always believing in me and challenging me to be my most authentic, revolutionary self.

Riverdale Avenue Books and Lori Perkins, thanks for being the first to publish *Juliet* and for teaching me so much about navigating the complexities of the publishing world.

Much respect to Walidah Imarisha and adrienne maree brown for hosting the Black and Brown Girls Write a New World workshop at the 2013 Allied Media Conference. Their workshop inspired the chapter "Ain't No Party Like an Octavia Butler

Writer's Workshop." It also gave me the confidence to believe in my wildest daydreams and make them come alive.

Love to everyone who read this book and offered insight or expertise on how to make it the best book in the whole world: Patrice Caldwell, Charlie Vasquez, Caitlin Corrigan, Laura Wooley, Key Jackson, and Glendaliz Camacho.

Habló Rodriguez-Williams, thanks for astral projecting into my life and being the best assistant and primx in the struggle.

To every library from the Bronx to Connecticut to Ohio to Portland, Oregon, thanks for existing. Libraries are sanctuaries. May we always protect them.

And finally, thank you to the universe for being infinite, majestic, and bubbling with joy.

Q & A WITH GABBY RIVERA

1.   What was your initial inspiration for *Juliet Takes a Breath* and how much of your own journey (if any) is reflected in that of Juliet's?

When they tell you to write what you know, do it. That's all this book is, me writing what I know.

I was nineteen when I fell in love with my first feminist book. I was nineteen when I took my chunky Puerto Rican ass out of the Bronx and landed in Portland, Oregon.

Nineteen when I came out. When I first fell in love. Nineteen when I decided my father couldn't control me anymore. Nineteen when I first realized the power I had inside of me, physically, emotionally, and spiritually. Nineteen when I decided to step into my dyke boots and never take them off.

This book is a snapshot of that time in my life, with a little bit of make believe, magic, and ancestral exploration.

2.   *Juliet Takes a Breath* has been many years in the making! If you were to relive the process, would you do anything differently?

Yeah, I would have taken up all my women/femme/non-binary author friends on their publishing offers. It would have been really cool to have that connection to deeply pro-dyke, pro-Latina, pro-feminist, anti-white racist publishers, you know? Like I clawed my way into publication, all on my own, and there were moments where people offered help and I was too scared to take it.

3. Why did you decide to set Juliet's story in 2003? Do you think her transformation would unfold differently if it took place today?

I was just trying to get everything I'd experienced down on paper. My own foray as a writer's assistant took place in the early 2000s and that's what I wanted to capture. Shit was fucking intense. There were color-coded terror threats every morning and George W. "Strategery" Bush was president. Gays couldn't get married in the U.S. and my mom still whispered when she said the word *lesbian*. "Magic Stick" by Lil' Kim & 50 Cent was on the radio and I didn't yet know the differences between gender expression and gender assigned at birth. This was the world I was becoming a young adult in and I wanted to catch a slice of it before it faded away.

4. The ways in which Harlowe fails Juliet are infuriating and heartbreaking, yet Juliet chooses to maintain their friendship. Can you talk a little bit about your decision to show Juliet forgiving her mentor?

Juliet forgives Harlowe because that's the next step in her journey. At the end of the novel, Juliet is more in touch with herself and her understanding of the world than she's ever been, but she's still got so much more to learn. I imagine that by the time Juliet is twenty-five, she's got a different relationship with Harlowe, and even more so by the time she's forty.

It's a process. And everyone's journey is SO SO DIFFERENT. Like, Ava, Juliet's cousin, is ready. Her politics and sense of self are so sharp and fully formed in the sense that she won't now or ever connect herself with anyone like Harlowe.

Personally, it's taken me a long time to realize that I can disconnect from harmful folks, from networks that elevate white people's comfort over the needs of Black people, indigenous people, all people of color.

Juliet forgives Harlowe for herself, so that she can move forward in her own personal journey through feminism and Bronx boriqua queerness. It's her way of being like, "Okay, so your words were important to me but actually I'm the reason I'm here." You know?

5. **The theme of ally-ship plays such an important role in this story. Do you have any advice for those who are seeking out allies, or who want to become better allies?**

Regarding ally-ship, everyone should read the article "Accomplices not Allies: Abolishing the Ally Industrial Complex" via Indigenous Action Media. Their main point is that we need "accomplices not allies."

For me, no one can be an ally. We can act in solidarity with tons of compassion and humility with each other. But allies are meaningless if we're not taking actions. A straight white actress posting a pride flag on her Instagram isn't gonna save LGBTQ teens from being homeless, you know what I mean? I wanna know if you're gonna take a bullet for us, if you're gonna put your body in the way of an assault and throw your vote on the line for better policies for Black Indigenous POC, LGBTQ folks, disabled folks, all of us. Walk through the storm with me, otherwise you don't deserve the sunshine on the other side.

We are the ones that have to show up for each other. We gotta share our money, resources, homes, energy, and histories with each other, no matter what.

6.   Growing up, did you always know that you wanted to be an author? If not, what was the turning point for you?

I've always been a writer but never thought I could be an author. That seemed like one of those fancy, lofty professions people only got to be if they were rich. Like rich enough to stay home and write and have all their needs met: housing, food, bills paid, etc.

The turning point was more like a multitude of tides rolling over me at different times. When my gender presentation went from tomboy femme to butch dyke, my whole world changed kinda. The same places that took my résumé beforehand were now not interested in hiring a visibly queer person. And by default, I was also failing as a Latina. Not hot, not high femme, and not trying to cater to any man or patriarchal system.

The recession tanked, and I had no damn money. I felt like the world was set up to crush me.

And then I made some promises to myself.

I promised myself that no matter what, I wouldn't hide. No

closets ever again. I wouldn't change my gender presentation to make anyone else comfortable. Whatever job I'd have in this stupid wild world would be one where I was happy, respected, and valued as a big fat bouncy Puerto Rican dyke from the Bronx. Punto.

7. Do you have any advice for aspiring writers, particularly those who are marginalized because of their race or sexuality?

Take all that pain and write it out, dance it out, fuck it out, love it out. And then let all the healing that comes from release be the beautiful balloon strings that keep you tethered to this earth. 'Cuz we need you, we love you. Our stories are life-saving.

And don't censor yourself for nothing.

8. Do you have any future plans for Juliet, or for more YA novels in the vein of *Juliet Takes a Breath*?

In my best daydreams, I write a novela dedicated to Kira and Juliet's summer love. Maybe it'll happen one day.

9. You've talked about how *Juliet Takes a Breath* is a love letter to books, especially to that one book that shakes up your worldview and changes your life. What book(s) have done this for you?

Aristotle and Dante Discover the Secrets of the Universe by Benjamin Alire Sáenz is one of those books that made me believe in love again. Like all types of love. That book reminded me that parents can love their kids without making them suffer through all their adult problems. It reminded me that everyone in your life can and should offer the utmost love and care to you as you grow. And the love that flourished between Aristotle and Dante reminded me that I don't ever have to shrink myself for anyone.

Palante: Young Lords Party—this collection of essays and reflections on the Young Lords Party offered me my first roots of Bronx revolution. It gave me the gift of seeing myself reflected in young Puerto Ricans living in the Bronx during my parents' time and how they rallied and fought against white corporate/politics interests and policies for a better life, for equality.

Queer Brown Voices: This book is another collection of essays and interviews with Latinos/as/xs who organized and protested against white supremacy and anti-LGBTQ violence in the U.S. from the 1950s and on. I learned from *Queer Brown Voices* that we've literally been fighting for our rights from day one in this country.

10.   If there was one quality of Juliet's that you could gift to every reader, what one would it be?

Curiosity. Juliet has questions, TONS of questions and that curiosity, to find answers and learn more, is what propels her out into the world and into her destiny. Without curiosity, you just end up scrolling past life waiting for something to happen. That's not enough. I want us all to be so curious that we don't tolerate anything less than the majestic for our lives. We all deserve to be living our wildest dreams right freakin' now.